Escape from Beckyville

Tales of Race, Hair and Rage

Nicole D. Sconiers

SPRING LANE PUBLISHING
Los Angeles, California

Spring Lane Publishing
8306 Wilshire Boulevard, #1239
Beverly Hills, CA 90211

Printed in the United States of America

ISBN 978-0-615-49544-6

Book design by Ljiljana Kovacevic

This book is dedicated to the memory of my great-grandmother, Sallie, who taught me the importance of storytelling. As a child, I sat at her feet as she dipped snuff, enthralled by the "speeches" she recited from memory.

8/2/11

Dear cousin Bev,

You are such a beautiful woman with a generous and loving spirit. Keep letting your light shine, and I'll see you at the top!

May God continue to richly bless your life.

Love you!
Nikki

Acknowledgments

I wish to acknowledge my mother, Lola Sconiers, for being a wise, comedic and fearless storyteller and for encouraging me to embrace a spirit of adventure and creativity. I also wish to thank Tananarive Due and Alistair McCartney, my mentors in the Antioch University Los Angeles MFA program, for understanding my quirky vision and challenging me to enter the territory of the brave writer. I especially thank Alma Luz Villanueva, whose tutelage inspired me to embrace speculative fiction and who always motivates me to dream on.

Many people have supported my writing dreams and encouraged me to stretch my imagination to the limit. I'd like to thank the sisterfriends whom I didn't have to hassle to read my stories, who believed in me when I didn't believe in myself – Toinetta Jones, Kim Rogers-Brooks, Bunmi Moore, Kenya Conway, Jill Yesko, Keyneica Jones, Rebecca Raphael, Edana Walker, Roque Herring, Glynis Childs, Jeannette Hollyday, Belinda Bass, Gabrielle Pascoe, Verna Jones, Olanna Mills, Kiki McKnight and Monique Johnson. A very special thanks to my sister for life, Carol King, who inspires me to be the best woman I can be and have fun doing it! I'd also like to thank my surrogate mother, Mollie Jefferson, who embraced me as her own when I didn't have family in L.A. and gave me the strength to believe I could overcome anxiety. Ms. Dorothy Wilder, you will always be the auntie who helped raise me, who cooked for me, gave me gambling money and kept stressing the importance of sharing my stories.

A dainty shout out to my editor, Kate Maruyama, who saw the importance of this book and created an order for the stories. Thank you, Kate, for strolling through the crooked lanes of Beckyville with me. A special thanks to Kit Reed for taking an interest in my career and for blazing a trail through her brilliant speculative fiction stories.

The Mighty Tropes, my cohort at Antioch University, will always occupy a special place in my heart – especially my girls, LaCoya, Brenna and Imani. We laughed together, stressed together, wrote together, partied together. Most importantly, we saw the artist in each other and helped her bloom. Ceeairrah VanCobb, Nancy Conyers, Jacqueline Jaffe and Heather Luby, thank you ladies as well for inspiring me with your wit and your beautiful words.

I'd also like to thank the Black Science Fiction Society for providing a forum for my work, especially authors Milton Davis and Charles R. Saunders, who are pioneers in the Sword & Soul genre.

And to the Jones women everywhere, who keep pushing back against the forces that seek to destroy your spirit, your fierceness, your hair – keep dreaming, and keep plotting your escape from Beckyville.

Table of Contents

Metamorphia

One morning, upon awakening from anxious dreams, Penelope Jones found herself transformed into a white woman. The arm clutching her pillow was as bloodless as a bone. Instead of the kinky twisted hair that she wrapped up in a silk scarf at night, the strands sticking to her cheek were long and flaxen. She tried to brush the hair from her face, but her fingers wouldn't obey.

What's happening to me?

It was no dream. Through the cascade of tresses, she saw the painting hanging beside her bed. A woman lounged in a hammock on the deck of a seaside house, her face turned away from the viewer, taking in the frozen blue waves, the pale ribbon of clouds unraveling across the sky. Penelope remembered the purchase well. She had ventured from her condo in the Miracle Mile to an African art store in Inglewood, so proud of herself for braving the unfamiliar streets, the men hawking essential oils and T-shirts on street corners. When she first saw the painting, she thought it was perfect. Not because she admired the artist's brush strokes or felt a kinship to the reclining woman, arm raised to her head, hand resting on a nest of knotty hair that mirrored Penelope's own. No. She simply wanted a portrait that accentuated her mahogany furniture and would make her friends think she was cultured.

Untangling herself from the covers, the white woman leapt to the floor. She frowned at the bed as if it had attempted to restrain her. Flicking sleep from her eyes, she closed them and opened them again.

"What in the world am I doing here?"

The stranger's voice startled Penelope. It was coarse and southern, and she had not expected such a noise to come out of her mouth.

As the white woman examined her surroundings, she lifted a hank of yellow hair and chewed it.

That's disgusting.

Penelope tried to spit out the offensive wisps that were as slippery as corn silk, but her tongue had turned traitorous and wouldn't obey. Penelope had never chewed on her own hair. Even when it hung down her back, before she took a pair of shears to it, excised the blonde highlights and the perm, she had never tasted her own tresses.

This is some kind of waking dream or some past-life regression I accidentally stumbled into. Serves me right for visiting that New Thought church.

She thought of her friend, Naomi, a devout Christian who attended Grimes A.M.E. mega church in Inglewood. Although Penelope had never felt truly comfortable amidst the swaying hips and storms of praise that drenched the stadium on Sunday mornings, never felt like an authentic believer, Naomi seemed to possess an inner peace and joy. She needed someone strong like that to pray for her.

I'll call her right now. Penelope couldn't dwell on the fact that she no longer had use of her hands.

"Where the fuck am I?"

Penelope winced. Gratuitous cursing irritated her. Even if she stubbed her toe or accidentally locked herself out of the condo, she never uttered anything more offensive than "Oh crumbs." She took pride in the way she spoke, taking years to erase the row houses and hand-me-downs from her voice. Since moving to L.A. from a small town in southeastern Pennsylvania eight years ago, she learned to tuck away her countrified qualities. She no longer pronounced "water" as "would-der" the way her mother still did, learning to say "wah-ter" like the other black women in Los Angeles she knew. Although she hadn't returned to the university since graduating from Hampton nearly a decade ago, she kept a journal entitled "Grad School Words" on her nightstand. Every time she spoke to her coworkers at Aesthetic boutique, she found ways to fold her new vocabulary into the conversation: "Marisol didn't mean to break the garment steamer. I really don't think she had any agency." "I love the way you paired a military jacket with that hoop skirt. It's such a subversive look."

Someone knocked at the door.

Oh, God. What now?

Her friends never dropped by unannounced. They respected her boundaries and called first before visiting. And who would drop by so early on a Wednesday morning? She was fearful and relieved at the same time. Fearful of how the visitor would react to her transformation. Relieved that help might be on the way, that someone could help restore her to her former self.

She tried to will her feet to move, but they wouldn't budge. She couldn't even wiggle her toes. The white woman stood in the same position. She stared at the window, as if oblivious to the knocking. Murky sunlight pooled on the sill beneath the venetian blinds. Somewhere down the block, a car engine stuttered then roared to life. It was a few minutes past 8:00. In another world, Penelope would be pulling on a pair of flare leg pants before heading to the kitchen to pack lunch for work.

The knocking grew persistent. The stranger looked down at the wrinkled Hampton University T-shirt and shorts she wore. The glare of those pasty legs shocked Penelope, and she wanted to cry out. Digging panties out of her butt, the white woman trudged through the open bedroom door, across the hardwood flooring in the living room, rounded the corner of the foyer and squinted through the peephole.

Penelope's upstairs neighbor stood there, her brow creased in irritation. She was a dumpy redhead whose bull terrier was always scampering across the floor in the middle of the night.

What does she want?

When the door opened, the woman gave a sheepish grin.

"Sorry to bother you. I live upstairs," she said. "Is the other girl home?"

"No," the blonde woman said.

Yes, I am. I'm right here!

"Really? I thought I saw her Jetta downstairs when I came back from walking Queenie."

"I guess she stepped out."

"Oh." She grinned that apologetic grin again. "Can I come in for a sec? Queenie knocked her blanket off the patio. I thought maybe it fell on the sidewalk, but when I went outside, I saw it hanging from your balcony. Mind if I just run and grab it?"

The stranger shrugged, stepping aside.

Hey. You don't live here. You can't invite people into my space!

Penelope's neighbor rounded the corner of the foyer, pausing as she entered the living room.

"It's almost identical to my place."

She examined the chocolate leather couch with a matching recliner, the étagère by the fireplace that wobbled when Penelope dusted it. One back leg was shorter than the other, but Penelope bought it, defect and all, because she was impressed with the word "étagère," and she thought it would add a regal touch to her home.

She cringed when her neighbor picked up an earthenware plate from one of its shelves. Penelope and several other single friends had vacationed in Barcelona the previous summer, so the cabinet was lined with crosses and other trinkets from the Monastery of Montserrat. Like countless other tourists visiting the Catalonian hillside, Penelope stood in line at the Shrine of Our Lady of Montserrat to get a glimpse of the famed black Madonna. Their guide, Ramón, a gap-toothed Spaniard with a wavy afro, explained several theories for how *La Moreneta* came to be so swarthy. The many burning candles and lamps used to venerate the Virgin had begrimed the wood, he said. Another belief was that the varnish had simply darkened with the passage of centuries. It was as if he wanted to assure the Italians and Australians and other Americans from the tour bus that no sculptor worth his salt would purposely depict the mother of baby Jesus as a black woman. But it was just as well because Penelope didn't really think the Virgin of Montserrat had African features. Instead, she resembled an English spinster who had emerged from a swamp.

"Fancy," her neighbor said, replacing the plate.

"Didn't you say you had to get a blanket?"

"Oh, right. I'll be just a sec."

The redhead drew back the lateral blinds and unlocked the sliding glass door. The morning breeze rushed into the room like chilly fingers. Penelope's neighbor (even though she had moved into the condo more than a year ago, she still didn't know the names of anyone in the complex) grabbed the doggie blanket from the railing and shook it out. It was a black fleece affair adorned with hot pink paw prints and a matching bow. The name Queenie was emblazoned in the center, encircled by a gold doggie bone.

The woman gave a grateful grin as she stepped back into the living room and pulled the sliding glass door shut behind her. Penelope had never been on the receiving end of such graciousness. Whenever she encountered the redhead in the underground garage or on the elevator, she was greeted with a curt nod or a tight smile. Even the terrier panting by its master's side regarded Penelope with the same haughty indifference.

"Sorry to bother you. Thanks again."

The woman headed toward the door, then turned around and said, "I haven't seen you in the building before. Are you her new roommate?"

I don't need a roommate, thank you. I can afford this place on my own!

"No."

"Oh." Taking in the stranger's wrinkled sleepwear and mussed hair, she said "Oh" again as if another more perverse scenario occurred to her.

The blonde smirked. "Ain't Queenie getting cold?" she said, and Penelope cringed at her coarseness, at her commonness.

Queenie's owner looked down at the blanket in her hand as if she had forgotten the purpose of her visit.

The white woman said, "Best get going before she knocks something else off the patio."

The redhead's eyes widened. Then without another word, she turned around and left.

The stranger closed the door after her. The deadbolt lock slid home with a menacing click.

"Dumb fat bitch," she said.

Although Penelope agreed with that assessment, she was nervous now that her neighbor was gone, unsure of what the woman who now occupied her body would do.

"Here I am. Rocked you like a hurricane!"

The white woman sang with fervor as hot water pelted her chest. Grabbing a bar of soap from the recessed shower shelf, she rubbed it between her palms.

Trashy.

Penelope never bathed without using a washcloth. The thought of running her bare hands over her breasts and between her thighs embarrassed her. Made her feel cheap. But the stranger soaped up with abandon, pressing suds into her armpits, lathering nipples like faded rose petals. She paused to inspect the birthmark on her right arm that Penelope had always regarded as a land mass, as a lone continent that had drifted away from its personal Pangaea. It now looked bruised against the milky skin.

She watched as those fingers – her fingers, with the trimmed cuticles and short, but polished nails – reached for a bottle of shampoo and squirted an apricot-scented stream into her palm. That eight-ounce bottle, along with conditioner and styling gel, had cost $135.

That's not cheap.

Penelope was surprised at the anger she felt, at the possessiveness, over an item she scarcely used. She never pampered her unprocessed hair the way she did when her mane stretched down her back. When her hair was longer, she had a standing every-two-weeks appointment with her stylist, Myaisha. Now, she rarely stepped inside a salon. When she cut her tresses into an inch-long afro more than a year ago, it wasn't because she felt a sudden longing to embrace her heritage. She was simply tired of looking like every other brown-skinned, long-haired black woman walking the streets of Los Angeles. She wanted to stand out. And stand out she did, just not in the way she imagined. When she entered Aesthetic the next day sporting the bristly crown of wool, her coworkers stared at her, and she was certain that her boss Veronique would force her to go up the street to Elgin Charles salon for a decent hairstyle.

If Penelope believed she was invisible before, she felt even more so *au naturel.* No black men looked in her direction. No man made eye contact with her at the Hollywood Farmer's Market or offered to buy her a cup of coffee as she sat in the Internet café around the corner from her condo. Even when she traveled to Spain and France last summer with her single friends, who convinced her that European men were practically proposing to every black woman they encountered, no men glanced at her abroad either, except for a few construction workers who called "Chocolat!" as she wandered through Père Lachaise Cemetery on the hunt for Richard Wright's grave. And when she finally found the writer's final resting place, not adorned with fresh daisies and orchids like Chopin's memorial, or even beer bottles of remembrance like Jim Morrison's tomb, but with a single rose, crisp with decay and time, she wept for the loss of beauty she had never known.

She felt like sobbing now, but no moisture filled the stranger's eyes. Even her melancholy was at the whim of a white woman, who was busy massaging her scalp with $55 shampoo.

Her visitor turned off the faucet with her toes, and the yellow bath rug squished as she stepped out of the shower in a cloud of steam. She rubbed herself with a towel hanging on the back of the shower door and then wrapped her wet hair.

If I woke up in a strange house, I would never take such liberties.

She would call the police first thing, afraid that the owners would return, appalled to find her on the premises. But the white woman opened Penelope's panty drawer as if she owned it. She pushed aside organic cotton bloomers and boy shorts, pulling out a pair of lacy red thongs with a matching bra. Penelope had buried the set in the bottom of her drawer, a sad reminder of the last time she had sex two years ago. Once clad in the lingerie, the stranger gave her hair a final rub with the towel then tossed it to the floor. She stared at her reflection, taking in the curvy hips and high buttocks, the full bottom lip. The girl's beauty was muted by the sullenness in her ice-blue eyes.

"How did I get to be such a fucking cow?" she murmured.

I'm not fat!

But Penelope didn't believe her own words. When she lived on the East Coast, she felt comfortable flaunting her 150-pound frame around, and black men – back when they looked at her with interest – called her "thick." But once she moved to L.A., she felt like a giant among all the skinny women. Veronique, who couldn't have weighed more than 100 pounds, always complained about how fat she was while rubbing her non-existent gut. So Penelope would suck in her belly fat and pull her jacket more tightly about her as she walked the streets.

As she reflected on these things, the white woman opened the door to the walk-in closet. She tossed wraparound skirts and pashminas to the floor, pushed aside cashmere sweaters and crepe dresses. She pulled a pair of jeans from a hanger and stepped into them. Not finding the top she wanted, she pawed through the dresser drawer, finally settling on a black baby tee that Penelope only wore when she cleaned.

Combing through her hair with her fingers, the stranger spied a brush lying on the vanity in the alcove. It wasn't really a brush. It was a detangling tool for natural hair that Penelope bought when she did the big chop. The teeth were littered with tufts of wool. Now the woman raked the detangler through her hair. Penelope envisioned the stubby black strands commingling with the flaxen locks, being absorbed, like a weevil in a field of wheat.

After a few minutes of grooming herself, the woman headed to the kitchen. Opening the stainless steel side-by-side Frigidaire that Penelope had purchased as a Christmas gift to herself, she stared at the dino kale and cabbage wilting in the crisper, the pungent jar of kimchi, the almond milk and cartons of tofu. She settled on a few bananas dappled with black spots and dropped them in a brown lunch bag. Her gaze fell on the Kate Spade purse on the marble countertop. She searched the bag until she found Penelope's wallet.

Get out of my things!

The white woman thumbed through the twenties and tens, counting out $90. Penelope rarely carried cash. She'd been planning on picking up her dry cleaning on her lunch break, but the Armenian man who altered her pants and fixed the zipper on her leather handbag, didn't accept credit cards. Now the white girl shoved the bundle of bills into the pocket of her jeans.

Thief.

Removing the license from its sheath, she stared at the photo. Her eyes narrowed, as if she had glimpsed something familiar but disturbing. Then she smirked.

"Penelope? What kind of name is that for a black girl?"

Shut up, Becky!

Grabbing the lunch bag and the keys from the counter, the white woman said, "Let's take that Jetta for a spin. I'm sure Penelope won't mind."

Then she unlatched the deadbolt and headed out into the courtyard, where sunlight fell weakly against a stone ledge.

She left my cell phone. My mom won't be able to contact me. Veronique will wonder why I never showed up. Somehow, the latter thought grieved Penelope more than the notion that she might never speak to her mother again. But in three years of working at Aesthetic boutique, she had never called in sick, not even when bronchitis flared up like a circle of fire in her throat. She felt as if she had to put in more effort than her coworkers, who thought nothing of taking a sick day to go to a concert or for a weekend getaway with a boyfriend.

I don't have any agency.

The white woman whistled, and the carefree sound reverberated in the empty corridor. Penelope's grandmother Sallie always said ladies should never whistle, especially not in public. She wanted to yell at the stranger who had commandeered her body, desecrated her memories and was walking nonchalantly toward the elevator.

Thief, she wanted to scream. But the words only echoed in her head.

After disengaging the alarm on Penelope's car, the white woman drove out of the subterranean garage and into the sunlight. She ejected the Vivaldi CD and flipped channels until she found a rock station. She peeled a banana and ate it as she cruised through the Miracle Mile neighborhood, gazing at the Spanish-style homes with arched entryways. Women walked miniature dogs or pushed designer baby carriages over broken sidewalks. Joggers trampled leaves from Jacaranda trees underfoot, white ear buds blaring music only they could hear. Back in Penelope's small town, the streets were usually empty during the day, because most folks were at school or work, but every day a steady stream of people flowed up and down the streets of L.A., regardless of the time.

The white woman squeezed the car into an empty spot adjacent to a park. She sat for a few moments, listening to the sound of the cooling engine. Elderly Korean men power-walked around the trails. Jewish women wearing skirts and mittens chatted with one another as they kept up a leisurely stroll.

"What a life," she said.

You should talk.

The blonde opened the car door, slipping the keys in her back pocket.

There was an open-air mall a few blocks away, with a department store, kiosks and high-end specialty shops. The blonde headed in that direction. Penelope knew a few salesgirls who worked at the cosmetics counter in the department store. She wondered if they would see the white woman approaching and notice anything familiar about her. She felt awkward in her body. Penelope stared at the ground wherever she went, as if an invisible weight were pressing against her neck. Even as a child, her grandmother admonished her to hold her head up. The stranger's walk was different. Her gait was sure, almost seductive, even wearing Penelope's only pair of flats. She breezed through the door of the department store, barely acknowledging the salespeople who greeted her. Had she walked into Penelope's boutique, she would have aroused suspicion – at least Penelope's, if no one else's. She carried no purse. Her hands were too free, unencumbered by shopping bags or wallet or any other emblem of civility. Although she walked with purpose, there was a furtiveness about her as if she had already stolen a blouse and was making her getaway.

How much of her is me?

The cosmetics department was a few feet away, and a veil of fragrances hung in the air. The white woman walked up to the display case, glancing at a container filled with lip liner pencils. Penelope loved makeup – the prism of eye shadows on the counter, the lipstick tubes standing at attention like dark soldiers protecting a crystal castle, the sparkling bevy of nail polishes arrayed like a linear rainbow. She felt like a different woman when she emerged from the makeup artist's chair.

"Good morning, miss. I bet you'd look hot in some lipstick from our new spring collection."

The white woman looked up from the case, eying the smiling salesgirl with disdain. Penelope recognized her as Sasha, a beautiful Filipina with an acne-scarred chin. Most of the women working at that particular makeup counter had bad skin that no amount of concealer or foundation could mask, as if they were sisters suffering from a disfiguring genetic disorder.

"No thanks."

Sasha, it's me.

The saleswoman craned her neck. "Your eyes are stunning," she said.

"The right shadow can really make them pop."

Don't you see me? It's Penelope.

"Not interested."

Not to be deterred, Sasha held a makeup brush aloft as if the blonde were a doll she wanted to play with. "A little blush can't hurt. Some color would really accentuate your cheekbones."

The white woman scowled, her face inches from the salesgirl. "I said I don't need no makeup. Got it? I ain't the one with bad skin." She strode to the door and out into the plaza.

Penelope was so shocked at her retort, and felt so sorry to see the hurt in Sasha's eyes, it barely registered that something hard was pressing into her palm. The white woman had swiped a lip liner sharpener. Now she shoved the purloined item in the pocket of her jeans. Then whistling, she walked along the cobblestone street of the al fresco plaza, as if it were a playground where only she belonged.

After an hour of window shopping, the blonde returned to the Jetta. She pulled not only the sharpener from her jeans, but a pair of shades, a rhinestone barrette, a paisley scarf and a satin eye mask that she had hidden in her panties. Penelope was startled by the number of objects that slipped her notice. Tossing her loot into the passenger seat, the white woman made a U-turn and sped off.

No wonder you only needed $90.

The chick was a petty thief. She felt a wave of hatred for the woman who was defiling her body. What if she had gotten caught? Penelope shuddered at the thought of being handcuffed and placed in the back of a squad car for those paltry items.

I've never even had a parking ticket.

Fear quickly supplanted her anger. It dawned on her that the woman behind the wheel was dangerous. Why had she stolen those trinkets that couldn't have cost more than $50 combined, when she had walked away from items ten times more expensive in Penelope's condo? She had nothing to lose. Nothing was of value to her, not even her freedom.

Penelope felt ill. The white woman could do something crazy, impulsive, maybe even drive into oncoming traffic. As if aware of Penelope's fears, she swerved into the right lane, and a horn blared behind her in annoyance.

"Fuck off!"

The woman jabbed her middle finger out the window of the Jetta, then turned right onto La Brea.

Are you crazy?

Penelope screamed, but it only echoed silently in her head. She never cut people off in traffic, never tailgated and certainly never flipped off other drivers, because she feared that the slightest injustice on the road would result in a bevy of bullets riddling her car. Even now, a 9mm could be trained on the back of her head. That was her worst fear: that she would die as a result of someone else's ignorance.

Tires squealed as the Jetta pulled into a McDonald's parking lot. Penelope was relieved when, after two minutes of idling in line at the drive-thru, the rear windshield remained intact. But she winced when the stranger ordered a double cheeseburger with large fries and a strawberry milkshake. Penelope hadn't eaten flesh or dairy foods in nearly five years, and the thought of animal products entering her body sickened her. But her body didn't belong to her anymore.

A sullen black woman handed the blonde her order. A pyramid of synthetic curls jutted beneath her McDonald's cap. Her lobes were weighed down with gold earrings so large that Penelope could have thrust her fist through the center.

"Thanks," the white woman said, reaching for her milkshake. "I like your hair."

Penelope was embarrassed for the cashier, as if the woman's tacky hair and jewelry were her own. She felt an urge to protect her from the blonde's gaze. She expected the white woman to utter some slur under her breath, but she didn't. She pulled forward into a parking space and opened her lunch. Very seldom did Penelope eat in her own car. The rare occasions when she did, she never made eye contact with passersby, focusing on her food instead. She didn't want others to feel sorry for her and wonder why she wasn't eating her meal at a table the way respectable people did. But the woman chewed with relish, picking cheese off the wrapper, licking ketchup from her fingers.

I wonder if she knows who she is.

Was it possible to influence the woman's actions, remind her of her former identity? As the blonde ate, Penelope repeated poems she had memorized in college: *Lias! Lias! Bless de Lawd!/Don' you know de day's erbroad?/Ef'n you don' git up, you scamp/Dey'll be trouble in dis heah camp ... Lift ev'ry voice and sing till earth and heaven ring/Ring with the harmonies of liberty ...* hoping some memory of blackness would fire in her synapse. But the stranger continued to suck strawberry milkshake through a straw, freezing Penelope's brain.

"Damn, that ain't do nothing. I'm still hungry."

The woman balled up her wrapper, dropped it in the greasy bag and tossed her trash on the passenger's side floor mat. With a loud belch, she started the car and backed out of the parking lot.

The stranger continued driving south on La Brea. Soon, the smoothie shops and antique furniture stores were replaced with liquor stores, chicken shacks and the offices of bail bondsmen.

Where is she going now?

Penelope rarely traveled south of Wilshire. Even though she had attended a historically black college, driving through black neighborhoods made her nervous. She couldn't pinpoint exactly where the fear lay. It wasn't like she was afraid of her people – except for gangbangers and little thugs who strolled around wearing cornrows with their underwear on display. Part of her uneasiness was the fear of not being truly accepted or considered "authentically" black. She couldn't dance, didn't know how to jump Double Dutch and rarely used slang. Growing up, the kids on her block teased her for speaking proper, "like a white girl."

This is one white girl whom I definitely don't speak like.

She struggled to hear herself over the din of rock music. The blonde sang along with gusto as if there was nothing on her mind but the pale blue sky. If there was a God, was this transformation some type of punishment? And if a white woman had to commandeer her body, why couldn't she be educated and classy?

Ever since moving to L.A., she'd been secretly envious of white women

– or maybe envious wasn't the right word. Bitter? Yeah, that was the feeling. The longer she lived and worked around white women, the more she began to resent them. The customers who breezed past her at the boutique as if she wasn't there, instead seeking fashion advice from Caitlyn and Madison. The saleswomen who ignored her at makeup counters or served her lukewarm food. The former coworker who inquired about every new hairstyle: "It's different today. Does it just naturally curl like that, or do you have a perm?" The woman on the sidewalk who tried her best to catch Penelope's eye right before threading her arm through her boyfriend's brown one. The women who marveled at her proper speech, who cradled their purses when she approached, who said, "I totally understand how you feel, because as a woman I …"

There's no way I can spend the rest of my life as Becky. I want to be me!

Becky. That was code. The name most black women she knew used to refer to an irritating or clueless white woman. It was a private slur – like nigger or kike but without the history or the bite.

Becky. Sometimes the label didn't apply, like the Jewish woman in accounting at her old job who complimented Penelope on her clothes, or her gynecologist, Dr. Romano, who had a surprisingly gentle way with the speculum. But the longer Penelope lived in L.A., it seemed that they were all becoming Beckies. The women who looked past her, around her and through her.

Maybe that was the real reason she had chopped off her long straight hair, so she would never be accused of wanting to be like them – desiring their beauty, their visibility, their freedom.

This must be karma for all the times I hated them, but envied everything they had.

The car slowed as the woman turned into a strip mall. Penelope, lost in her ruminations, tried to get her bearings. They were somewhere around Heliotrope Boulevard. Why in the world had the woman come to this neighborhood? What was of interest to her in this small plaza that was home to a check cashing joint, a Chinese restaurant with a red C rating glaring from the window, a salon and a beauty supply store advertising "100 percent Indian hair!"

She's messing with me. There's nothing for her down here. She's no wigger. The blonde squeezed into a tight parking space. *Wherever she came from, I doubt she even has any black friends.*

It was a few minutes before 1:00 in the afternoon. The stranger hopped down from the Jetta and headed across the parking lot, which was littered with beer bottle caps, cigarette butts and a discarded black plastic bag. She stopped in front of a plate glass window, which spelled out Pearline's Elegant Tresses in cracked gold lettering.

A jangling bell announced the stranger's entrance. Pearline's shop was poorly lit. Although it was still bright outside, Penelope felt as if they were entering a cave. The smell of lye and burning hair filled her nostrils – a chemical stew. Three women sat beneath hooded dryers, and they looked up as the blonde walked in. A woman with a copper complexion and a small pompadour sat behind a counter near the door.

"Do you have an appointment?" She ran her eyes over the white woman's jeans and halter top, stopping at her yellow hair.

"Naw. You take walk-ins?"

"Yeah. It's gonna be about an hour though."

"I'll wait. I don't have nowhere to be."

In addition to the three women reading magazines beneath the dryers, there were two more patrons being shampooed at sinks near the back of the shop.

The woman with the pompadour, presumably Pearline, called to one of the stylists. "D'Ondra? Can you take a walk-in?"

D'Ondra looked up from the head she was washing. She had long purple nails, and she scrubbed her customer's scalp so vigorously, Penelope thought it would bleed. She never understood how some stylists could do hair with dragon nails.

"Yeah. Let me blow dry my customer and get my 1:30 perm started, and I'll take her."

If the black women in the shop were surprised to see a white woman in their midst – in their territory – they didn't show it. As the blonde took a seat on a bench by the window, Penelope was reminded of the one time she had visited a white beauty salon. It was a few months after she had done the big chop, and she didn't know how to manage the woolly locks that were growing in. Her hair was curly in some places, nappy in others and of varying lengths. In desperation, she took a lunch break and headed to the salon down the block down from Aesthetic. Her coworker, Caitlyn, was a regular customer, and her short, spiky hair always looked nice. A blonde with big teeth and quick green eyes looked up from her appointment book as Penelope opened the door.

"Do you accept walk-ins?" Penelope asked.

"Walk-ins for what?"

Several other black-smocked stylists glanced over at her. Penelope felt embarrassed, as if she had walked in wearing a diaper on her head. She lowered her voice.

"I'd like to get my hair done."

"I'm sorry, but we don't really have experience styling hair texture like yours." Penelope stole a look at the other beauticians, but they had gone back to blow drying and sudsing more manageable locks. "Maybe you can try Elgin Charles. It's not far from here."

As humiliating as the experience was, she'd left the salon not hating the blonde woman and her dismissive attitude, but resenting her own hair that did not blow in the wind, that could not be tucked behind an ear.

Now the white owner of her body flipped through black hair magazines, pausing at various styles.

What kind of style is she going to get? Cornrows? Two-strand twists?

It occurred to her that the stranger did not have much money. She had stolen $90 and spent nearly $10 of that on lunch. Penelope wasn't sure what they charged at Pearline's, but her former stylist, Myaisha, charged between $45 and $55 just for a cut, and that didn't include any other services, such as shampooing and styling.

What is she going to do for money? I hope she doesn't get her hair done and then try to run out of here, because sisters don't play, especially when it comes to Becky. They will catch her and beat her ass.

Beat my ass.

"You can come back now."

D'Ondra stood a few feet away, beckoning with a rat-tail comb. The heavy black smock she wore was flecked with water. The smock wasn't as sleek as the ones worn by the women in the salon who had turned Penelope away. It was a heavy, pleather material.

Like something someone around here might wear to the prom.

To her surprise, the white woman tittered.

Did she hear my thoughts, or am I thinking hers?

D'Ondra blinked. "What's so funny?"

"Nothing. Private joke."

She followed the stylist back to her station. Penelope felt embarrassed to see the fat rolls on the back of her neck, the kinky balls of hair at her nape. She wondered what the blonde woman was thinking, if she considered D'Ondra typical of black women – fat and unkempt with long fake nails bloated with acrylic.

Why do I always worry about what white women think? For once, I'd like to have the luxury not to give a damn.

D'Ondra gestured to a swivel chair, and the blonde sank into it. At her station, several styling tools soaked in a glass bottle of blue liquid. Tufts of woolly hair littered the maple laminate cabinet, and D'Ondra fanned them to the floor. Several twenties unfurled beneath the pronged attachment of a blow dryer.

Please do not steal that money.

D'Ondra said, "I didn't get your name."

"Becky."

"What you having done, Becky?"

"I want my hair cut."

"That's it? You don't want me to wash or condition it?"

"How much is all that and the cut?"

D'Ondra put a finger to her lip as she calculated in her head. "About $60. Plus tax."

"Naw. That's alright. Just the cut. You don't have to style it."

D'Ondra shrugged as she shook out a lavender apron and tied it around the white woman's neck. "Suit yourself. How short you want it?"

The blonde raked her fingers through her hair, which tumbled down past her shoulders. She pressed the blade of her hand against her earlobe.

"Take it up to here."

In the mirror, Penelope saw D'Ondra's eyes widen. Like many black women, the stylist considered long hair something to be cherished, a badge of honor, something to be grown out as long as possible. She parted the blonde's hair with the rat-tail comb.

"You sure about that? Once it's gone, it's gone."

"It's just hair. I can always grow it back … or get me some extensions."

The black woman giggled. "Ain't that the truth." She pulled a pair of shears from the bottle of blue fluid and wiped them on a towel. "Alright. Say goodbye."

"Goodbye." Flaxen tufts slid down the lavender apron, and the white woman shook them to the floor. After a few minutes of watching the rain of yellow tresses, she said, "You ever do a white woman's hair before?"

"Yeah. I have several white clients."

"You go to them, or do they come here?"

"Both. Why?"

The blonde shrugged. "Just asking."

"Hair is hair," D'Ondra said. Her scissors clicked, and another lock fell. "Lot of different types, but you work with it the same way. If you a good stylist, you can do all kind of textures."

"What kinds of textures you like working with the best?"

D'Ondra chuckled again, a low rumble in her chest. "You ask some funny questions, Becky. Well, if you must know, my preference is thick hair. The kind of hair my mama used to call cantcha-dontcha."

"Cantcha-dontcha?"

"Cantcha comb it, dontcha try." Another hank of hair slid to the ground. "Nappy. Knotty. That's the kind of texture I like to style. Our hair is versatile. Strong. To me, ain't nothing in the world prettier than a black girl with a press 'n curl."

Penelope watched the white woman's metamorphosis in the mirror. Part of her had been hoping that, somehow, the excising of the yellow locks would reveal nappy roots. But D'Ondra parted and snipped, parted and snipped, and the hair collecting in the teeth of her small-toothed comb was straight and blonde and fine.

Penelope felt as if her life were being blotted out by a growing darkness. Nearly six hours had passed since she woke up to the flaxen strands sticking to her cheek. She wondered if she would ever return to her own world, and how she would make her re-entry. Would she ever start up a blender again to make a smoothie? Would she ever paint her toenails again? Would she ever again hear the sound of her own laughter? Even though she hadn't put much effort into styling her kinky hair, she thought of the silk scarf left behind in her condo. She bought it because regular cotton scarves broke her hair off, and it was the one thing she did to protect her fragile tresses. Now, as the blonde fingered her remaining hair, Penelope longed to feel her own coils. She no longer saw herself as inhabiting the body of a white woman who had inhabited her body. She saw herself confined to a small, dark place with no power over her limbs, no ability to come and go as she pleased, no voice, no language, no tribe, no song. Her own private diaspora.

"You sure you don't want me to style it in any way?" D'Ondra asked.

"Look like you just put a bowl on my head and cut around it." The blonde smirked. "Just cut it all off. Leave me an inch or so."

D'Ondra glanced down at the mound of golden hair circling her feet like discarded hay. Other customers looked over as well.

"You can gather that up and make extensions with it," said a gap-toothed woman with rectangles of foil in her hair. The other patrons giggled.

"It's only hair," the white woman said. "Besides, according to D'Ondra, it'll never be as pretty as a press 'n curl – whatever that is."

Penelope envied the easy way the stranger joked with the other women. She never felt that comfortable, that free. She had never experienced the beauty shop camaraderie born of long hours in a chair, gossip, and the emergence of showy styles. Now, she'd have to experience her life second-hand, filtered through the eyes of a white woman.

D'Ondra untied the smock and shook it free of hair. Then she brushed off the blonde's neck and shoulders. She fluffed up the shorn locks with her dragon nails and handed the white woman a mirror.

She said, "Look okay?"

"I guess. I wasn't looking for no particular style. I just wanted something different."

D'Ondra smiled. "You sure are the funniest client I've ever had, Becky," she said, taking the mirror. Then she wrote out a receipt and handed a copy to the blonde. "That'll be thirty bucks."

Without protest, the white woman reached in her back pocket and pulled out the wad of bills. She peeled off two twenties and handed them to the stylist.

"You need change?"

"Naw, I'm good. Thanks."

"Thank you, Becky. Come back and see me some time. I can do a lot of cute styles with your hair that length."

The blonde peered at her features in the larger mirror of the station as if she had never seen her thin lips and ice-blue eyes before. "Not sure where I'm headed, but I don't think I'll be back."

"Well, be safe." D'Ondra took the bills and folded them in with the other twenties on her station. "But before you leave town, tell your black girlfriends to come see me. I give a ten percent discount to new clients."

Becky fingered the dark birthmark on her arm. Then, pulling keys from her back pocket, she headed toward the door.

"I don't have any," she said. "I ain't close to any black women."

The bell over the door jingled as she stepped out into the sunlight. She stood in front of the Jetta for a few minutes, watching a Buick slow for the light on Heliotrope.

Where are you going, Becky?

The blonde twirled the keychain around her finger. Then she passed Penelope's car and walked out of the strip mall.

What are you doing? You can't just walk away from my things.

The blonde headed south on La Brea, the breeze whipping through her cropped locks. Men whistled and catcalled out the windows of several cars, but she didn't turn around. She kept going.

Do you hear me, Becky? I'm not a trashy white girl. I'm Penelope Jones. I won't let you own my life.

The white woman thumbed the keys she was holding. She tossed them in a patch of grass near the railroad tracks.

"Penelope? What kind of name is that for a black chick?" she said. Humming to herself, she headed down the hill, following the tracks.

Three-Fifths of a Woman

Every morning after dropping her daughter off at daycare, Prostheta Jones returned to her apartment, pulled off her human face and hung it on the Styrofoam stand on the top shelf of her closet. She tried wearing the mask for a few hours longer today, but she felt suffocated. The moist flesh of the mask tickled the blurred remnants beneath.

Now she sat at her desk, writing up a press release for a client. The branch of a live oak tree thumped against her window, casting shadows across her vertical blinds. A skateboarder cruised down the block, wheels rumbling on the uneven pavement below. She was lucky to have found a job as a consultant for a small public relations firm, which allowed her to work from home, drafting press releases and bios in the dark cave of her office. It made her laugh – and saddened her – to think that she was part of a team responsible for shaping a celebrity's image, when she could not show her real self to the world.

After a few hours at her computer, she went to the kitchen and put on a pot of coffee: vanilla nut pumpkin pie, her favorite. She stood by the fridge while it brewed, looking at the magnets featuring her daughter's face that lined the door. Grace was four and precocious, her face squished into a smile in every photo. The child had Prostheta's nose, which was turned up slightly, and her hazel eyes. Her small ears were recently pierced, and Grace loved her yellow butterfly earrings. Her reddish-brown skin was clear. Intact.

Every night when Prostheta bathed her daughter, she examined her face, as if studying a porcelain doll for cracks. She almost wept to discover that there were no fissures, no erasure of epidermis. The child's features were solid. But she also touched the nose, the lips, the cheeks because it had been years since her own face was whole, and the memory of her features was fading fast.

"Mommy, I'm cold. I want to get out." Grace dreaded those nighttime rituals.

"Almost done, honey. You don't want a dirty face, do you?"

"No."

"Then hold still."

Prostheta never allowed her daughter to see her without the mask, reluctantly pulling it on when she arose and before picking Grace up from daycare. She wouldn't allow the child to sleep with her, always answering her tears with "I thought you were a big girl, and big girls don't sleep in bed with their mommies." Little kids were easily frightened, and she didn't want to scar her daughter's dreams. *In time, I'll show her.* She poured coffee into a waiting mug. The smell of spiced pumpkin wafted through the kitchen, causing the gash where her mouth once was to water. The twin holes comprising her nose still retained a keen sense of smell, as if the erosion of her other features had sharpened this faculty.

Mug in hand, she returned to her office and to the files of Becky Bradshaw, the firm's newest client. A teen singing sensation, Becky's video had gone viral, making her a household name a week after the release of her first single.

She's more famous for having a horrible voice than for any true talent.

But work was work, and Prostheta was happy to have a job, even if the bulk of clients were beautiful but banal.

At one time, she dreamed of becoming an actress. In kindergarten, she played the role of Clementine, the miner's doomed daughter immortalized in the folk ballad. Prostheta felt the remains of her lips curving upward as she remembered the gusto with which she had hurled her five-year-old body to the ground on cue:

Drove she ducklings to the water
Ev'ry morning just at nine,
Hit her foot against a splinter,
Fell into the foaming brine ...

Oh my darling, oh my darling,
Oh my darling, Clementine!
You are lost and gone forever
Dreadful sorry, Clementine ...

As a child, she sat on the stoop of her row house in Baltimore, creating movies in her mind. She saw herself onstage, in the spotlight, hearing the rush of applause from her adoring audience. At age ten, she told her mother she wanted to be an actress.

"No." Deborah Jones never looked up from the sink where she stood, washing dishes. That one word, and her mother's back, drove a stake through Prostheta's dreams. The lights faded. The applause was lost to her forever.

But I still moved to L.A., land of reconstituted dreams.

She studied Becky's head shots. Prostheta hated to crack on anyone's looks, but the white girl had a charming ugliness – fat cheeks, clumpy makeup masked budding pimples, bright vapid eyes peered out from beneath patchy brows. The singer did have a nice cleft in her chin and a head of curly red hair. In spite of her homeliness, she was more visible than Prostheta would ever be.

By the time Prostheta glanced up from her computer, it was nearly 3:00. Outside her window, a cawing crow competed with the incessant blare of a car alarm. She had to stop by the cleaners before picking up Grace. It saddened her that she couldn't take her kiddo to the playground often or encourage her in ballet or piano lessons. She didn't feel comfortable staying outside her home for long. She didn't have any close female friends and was resigned to living a solitary life in her apartment. *My lair.* She headed to her bedroom closet. Most activities she could complete online, like banking and clothes shopping, but she had to leave the house for some things. Although the mask was secure and lifelike, she still felt like she was being scrutinized. The feeling was worse than the apprehension she felt when she first moved to Los Angeles nearly six years ago. When her skin was unbroken, it seemed as if she were passing through a wall of eyes daily. She was casually assessed by passersby as she walked down the street, her face raked over by salesgirls and shop owners. She felt like less of a woman now, knowing the face that was gazed upon – but never seen – wasn't even her own.

She pulled her facial covering down from its stand, studying the features. The mask was the same russet color as her skin. Sometimes she was amazed at how realistic it looked. She pinched the petite nose. The bottom lip dimpled under her touch, then sprang back once she removed her finger. Prostheta pulled on the mask, the inside of which smelled of antiseptic. There was a quick suction movement as it warmed to her face and adhered itself. She pressed the flesh against her temples and jaw line, making sure there were no telltale creases. Satisfied that the covering was firmly attached, she whisked pressed powder over it and applied red lipstick – the brighter the better. *At least I still have my natural hair.* She pulled the short chunky plaits down around her ears and forehead.

"I almost look like the real deal," she said to her reflection. When she did her monthly grocery shopping, black men passed her in the aisles and whispered, "Hey sister. I like that natural look." She shot them quick smiles and then focused on the contents of her cart. It would be nice to have a boyfriend. Sometimes, when Grace was asleep and Prostheta was alone in her bedroom, she wanted to be touched, to be desired. But there was no man she could call; not even to come over in the middle of the night in the sanctity of darkness. Who would date a faceless woman, much less have sex with her?

A few months after moving to L.A., her facial skin began to bubble and crack. It grew hot to the touch, as if lit by an inner fire. At first, she blamed it on the sun, then smog, then the stress of trying to find a job and a decent place to live. But even after she got settled into her North Hollywood apartment and began using sunscreen for the first time at twenty-five, the fissures deepened. She returned home after finishing her assignment at the temp agency and noticed strips of flesh, some the size of a thumbprint, missing from her jaw line. She smoothed on foundation gingerly, afraid she would tear the remaining skin. Prostheta didn't have health insurance and couldn't afford to pay out of pocket for a dermatologist. She tried patting brown Vaseline on her face, then extracts of lavender and splashes of rose water – home remedies she remembered her grandmother using to keep her skin healthy – but to no avail. The peeling worsened. She had toned arms, a flat stomach, thighs that former lovers called "thick." Everything below her neck was beautiful, but her face was shredding away.

At night she lay on her back and wept, imagining life as a fractured woman. She couldn't wail the way she wanted to for fear of ripping the fragile flesh. Even when she was careful – when she held in those sobs of fear and rage – she still found bits of skin on her satin pillowcase in the morning.

One night, in desperation, she called Erick, a man she met at the club and half dated. He was decent looking, dark-brown skinned with a goatee. He had a steady job as a used car salesman, but she knew they'd never have a true relationship because he didn't read, didn't even own a library card. He arrived at her apartment in a wrinkled button-down shirt, a Bic pen still clamped to his breast pocket. She undressed him right there in the foyer and they rutted in the dark on the hardwood floor. Then, when he rose to search her refrigerator, wearing only socks, she told him to get dressed and get out. She never called him again, not even when Grace was born.

I was so desperate back then. She shook her head as she grabbed her keys from the kitchen counter and headed out the door.

The dry cleaners were located two blocks south of her apartment, but she preferred to drive and park behind their building. Judy, the Filipina co-owner of Green Elegance, was ringing up a customer when Prostheta walked in. Prostheta studied the contents of her wallet as the redhead paid for her clothes. The woman glanced back at her and then draped the plastic garment bag over an arm.

"See you next week, Judy."

"Thanks, Lisa. Bring in the tote bag you were talking about, and let's see if we can fix that zipper."

Lisa nodded as she left the counter, her plastic bag brushing against Prostheta's blouse.

"How's business, Judy?" Prostheta asked, approaching the counter.

Judy frowned, a thick shock of hair covering her brows. "Slow, but what can you do in this economy? People wash their own clothes now or walk around smelly."

She laughed, and Prostheta joined in, trying not to look at her watch.

"Well, you know I'm a steady customer." She handed Judy her claim ticket. "Most of my clothes can't be thrown in the washer. They have to last."

"You have good, quality things, lady." Judy, like most people, could never pronounce her name. "How's the job?"

"Same songs, different faces," Prostheta replied. "I'm running late now. Have to pick up my kiddo."

Judy pressed a button, and the clothing rack hummed to life. Transparent bags filled with dresses and slacks and suits moved toward her. Prostheta made it a game to guess the owner of the respective item of clothing. A pair of dark-blue designer jeans? Some skinny BMW-driving blonde chick with a maid, too lazy to clean or wash her own clothes. A cheap-looking gray suit? Some unemployed middle-aged guy who smoked Marlboros and was always looking through the classifieds, half wishing he wouldn't find work.

Then her things made their way around the conveyor belt, and Judy flipped off the switch. She laid out the black slacks, black suit jacket and black camisole on the counter.

Who do these things belong to? A high-powered businesswoman? An industry executive? Or a lady on her way to a funeral?

Prostheta sighed as she paid for her things and headed out the door to pick up her daughter. She rolled down the window as she drove toward Grace's school. It was a sunny February afternoon, those brilliant winter days that belie the season. She loved feeling the wind on her face, but now could only sense it around her eyes. She touched her mask. It was sealed tightly to her remaining flesh. It would not blow out the window and down Lankershim Boulevard. She felt an urge to rip off the false face and allow the breeze to massage the horror beneath. *If only I were that brave. But I do still live in L.A.* People on the sidewalk would gawk at her, would lower their designer shades to get a better look at the solid blur that comprised her face, the whizzing of tissue and blood, like rapidly shifting land masses on a lone continent.

"Your facial skin is erasable," Dr. Esther told her. Prostheta was six months pregnant at the time. She sat on an exam table in a storefront office, hands clasped over her expanding belly. She'd done an Internet search on "black skin issues Los Angeles" and found the naturopath's advertisement after scanning pages and pages of results. "Plagued by peeling skin? Feel like your looks are fading? Let Dr. Esther help restore your beauty – naturally!"

"Erasable? I don't get it."

The woman touched Prostheta's face, smiling sadly. She was big bosomed, but the legs beneath her lilac skirt were thin. Dr. Esther looked to be in her sixties, but she had lineless plum-black skin. The strands of hair peeking out from beneath her head wrap were as black as Prostheta's.

"Baby, I've seen this condition before – Black Facial Erasure. Not as advanced as yours, of course. I get a lot of girls your age in my office, crying, wondering why their face seems to be vanishing."

"What's wrong with me?" Prostheta felt like crying too. The remaining skin had begun to blur, as if smudged by an angry artist. She had to buy a wig with bangs and didn't leave the house without a floppy hat. No telling what her face would look like in three months when it was time to have the baby. She would have to deliver the child herself, too embarrassed to go to a hospital.

"Some women are more sensitive to the gaze."

"What gaze?"

Dr. Esther walked to the window where she stood next to a wall filled with brown bottles of herbs and tinctures, looking like a chemist. Traffic rumbled by on Heliotrope Boulevard, and a passing SUV blasted hip-hop through worn speakers. Outside on the corner, a man sold incense and essential oils. The naturopath closed her blinds.

"I'm sure you know how it feels to be seen and not seen at the same time," Dr. Esther said. "It erodes the flesh, if you're exposed to it long enough."

Prostheta thought of snooty salesgirls and even some of her former coworkers at the temp agency studying her when they thought she wasn't looking. The corrosive glances. She said nothing.

"Not an herb or ointment in my office can reverse this condition," the older woman said. But she rubbed Prostheta on the shoulder as she spoke, as if to soften the pronouncement. "I do have a remedy. Now it won't cure the dissolving, but it'll help you feel as close to whole as possible."

She disappeared into the back room. Prostheta felt the baby kick and rubbed her belly. *She doesn't deserve this. I don't want her to have a damaged mother. It's not fair.* Even as she thought those words, she felt her skin shifting, changing, blurring.

When the naturopath returned a few minutes later, she carried a white container the size of a shoebox. She pulled off the lid and Prostheta covered her mouth. She thought she was staring at a beheaded black woman. Dr. Esther reached in her pocket for a pair of rubber gloves. After rolling them on, she lifted the mask out of the box, proud of her creation.

"Feel that. It won't bite," she said as Prostheta shrank back. "One hundred percent human."

"From dead people?"

"I have vendors," Dr. Esther answered. She would say no more, instead urging Prostheta to touch her handiwork. The mask was cold and stiff – like a piece of chicken left on the counter to thaw. But when she jabbed it with her fingertip, it grew warm. There was a suction-like movement as the flesh tried to enclose her finger. She snatched her hand away.

"It won't bite you, baby," Dr. Esther repeated. "It warms to your skin. Won't need glue or anything like that. This mask has special adhesive properties."

Could she wear a facial covering? The naturopath had obviously sold them before. Here she was hawking human faces in a storefront clinic with the ease of an inner city beauty supply owner selling human hair. What other option did she have? Resigned, she let the doctor slip on the mask.

"It's durable," Dr. Esther said, as she patted the skin into place. She stood back, beaming at Prostheta. "You look just beautiful. Can't even tell the difference."

As the doctor rang her up, Prostheta studied her reflection in the mirror behind the counter. It was like looking at the face of a long-lost relative, someone you've never met, but feel a kinship with on sight.

Dr. Esther placed the white box in a bag along with the receipt. She bent down and opened a compact fridge to the right of the cash register. When she rose, she was holding a small purple bottle with a black cap.

"Keep this refrigerated. It's my special antiseptic for the mask. You have to treat it once a week. Directions are on the bottle," she said, placing the elixir in the bag. "Now if you have any other skin issues, just come back and see me."

It will have to do. Prostheta shoved the debit card back in her wallet and took the bag from the naturopath. Her new face. *I'll be a mommy soon. Don't want my baby girl to be ashamed of me.*

Prostheta arrived at her daughter's daycare a few minutes past 3:30. She parked near the curb at the end of a queue and sat in her car, listening to the falsetto of a gospel singer on the radio. She didn't crowd the front entrance like the other mommies, who fawned over their kids. Those were the children who cried for an hour after being dropped off. She wanted Grace to be strong, to be her own person, even at four. What would her child – who loved to draw and dress up in tiaras and sparkly shoes – grow up to be? An artist? A lawyer? Prostheta thought back to her mother's "no" when she was ten. *I'll never discourage her dreams.*

Prostheta hadn't returned to the East Coast since she fled for Los Angeles more than six years ago. There was nothing in Baltimore for her. No job. No man. No close relatives. Deborah Jones had passed away when she was twelve. "Passed away" was the euphemism her mother's first cousin Pearl whispered as they stood before the closed casket at the funeral. Prostheta didn't know her dad, so she went to live with her grandmother until she left for college. But when she was a sophomore at Hampton University, she received a handwritten letter from her mom's best friend that shocked her. She read it several times until the paper was thin from her tears.

"Hung herself," Miss Shirley wrote in wobbly curlicues. "You're old enough to handle it now, and I couldn't let you keep believing the lie that she died of a heart attack. Your mama was a strong lady, one of the strongest ladies I knew, but certain things can break even the mightiest of women."

What would our relationship be like now if she had lived, now that I'm a mother too? Prostheta wondered as she snapped off the radio. She opened her car door and stepped into the sunshine. The herd of moms had thinned, and she was anxious to see her own child.

Her memory of Deborah Jones was hazy. She remembered her mother bustling about in their row house – standing over a stove, washing dishes, reaching up to hang wash on a line. She always showed Prostheta her back. Even when she crushed her dreams of becoming an actress, she didn't turn around.

Prostheta tasted the pumpkin coffee on her tongue as she entered the daycare. Her mouth watered as it did when she was about to vomit. What had broken her mother, caused her so much pain that she took her own life, leaving behind a daughter on the verge of puberty? *Mom was always hiding her face from me … and then she was gone.* Her smile was steady as she greeted the young woman at the front desk, but her hand shook as she signed in.

Grace sat on a bench in the play area, her head bent over something she was drawing on construction paper. Poufy strands escaped her pigtails and Prostheta wanted to smooth them down, tame the unruly edges. Her knees wobbled as she approached. The child hummed to herself, some nameless tune she made up.

"Grace?"

The girl turned, and Prostheta wanted to drop to the floor. Her daughter's brown skin was whole. It was solid. It was beautiful.

She said, "Mommy, why are you crying?"

"I'm just happy to see you, honey." Prostheta kissed the intact skin, nuzzling her daughter's cheek as best as the mask would allow. "Ready to go home?"

Grace nodded. Prostheta turned, stifling an audible sigh. She grabbed Grace's jacket and lunch bucket from a cubbyhole near the door.

"I made this for you, Mommy."

The girl held up the picture she'd been working on. Two stick figures held hands. The larger faceless form loomed over the smaller one like a dark, frail tree. The shorter figure had eyes, a nose and a thin semi circle mouth. Grace had dotted the skin with a red crayon.

"That's beautiful, baby. Is that you and me?"

The child nodded, proud of her handiwork.

"I thought so. That little girl looks just like you. Does she have the measles?"

Grace shook her head. Pointing a chubby finger at her creation, she said, "She doesn't feel good. Her face burns."

Here Come the Janes

Someone got the notion that a black woman's hair contains blood and magic. That's how it started. At first, I tolerated questions about how often I washed my hair, if it was real and even if I could plant a strand and grow my own knotted forest. Although I grew tired of the questions, I preferred them to what happened later, during the Rebellion.

Before the dark time, when it was still safe for us to go outside without wearing scarves, I had a thick, unruly mop of hair that stretched down to the middle of my back. Black as lust and just as heavy, my hair attracted stares as I walked the streets of L.A. It wasn't unusual for a lady standing behind me in line at the organic market to ask, "Can I touch your hair?" Then, without waiting for my reply, she would pet the glossy strands as if stroking a dying seal right before the club descends. Looking back, I'd gladly endure those tiny acts of boldness than suffer the outright plunder that occurred in the end.

I was raised by my grandmother, Lucille Jones, and in her own way, she tried to prepare me for what was to come.

"Baby, your hair is tougher than uncooked collards," she would say as I fidgeted between her knees, trying to escape the straightening comb. That metal tool symbolized heat, pain and silky hair.

"Nana, I don't want collard green hair," I told her. "Nobody likes it."

"Oh, they like it, Thessie. They just don't know it yet. But one day, they'll be hungry for it."

The Marcel wand clicked its complicated metallic language as I squirmed.

I rarely saw my grandmother's hair. She was a laundress, and few strands escaped the indigo scarf she wore as she washed other people's clothes. She swapped the sweaty head wrap for a clean one as she climbed into bed for the night. Even though she took the Marcel wand to my head once a week, melting my kinks into benign curls, she also taught me that that nothing on this earth is more powerful than the coil, than the tapestry of knots springing from a black woman's scalp, defying even layers of lye, and years and years of fire. I often walked around our small Baltimore row house with a burned ear or scalp. Tender-headed, Nana called me. That was the term used to shame a girlchild who was not yet immune to the weekly assault on her locks. In time, I became immune, but then the first Jane snaked into my house to assault me in a far more vicious way.

I was showering at the time, watching bubbles skitter around the drain as I rinsed. My thirtieth birthday was a month away, and I was trying to decide whether to continue straightening my hair or to go *au naturel*. After a lifetime of hot oil, curling irons and pressing combs, most black women have an uneasy relationship with heat, and I was no different. Follicles have memory. Every two weeks, my hair resisted the illusion of silky straightness, preferring instead to return to its original spiral.

A rumbling sound in the living room interrupted this eternal inner struggle. *Just my luck to be naked and wet when an earthquake strikes*, I thought as the water drained away. In the silence, the screen over the fireplace jangled. I lived alone in a rented two-bedroom house in North Hollywood. But I was no longer alone. I heard something slither across the hardwood floor in the other room.

I climbed out of the shower and wrapped myself in a towel, trying to still my shaking hands. I didn't own a gun, had no knife to protect myself. The only weapon I had was a rat-tail comb lying on the sink. I had used it earlier to detangle my hair, and a few strands remained in the teeth. Holding it business end first, I tiptoed to the bedroom door. It was a flimsy weapon, but I would be able to gouge out an attacker's eye. If I could find the courage.

I opened the door to the sound of coughing. That low wheezing noise somehow heartened me – an intruder with a handicap. I leapt into the room and onto a sooty figure sprawled by the fireplace. Hands reached for my throat, and we wrestled so wildly my towel was nearly ripped off in the struggle, but then a muffled voice cried, "Stop stabbing me, Thessie."

The prowler knew my name. The comb clattered to the floor as I pulled myself up and turned on the lamp. I knew the voice. It belonged to Jane, my coworker from the real estate firm. She lay in a blackened heap by the mantle.

"Jane? Are you okay?" I tried to keep my voice steady as I helped her to her feet.

She nodded, spitting soot. Her blue eyes were raccooned with dust. I glimpsed the pinkness of her scalp through yellow hair that hung down like rotting twine. Yeah, it was Jane.

"What in the world are you doing here?"

"I saw the light on in your bathroom, and I figured you were taking a shower ..." she began, wiping ash from her face.

"And?"

"And ... I just wanted to see what your hair looks like when it's wet."

She stared down at her dusty stilettos. *How she managed to climb up on the roof in those, I'll never know.* Jane was slim and stylish, the kind of woman who could throw on jeans and a button-down shirt and look sexy. But now her black dress was torn and streaked with ash. And her face, usually frozen into a toothy smile, twitched with desperation. Water from my hair dripped onto the hardwood floor, mixing with her soot, forming murky tears.

Few people outside of my immediate family and my beautician have ever seen my hair wet. Whenever I go to Venice Beach or Malibu, I prefer to sit on the sand, far from the briny fingers of the Pacific. Each rainy day poses a threat greater than traffic jams and slippery roads. At the slightest bit of moisture, my hair swells into a thundercloud of naps, taking hours to tame. Why did Jane want to see me at my most vulnerable?

I said, "You broke into my house to observe my grooming habits?"

Her eyes regarded me slyly, like the whisper of a ribbon being pulled from someone's locks. Jane and I had been working together as research assistants for three years. We were close enough to grab a latte on our afternoon break, but she'd never been to my house. I rarely had visitors. What the hell was she doing in my place? I sat on my coffee table, waiting for her reply.

"I just love the texture of it. It seems so strong and healthy." She reached out to touch me, but then thought better of it, wiping off her dress instead.

Beneath the smudges, her skinny legs were bloodless as cauliflower.

I wasn't sure who to call – the police or mental health services. As I twirled wet tendrils around my finger trying to decide, Jane looked up, like a dog waiting for scraps to fall from the table. She held out a hand, and I stared at the bulging map of blue veins.

"Can I touch your hair?"

"It's late, Jane. I think you should go now."

I no longer cared about the jumble of firewood and dirt on the floor or the reason she gave for breaking into my home. I didn't care what happened to her. I just wanted her out. But she made no move toward the door, and I swallowed the ball of nervousness in my throat. Maybe I did need a weapon, The plastic comb lay in a puddle on the floor, and we both stared at it. A clump of woolly hair seemed to be growing from the teeth.

"It seems so healthy. So full of life," she said. Touching her own hair, which was stringy and thinning, she said, "Mine has never been that strong."

I'd had enough. I rose, making sure the towel was tight against my body, and backed toward the front door. "You really need to leave now."

"Alright, I'll go," she said with a sigh. "Sorry about the mess. Maybe I can ask my housekeeper to come –"

"Goodnight, Jane."

She bent down to retrieve her clutch from where it landed near the coffee table. As quick as a fox, she pounced on the comb, pulling strands from the tines. Her blue eyes gleamed.

"See you tomorrow, Thessie,"

Her stilettos clacked as she passed me, clutching the wiry strands of my hair. She walked down the driveway and into the night. Like a snail, she left a sooty sludge behind her.

After Jane shimmied down my chimney, I avoided her at work, busying myself with the mundane tasks of setting appointments or researching properties for my boss, Brent. Sure, I thought about going to H.R. or letting Brent know about Jane, but I didn't want to be seen as the angry black woman at the job. After all, I was the good one – the one who showed up on time, stayed late and never complained. And besides, who would believe me? One thing was certain though; I would never be able to grab a coffee with Jane again. How can you possibly strike up a casual conversation with a lady who steals your hair?

Around the same time, I noticed a change in my other female coworkers. I was the only black woman in the office, and we didn't really mingle, exchanging a few words in passing about clothes or difficult clients. But as I sat at my desk, I heard murmuring behind me. Two or three women huddled at the entrance of my cubicle, staring at my back with their Botoxed eyes. Another time, engrossed in paperwork, I felt someone's breath on my neck. It was my coworker Becky, a slim redhead with big teeth. She dropped a folder on my desk, then her fingertips trailed along my shoulder, plucking something from my blouse. I wasn't sure if I was imagining things, but I rearranged my cubicle so my back was no longer exposed.

I tried to get on with my life, but a few weeks later, I ran into Jane, or should I say, she cornered me in the restroom. After peeking under the stalls to make sure I was alone, I locked the bathroom door and studied my reflection. My birthday had come and gone, and I decided, once again, to straighten my hair. My stylist, Myaisha, cut my bangs on a slant that covered my left eye and half of my cheek. "It makes you look sexy and mysterious," she said as I sat in her salon chair at Sexy Shearz, but I didn't feel pretty. All I saw was a big nose and big pores. Stubby lashes bordering hazel eyes. Well, I did like the color of my eyes. They're the same brownish-gold color as Nana's. I hated myself for not being strong enough to go *au naturel*. I hated that I had to be tough as uncooked collards to love my hair. I felt guilty after leaving the salon, the smell of burnt hair still lingering in my nostrils and on my jacket as I headed to my car on Melrose, guilty for wanting locks that blew in the wind, that could be tucked behind an ear. But nappy hair wasn't sexy enough. At least not in L.A.

Standing in the mirror, I fussed over my bangs with a new rat-tail comb. The other one ended up in my trashcan. I had nightmares of Jane's veiny hand gripping the narrow handle, raking my scalp until it bled, until the weary follicles surrendered their bounty.

In the mirror, I saw a blur of movement over my shoulder. As I turned to watch, two shiny red pumps dropped to the floor of a stall. The door creaked open, and Jane's coy eyes met my own.

"Are you crazy?" I tried to keep the tremor from my voice. "Why are you hiding out in the bathroom?"

"You've been avoiding me, Thessie." Her voice was stern, unlike the smooth giggles that usually punctuated her Valley Girl twang. "I figured this was the only way to catch up with you. Are you mad at me?"

My hip hit the edge of the sink, and water seeped through my silk blouse. My fingers tightened around the comb.

"I'm not mad. I've just been busy."

Jane flashed a smile, bovine and wanting. Was it my imagination, or were her eyes a deeper shade of blue? The lines in her face that she always complained made her look five years older than thirty-two (I thought ten) had vanished. Her yellow hair was thick and glossy. I could no longer see the pinkness of her scalp. She met my gaze, her fingers twitching at her side.

"Let me touch your hair, Thessie."

"I've got to get back to work." I unlocked the door, trying to keep my hand steady.

I'd gotten so paranoid about the other women, I half expected to see them out there in the corridor, in their form-fitting dresses and peep-toe shoes, blocking my escape. But no one stood there. I glanced back at Jane. She crouched by the sink, her skirt sweeping the floor, as she plucked strands from the dirty tiles.

I quit my job the next day.

I couldn't stomach the thought of Jane crawling around my cubicle when I left work for the evening, hunting for more wisps of my hair. If she were foraging in my hamper, sniffing my dirty panties, she couldn't have violated me more. And whatever the nature of her hunger, it seemed to have infected the other women at the firm. It wouldn't be long until they started stealing strands as well. If they weren't already.

No longer able to afford my rent, I moved to a studio apartment in Inglewood, at the intersection of Heliotrope and Maple. The main boulevard was filled with chicken shacks and check-cashing centers. Beauty supply shops with Korean proprietors advertised "100 percent Indian hair" next door to the ninety-nine cent fish joint, which always had a line stretching out the door and down the block. No women in designer skirts and $600 shoes would follow me here. So I thought. But I was wrong. It was too late by then. It was as if Jane had cloned herself. Everywhere I went, I felt a predatory gaze on my back. Ladies still fondled my locks as I stood in line at the market, but as I combed my hair in the mirror afterwards, I noticed something frightening. There were jagged sections throughout, as if something had been gnawing on my hair.

Although my apartment was on the second floor and I had a deadbolt lock installed, I didn't feel any safer. As I rode the metro to job interviews, I examined the heads of other black women. I noted the broken strands, the helpless scalps peering out through bushy manes. I wondered if they too felt fingertips brushing their shoulders before some pale woman asked: "Can I touch your hair?"

After a while, I wouldn't leave my apartment without wearing a scarf. I still hadn't found a new job and lived off my savings. When I ventured out to stock up on groceries or to wash my clothes, I noticed there were fewer and fewer black women on the streets, their absence shouting from beauty salons and nail shops and swap meets. The few that I encountered were similarly scarved. We shot each other furtive glances. "What's happening to us?" our expressions said. For most of us, style is sacred, a way of worshipping a fickle deity for bestowing texture that is both curse and blessing. The intricate braids, layered coifs and towering curls provide all the drama of high praise; but the showy styles had been silenced.

Even though we were being careful, the Janes grew violent in their hair lust.

One afternoon, while riding the bus through downtown L.A., I happened upon a scene of what would later become routine brutality. Three Janes attacked a woman on the sidewalk. Although the victim looked to be nearly 300 pounds, the predators, with their long lustrous hair and thin arms, easily held her down, ripping knotty chunks from her scalp as she screamed. People gathered in the doorways of taquerías and jewelry shops to watch the assault, but no one tried to stop it. The bus continued its slow drift through streets clogged with fast food wrappers and homeless people, leaving behind the wails of that wounded woman. I pictured the bloody roots, the arc of pain that shot through the woman's head, and tightened my silk scarf.

Every morning, I scanned the newspapers but I never read about that incident. I never read once about a Jane being arrested for the rape of our coils. I had to learn about the ongoing violence underground.

"Wanda's Palace of Curls closed up last week. It's a bad time," my neighbor Philomena told her friend as they stood by the washers in the laundromat. She was in her fifties, and she kept tucking in strands that escaped her faded black scarf. Philomena knew all the gossip, usually right as it was happening. I took my time folding clothes, trying to confirm what I already suspected.

"Ain't that the truth. Look at this." Her friend lifted her shaggy wig to reveal a swath of scalp dotted with keloids. While Philomena gasped, I grimaced, turning back to my shirts.

"Whoo, that looks painful. Was it them?"

"You don't even have to ask."

"Too bad you can't go to the hospital," another woman chimed in. She closed her dryer with a thud.

"But did you hear what they did to Wanda?" Philomena tried to draw the attention back to herself. By then, several women raised their heads to listen, no longer bothering with the pretense of folding clothes. Satisfied that she had an audience, she continued. "One day when Wanda was taking out the trash at the salon, up pops two or three of those things. Well, Wanda had her head wrapped tight – you know she been wearing that press 'n curl for the past fifteen years – so they couldn't get to it, but they grabbed the bags she was taking out to the bins. She ran inside and locked the door, but she watched from the window. Said they tore right into that trash just digging out hair."

"Thieves," someone said, and a murmur went up in the room. I grabbed my basket, nodded to the women and then headed back to my studio.

As I put my clothes away into my dresser, I thought about why no one was reporting it. Maybe because our hair had so little value to begin with that its plunder could hardly be classified as a crime. I thought of all the ads and billboards for taming black hair, de-frizzing it, making it silkier, more manageable, more human. But it was obviously of value to the women who were … feeding on it. I never knew what exactly they did with the looted hair. *Maybe they're making a cosmic voodoo doll to zap us of our strength,* I joked to myself. I untied my scarf to give my scalp a chance to breathe, raking my fingers through the stubby strands. All I knew was that as our enemies grew bolder, we were growing brittle, like palm fronds littering a road.

By November, a group of women in Inglewood decided to put a stop to the violence against our locks. It's been said that real revolution in Los Angeles takes place south of Wilshire Boulevard, unlike in The Valley or on the Westside, where the major protests involve pesticides or puppies. One evening as the sun was setting, I gathered with seven other women in an abandoned beauty shop on Heliotrope. As we snuck up the alley and broke in through the back door, I noticed that on the wall behind the salon, someone spray painted "Beware angry black woman" in watery red letters. The place smelled of strawberries and bleach, and we coughed as we walked across a tile floor thick with dust. Several lavender smocks were flung across stations, as if their owners had ripped them off before fleeing. I wiped off a salon chair with my sleeve, and the other women did the same. In the growing darkness, we discussed strategies to combat the Janes.

"We could go bald," said an earnest young woman named Daphne. She rubbed the birthmark on her cheek. "Just chop it all off, so there's nothing left for those bitches to steal."

The rest of us fidgeted in our chairs, avoiding her eyes. I stared at the plate glass window. The name of the salon was written in a semicircle of peeling gold letters: Pearline's Elegant Tresses. Even though we were losing our hair at the hands of others, willful baldness terrified us. We had endured a lifetime of barrettes, lye and cooked flesh in the pursuit of an elusive beauty, memories not easily borne away. But a thing is never truly loved until it's threatened. The onslaught of hair-lusting zombies that the law couldn't stop made us love our roots more.

Sharice, a single mom, suggested that we buy football helmets, but we laughed at the idea. "My head is big enough already," said Velma, a woman with a scar under her eye who looked as if she could move the building if she wanted to. A helmet meant hiding our faces, and I wasn't ready to do that. No one was.

I was the one who thought of fire. Maybe because I was the daughter of smoke and heat, and the Marcel wand's dual barrels of iron had been seared into my consciousness since I was old enough to sit between my Nana's knees. But if a black woman's hair contained blood and magic, then, despite our ragged demeanors, we possessed the strength to reclaim what was rightfully ours. The magic that the Janes leeched from our locks was the same magic that would destroy them.

"We need to lure them out with this," I said, tugging on a hank of hair that had escaped its silken prison, "and burn them."

"Girl, I can't do that. I've never hurt anyone in my life," said Ava, readjusting the cowboy hat she wore on her tiny head.

"Aren't they hurting us? We have to send a message to the Janes that they can no longer get away with this theft."

It was the first time that I had publically named the thing I feared, but I could tell by the women's expressions that it was just the right term. A few scattered handclaps met my little speech. I was terrified, but proud. It was the first time in my life that I had taken a stand, and wouldn't you know, "Survival of the Tresses!" would be my battle cry? Beneath my head wrap, the unruly mop that once stretched to the middle of my back now hung in uneven wisps, only as far as my collarbone. The Janes could steal the rest of my hair, but I wouldn't let them leech my DNA without a fight. With the memory of Nana's gnarled fingers on my scalp, I was reminded that one day everyone would crave collard green hair. Maybe my grandmother had been planting seeds for this very time.

Daphne was the first to rise. About nineteen or twenty, she only came up to my shoulder, but her spunk made her the tallest woman in the room. She lifted the Lakers cap from her head and dropped it on the floor. Her reddish-brown highlights were clumpy and brittle, but whether the damage was caused by the Janes or just by chemicals, I couldn't tell. Around the room, scarves, baseball caps and church hats were being yanked from heads. A big-breasted woman named Serita peeled off wefts of synthetic hair that were glued to her real hair and tossed the artificial locks to the floor.

"I'm free," she said. "No more weave."

Khadija, who was close to my age – thirty-two – sucked her teeth. "Serita, if the Janes disappear tomorrow, I know just where to find you."

Nervous laughter filled the salon. It felt good to be among friends and to finally have a plan. This was the beginning of the Rebellion. If I ever survived it, I vowed never to straighten my hair again. Several women made similar pledges.

In the waning fall light, we solidified our plans. We would take exactly one week to collect our supplies: gasoline, rags, bottles, lighters. We would set shaggy traps throughout Los Angeles, and when the Janes sniffed out what they thought was easy prey, we would ignite them. I felt anxious. I had never taken a life. I hated to kill spiders or water bugs, and I was certain none of my comrades had ever laid their hands on another person in violence, but the Janes had become inhuman in their lust. It was either their survival or ours.

As a visible testimony to our sisterhood and to our mission, we burned our scarves and hats in a rusted sink, where Pearline or other stylists once shampooed hair. I wished the owner could see that her deserted storefront shop on Heliotrope, where women once read magazines under hooded dryers and preened before mirrors, was the birthplace of a revolt. We walked each other to our respective homes to make sure that we made it back safely. Later, as I sat on my bed with a cup of herbal tea, I wondered what I was getting into. Even locked inside the walls of my studio, I knew that I wasn't truly safe. None of us were. Not that night, and certainly not in the rampage to come.

That night, I dreamed of Jane.

I was washing my hair in the shower, and the smell of lavender filled the tiny bathroom. My locks were long and knotty, and the texture felt good against my spine. As I leaned forward to rinse out the shampoo, the water flowed crimson. I tried to stop the sticky spray, but both hands became tangled in my hair. I tugged and tugged, but my fingers turned into stalks, like dark trees taking root in my scalp.

From the living room, there came a rumbling sound, as if the earth beneath my building had cracked open. Something slithered across the hardwood floor.

I slid to the bottom of the tub, my hands still knotted in my hair. A steady red stream from the showerhead pelted my belly and legs.

I tried to scream, but could only whimper. Urine mingled with the blood filling the tub, a slimy reservoir. The bathroom door creaked open, and the stench of smoke and charred flesh overpowered the lavender scent of my shampoo.

A pale hand streaked with ash groped along the wall and then its owner came into view. Jane, my Jane. Her blue eyes met mine. Beneath the soot, her face was seared. Flame had eaten away at her nose, and something dark and glistening wriggled in the cavities. Her skin hung down in blackened strips, falling on my floral rug. Despite my fear, I couldn't look away from her hair. It was shiny and thick and hung to her waist in monstrous yellow curls.

She pulled back the sliding door of the shower and stood over me. Soot sifted down onto my skin. I hunched over onto my side, my fingers still plaited into my tresses as a voice whispered, "Can I touch your hair?"

A hand fell on my shoulder.

Bolting upright in my bed, I gripped the pillow. In the darkness, I could make out the easel near my closet door. I never had a knack for painting, but during the long idle days that I spent in hiding, I did watercolors – simple scenes of lakes and fruit bowls. Something to calm me. Adjusting the towel that I pinned to my head nightly, I rose and turned on the lights. I peered behind the bamboo room divider, half expecting to see her there. But I was alone.

Opening the blinds, I stared out the window at the street below. There was an ad for oil sheen above the liquor store across the street. The familiar pink bottle, a beauty staple from my childhood, taunted me. *No need for styling gels and smelly elixirs now*. It was after 4:00 in the morning, and the block was nearly empty. Two men walked past my patio and disappeared into the alley behind the building. I wondered why they were immune to the Janes' attacks. We shared the same hair texture. I envied these men their freedom, their ability to walk the streets unscarved and unmolested, but maybe it was only a matter of time before the Janes came for them.

With a sigh, I jiggled the handle on the sliding glass door to make sure that it was locked. As I did, something trapped between the outer door and the jamb caught my eye. Strands of hair, long and flaxen, flapped in the breeze.

On Thanksgiving Eve, Los Angeles burned. Eight women armed with makeshift bombs reduced entire buildings to ash.

The morning of our attack, we gathered at Pearline's Elegant Tresses to stockpile our supplies. Daphne pulled a pair of scissors from her purse, and we formed a circle, snipping locks from the head in front of us to provide the traps that would lure the Janes. My hair was now no longer than the second joint of my finger, the shortest it had ever been. As I gazed at myself in a dust-streaked mirror, I was pleased with the renegade staring back at me. For the first time in my life, I felt beautiful.

A slim woman named Ophelia, who had been a ceramics teacher in Watts before going into hiding, fashioned handmade helmets for us. These weren't the kind that would hide our faces. The clay headdresses swirled with yellow and purple paint. They were inlaid with crystals, which Ophelia said would protect our minds and spirits and ward off our tormentors. We donned our new headgear with joy, feeling like warriors.

Beverly Hills was our first target. The area stank of perverted glamour, a musk both feared and desired. It dripped from the couture boutiques, cosmetics stores and designer jewelry shops that dotted Robertson Boulevard. Before the Janes disrupted my life, I rarely ventured to this side of town. It seemed that even the mannequins with their pouty sneers and flowing yellow locks had more right to be there than I did. But now, in the middle of the night, we sprinkled strands along the sidewalk, like priestesses performing last rites. The stores were all closed, so it was less likely that we'd harm any innocent bystanders.

With two women to a car, we parked in the shadows, waiting. I shared an old Buick with Daphne, and the smell of gasoline from the bottles in the backseat was cloying. She sat behind the wheel, scraping polish from her nails. From time to time, she scanned the street.

"Are you scared?" I asked, watching as she tried to steady her hand.

"Yeah, but it feels worse to be in hiding. Just wish things could go back to normal."

"What were you doing before all this?" I asked.

"Going to cosmetology school to do hair," she said with a wry laugh. "No need for a license now."

"There will be, one day," I said, not sure if I really believed this. I glanced at the brick façade of a boutique. Two bald mannequins stared back.

"I hope so. I didn't move to L.A. to hide out. Shoot, I'm young. I want to date, go clubbing. I'll be twenty-one in a few months, and I was looking forward to going to Vegas with my girls, taking my first shot of tequila. Legally, that is."

"You think the Janes are in Vegas, not just in L.A.?"

"The Janes are everywhere – at least that's what my people say in Philly. But not as many as there are here. Women are weaker on the West Coast. They don't stick together. Lots of lonely black chicks in L.A.," Daphne said. "I don't think the sisters back home – at least not in Philly – would stand for someone stealing their hair."

"Especially not in Baltimore. They would have rioted by now." I thought of the stiff beehive styles that put any peacock's plume to shame. We both laughed, then Daphne grew quiet as headlights shone into the Buick. We both slid down in our seats until the car passed.

"We're supposed to be the strong ones," she said finally. She adjusted her helmet, her nails scraping the rose quartz. "How did we let them get so out of control?"

"Maybe they've been transformed by hate – theirs and ours."

As soon as the words left my lips, I thought I really understood Nana's saying about collard greens. I saw our enemies feasting on something powerful, but bitter, ingesting the pungent strength springing from our scalp, a force we tried to douse daily.

"Whatever they are, I just want them gone," Daphne said. "I'm tired of looking over my shoulder."

As if summoned, a figure crept down the sidewalk on all fours.

Then another appeared.

And another.

The Janes.

Daphne and I ducked down in our seats, reaching for each other's hand. I wondered if our sisters parked up the block felt the same greasy fear. Peeking in the rearview mirror, I glimpsed what I had suspected all along.

The Janes were eating our hair.

All of them wore pencil skirts, their uniform of choice. All had yellow hair hanging down in shiny tangles. One had locks so long and matted they swept the sidewalk when she stood, and she nearly tripped in her heels. She held the woolly strands up to the streetlight before they vanished into her mouth.

Something flipped in me. I was angry at my helplessness, angry that we were being hunted. What would our enemies do when the last follicle was defiled, when the blood vessels constricted and our scalps smoothed over, as unyielding as stone? Would our lashes be next? The downy lining of our nostrils? Or worse, the weedy hair of our vulvas?

I hurled the first firebomb.

I saw the golden tongue of flame before I heard the bottle shatter on the sidewalk. A matted-haired monster was engulfed by the blaze, and the stench of cooked flesh reached me through the open window. I turned my head, but not before my eyes met her blue ones, and in them lay a mixture of fury and something else, perhaps relief. Daphne gunned the engine of the old car. She swung a U-turn at the end of the block, clipping a parked Benz with a boot on the tire. I handed her a whiskey bottle filled with fuel. She lit it and tossed the bomb at a group of Janes across the street.

"Give me another one," she said, high on her own fear.

I passed the bottle to her. She set fire to the dangling cloth before hurling it through the plate glass of the couture boutique.

"That's for messing up my bob!" she yelled out the open window.

Flame blackened the brick façade of the boutique and would soon dissolve the sneers of the mannequins. Feeling the release, I laughed as the inferno on Robertson raged. An explosion sounded up the street. I turned to see Serita and Velma, who'd been parked in a silver Honda, tossing bottles at the monsters. From another car, Ophelia's thin arm, laden with handmade bracelets, shot out like an arrow, and another yellow-haired beast wailed as flames licked her body. My joy soon shifted to sorrow, and I began to cry. Through my tears, I saw two Janes overtaking our car. Lighting the rag dangling from the top of my makeshift bomb, I hurled the glass at them.

"That's for petting my hair while I was in line at the organic market!"

"That's for asking how often I wash my hair!"

"That's for asking if my hair is real!"

"That's for asking if you can touch my hair!"

"Can I touch your hair?"

"Can I touch your hair?"

"Can I touch your hair?"

We shrieked as we sped down the block and away from the sickening sweet scent of burning flesh.

Brentwood was next on our hit list, but we never made it.

Before the flashing lights overtook Daphne's Buick, I was still taking in the eight or so Janes we had destroyed, about one for me and every one of my comrades. We headed west toward a city already infamous for a bloodbath on Bundy.

"What's our next move?" Daphne asked. Her hand shook as she steered.

"Brentwood, remember? Khadija said we'd meet up there."

"No, I mean after tonight."

"I can't even think about the future right now," I said, leaning back into my seat. "We got rid of some, but what about tomorrow? We still can't leave our homes without scarves. We're still not free."

"Scary as hell, but it feels good." Daphne turned on the radio, and the mournful strings from a folk song filled the car.

"Yes, it does," I said.

"Like we won something."

As we left the tree-lined expanse of Beverly Hills and entered Westwood we heard the familiar whine of sirens.

"Damn. What do I do now?" Daphne said, glancing in her rearview.

"Don't pull over, unless you want to explain the explosives in the backseat."

She gave me a tiny smile. "Maybe we can tell the cops we're just protecting ourselves."

My helmet hit the headrest as Daphne floored it. We raced down Wilshire, tires squealing. The bottles in the backseat tinkled a frantic melody as we ran stoplights, swinging the Buick down dark side streets. The car stank of spilled gasoline, and I knew that if the police didn't catch us, we would probably end up ablaze. But even that option was somehow more bearable than ending up in the hands of the Janes.

The propeller of a helicopter sliced through the night, and a gash of light from the sky illuminated the road in front of us.

"It sucks that my mug shot will be broadcast on TV with my hair looking all jacked up," Daphne said. Her lips twisted to the side in a smirk, but her voice trembled beneath the bravado. "What will my people in Philly think?"

"That L.A. went to your head?"

As we passed a house with an American flag on the porch, its fly end shuddering in the breeze, an old dog appeared from behind a parked car. He looked as startled as we did. Tires whined as Daphne swerved to avoid hitting the mutt. I closed my eyes as she bore down on a telephone pole. The last thing I remember was being thrown from the open window. There was an explosion and my head struck something metallic, the clay helmet clanging as the inner darkness spread.

I awaken to the pulse of an EKG machine, which my groggy mind mistakes for sirens. I try to sit up, but a fierce burning in my ribs forces me back against the pillow. Slowly opening my heavy eyelids, my gaze settles on a man in a police uniform reading a newspaper by my bed. On my sharp inhalation, he looks up, his bushy eyebrows knit together in a frown.

"Welcome back, Sleepyhead," he says, standing over me. It is only then that I notice my right arm handcuffed to the bedpost. An IV drips from the other arm. I turn away from the officer, focusing instead on the bag of clear fluid keeping me alive.

"You've been out for a while, girlie," he says, ignoring my snub. "Shame about your friend. That helmet thing you had on probably saved you from brain damage ... or worse. But brain damage is the least of your worries now."

He steps outside, leaving the newspaper on a tray stand beside my bed. I can't look at the paper. Daphne is gone, and who knows what happened to my other comrades? It hurts to breathe, let alone move or pick up a newspaper and read. I already know what the paper says, waxing on about the murderous rioters who tried to burn down the high-rent district, never mentioning the women who were hungry for our hair.

I'm still gazing at the IV bag with its steady drip when the slither of shoes down the corridor breaks my reverie. Sensing a presence outside the door, I turn to face my visitor, wincing from the pain.

A nurse stands in the entryway. She walks into the room, stilettos clicking. Her legs are shapely, but as pallid as bone beneath her fitted skirt. A white cap sits jauntily atop a tangle of lustrous blonde hair.

There is no blood and magic. There is no blood and magic. The EKG machine thumps a staccato rhythm as she hovers over my bed. I don't even bother reaching for the call button, for I know there is no help in the hospital, for I know that I will probably summon a cadre of Janes to the floor.

The nurse stares down at me, a smile crinkling the corners of her sly blue eyes. One veiny hand grips a rat-tail comb.

"Time to do your hair," she says.

Textured

Capricia Jones kept a black plastic bag filled with hair in the bottom of her closet. It was the anonymous type of bag in which Korean proprietors of inner city stores packaged the hair that lined their walls like artifacts from a museum of forgotten beauty. Those proprietors knew black women didn't like to be seen carrying someone else's tresses through the parking lot to their car, and the bag provided a certain masked dignity.

This particular bag in the bottom of Capricia's closet was home to a bundle of straight hair, with a piece of black thread still clinging to the weft; a hank of curly reddish-brown hair, and a weft of kinky hair that she bought for those occasions when she was feeling particularly bohemian. Each different texture transformed her. When she wore her hair curly, she felt like a biracial Valley Girl – although she lived in Koreatown and both of her parents were black. She loved getting caught in the rain, or going to the sauna or having the white women at the production company where she worked stop her in the bathroom to say, "Look how it bounces. Can I touch it?"

When Capricia sat in the salon chair at Sexy Shearz to have the straight hair sewn in, she felt very feminine, accentuating her store-bought tresses with glittery headbands and butterfly barrettes. She wore white button-down shirts, so anyone watching from afar would notice the length, would see the contrast of the black hair against the white shirt.

The kinky hair she wore least of all. It drew attention to her thick lips and chubby nose, but since more and more black women were wearing their hair free of heat and chemicals, she didn't want to get left out of the trend. So she tried to spruce up the knotty chin-length locks with flowers and head wraps and accentuated the look with a peasant top so people would view her hair as part of the ensemble, a nappy performance piece.

But Capricia was in crisis. One day, she severed the last thread connecting any trace of artificial hair to her scalp and dropped the cluster in the bag to join its sisters. As she slicked back her thinning hair – which was shoulder-length, permed and in need of a good trim – the textured locks began to war amongst themselves.

Won't be long before she wears me again, said the straight hair. I make her feel pretty and sexy.

I make her feel like she could be any race – or at least mixed with white or Latino, the curly hair chimed in. She gets, like, way more play from black men when I'm around.

You can have the brothers. White men notice me the most, and she's trying to keep her options open.

Who do you attract? they asked the kinky hair.

I'm not trying to attract anyone, Kinky Hair said. I just enhance her natural beauty.

She doesn't have any, Straight Hair said. She's average without me flowing down her back.

She's way homely without my bouncy ringlets framing her face.

She's invisible without hair that blows in the wind.

Dude, I blow in the wind too.

I'm human.

I'm human, too. And I cost more.

The kinky hair said nothing. She believed she was more intelligent than her textured counterparts, more conscious. But she was saddened because Capricia had only worn her for a short time. I have lain close to the real hair that springs from her scalp, and we are from the same root.

The straight hair was silent too, thinking her own thoughts. She had been with Capricia the longest, saw her change from a plain production assistant to a goddess. Her shapeless dresses and flats were replaced with miniskirts and stilettos. People often asked if she was an actress or model. Capricia just smiled and toyed with her hair or tucked it behind an ear and answered, "No, I came to L.A. to write."

She'd be writing all day long – at the check-cashing joint on Heliotrope Boulevard – if not for my intervention, Straight Hair said. She knew the glamour that lay in her dead, processed strands, the ephemeral beauty that blew in and out of Capricia's life like autumn leaves.

Curly Hair fidgeted in the bag, trying to separate herself from the other textures. She didn't like Kinky Hair's coarse strands mingling with her own, and Straight Hair smelled musty, like rancid cocoa butter. Although Curly Hair hadn't been with her owner as long as Straight Hair had, she knew she was the more valuable purchase. Capricia felt exotic when she wore her, often twirling the silky ringlets around her finger as she spoke with the twang of white girl stoner. She knew that growing up, Capricia wanted to be mixed. Anything but black. The girl ran home from school one day when she was eight asking her mother if she was Chinese because the kids in her third-grade class teased her about the slope of her eyes. I make her feel better than she is, less invisible. Salesgirls smiled at Capricia in boutiques instead of trailing her through their aisles. They thought she earned more money than she actually did as a PA. Men of all races honked as she walked down Sunset, when they would have otherwise driven by her common-haired self.

She wears classier clothes with me, said Straight Hair.

She's less black with me, Curly Hair said.

She realizes that I'm the most powerful piece she owns because I am the closest to her real texture. I am not processed.

You're synthetic, Straight and Curly said, their violent movements shifting the bag. Straight added, No black woman alive would cut off her real hair for another black woman to wear. Black women are stingy that way, have to hold on to every last strand, no matter how rough it is. But feel me. I was imported from India.

I was imported from Brazil.

Kinky Hair didn't know her person of origin – if she had one. All she remembered was being grouped together with other nappy hairpieces beneath a glass case at the back of the Korean family's storefront on Heliotrope.

But I am the prettiest hair of all because I resemble her roots.

I make her feel like she belongs in L.A.

Dude, she can travel anywhere in the world with me.

I set her free.

The three hairpieces heard a rustling sound. Capricia's pinched cheeks and sunken hazel eyes appeared at the opening of the plastic bag. She sprinkled something thin and prickly onto them and then sealed up the bag again. The hairpieces whimpered, even Kinky Hair, who was used to being tossed aside. They were covered with the strands of their owner's real hair.

The bag had lain in Capricia's bedroom closet for the past nine months. Now she carried it to the kitchen and stuffed it into the garbage can by the fridge. On her way back to her bedroom, she glimpsed her reflection in the mirror over her couch. Her hairdresser, Myaisha, a dimpled brown-skinned woman with a pink-purple mohawk, always said, "Not everyone can rock a teeny weenie afro; you have to have the right shaped face for it." Capricia thought her chin was too long and her nose too big for the cut, but she didn't feel ugly. She hadn't felt her real hair texture in over twenty-two years, since she was ten, right before her mom gave her the kiddie perm that was the portal to years of heat, hot combs and lye. Now she fingered her shorn locks. The wiry coils felt strong and alive, belying the cancer.

Too late to love it. At least she would wear this new texture with pride until her follicles gave up the ghost, as her eyelashes and brows had, until the long-neglected roots finally withered away.

Happy Black Bitches Club

Beware angry black woman
—Graffiti on the side of a beauty salon

The streets of Los Angeles were filled with smiling black women. A happiness epidemic seemed to infect the land of smog and starlets. Women grinned as they were ignored at makeup counters in Sherman Oaks or cut off in traffic on the 405 Freeway. They smiled as they were followed around boutiques on Melrose or called "black bitch!" from passing cars as they power-walked through parks in North Hollywood. They laughed as they jogged up Wilshire, trying to catch the bus as it pulled away from the curb, or as they brushed off catcalls from men loitering outside of liquor stores on Crenshaw.

On rare occasions, one might encounter a woman who wasn't so cheerful. Before the crackdowns, she may have been the silent type, unsmiling and reflective as she went about her day. Such a woman as this was dangerous. The California Anger Patrol slowed as they cruised past these outlaws. Although the offender might flash a smile at the sight of the red-and-black patrol car, a deadened kind of glee, at that point, it was too late. Her true temperament had already registered on the Rage-dar. Depending on the mood of the officer, she might be taken in for questioning or at the very least, given a ticket for Anti-Cheerful Behavior. These encounters often ended in an outburst, for few black women were able to contain their emotions while being harassed. Their eyes lost the veneer of merriment. They cursed. They cried. The lucky ones were taken to jail. The unlucky ones wound up in deprogramming facilities.

Even before her temper was outlawed, Nia Jones was known as one of the brooding ones. As proof of this, her mother would open her wallet and pull out the picture of a brown-skinned tot with uneven pigtails and pursed lips, her hazel eyes narrowed in boredom. Now twenty-seven, Nia found it hard to mask those streaks of malaise. It was hard for her to smile when she wasn't happy, even if her freedom depended on the outward appearance of joy. Nia's mother begged her to get diagnosed for a mental health disorder. "The authorities'll understand if you're clinically depressed or bipolar," Loretta Jones said. "At least, you'll have a doctor's note if you get pulled over."

A medical excuse was a paltry weapon against the CAPs, and Nia knew it. She'd read in the *Times* that they were cracking down on mentally ill black women as well. Everyone with a mouth and dark skin was a threat. Yet, amidst this oasis of happy faces, suicide was on the rise. Nia attended church with two women who could no longer endure the policing of their emotions – one hanged herself in her apartment and the other slashed herself out of existence. As she passed the open caskets at their funerals, she noted that the lips of the deceased were arranged in a crooked semi-circle. Even in death, they dared not defy the Rage Patrol.

But black women had to vent in some way, as reckless as the activity was. It was unnatural to think that after decades of being called "angry bitches," "sapphires" and "castrators," a law would force them to tuck away their rage. They devised new ways to stoke their ire, to keep it crackling just beneath the skin. Speakeasies for women of color cropped up in Inglewood and Watts. In these forbidden dens, black women could curse, gripe and even fight, if they could find a partner willing enough or drunk enough to indulge them.

"Sounds like a joint we need to check out," said Nia's friend, Cami, as they drove home from a restaurant in Hollywood one night. Cami was a grad student, and someone had pulled her aside after her Women's Studies class and given her the name of a speakeasy on Heliotrope Boulevard.

"Girl, I'm full and tired. I just want to go home," Nia said as she dragged her fingers through her bobbed hair, hiding the side of her face. She was relieved that they were nearing the on ramp for the 101 Freeway so she could lean back in her seat and relax. Freeway driving provided a certain invisibility that regular street driving did not.

"Let's just go for an hour," Cami said. "A club exclusively for angry black chicks? That's some radical shit."

Nia didn't want to admit that she was afraid. *I don't need to go looking for trouble. I should just go home and write.* But Cami kept taunting her about being too bourgie to go to the hood, so she relented. Thirty minutes later, they cruised past a strip mall on Heliotrope, parking on a darkened street a few blocks away. Nia quickened her steps as she followed Cami down an alley. Her friend was short and heavyset, but she moved with the grace and assurance of a much thinner woman. Nia was afraid of the inner city, especially at night. *Just my luck to be walking down the street, minding my own business, and get shot in a driveby.* It was nearly as frightening as the thought of being raped by some patrolman. She'd heard horror stories of black women who had been fondled or worse by officers who threatened to haul them in on trumped-up rage charges.

"I think this is it," Cami said, pausing at the back door of a brick building with a dusty purple awning.

After Cami gave three short raps on the door, a chipper voice from within said, "Rainbows or unicorns?"

"Sunshine," Cami said.

A woman wearing a yellow head wrap opened the door with a wide grin, as if welcoming them to a potluck. After gazing around to make sure her visitors were alone, she dropped her cheerful pose and led them down a dark hallway. The place smelled as if it had been scoured with salmon. They walked past rusted sinks and faded mirrors. A yellowed poster above a chair featured the smiling eyes of a brown-skinned woman. A lock of hair was strategically placed to cover her plump nose. The lower part of the poster containing her pearly whites had been ripped off. They were in a beauty shop that had not seen clients for many years. The bass of a hip-hop song blared from below, and the floorboards vibrated beneath their feet. Nia and Cami tiptoed down stairs bathed in green light to a basement where twenty or thirty morose black women congregated. It was like a house party without the weed, merriment and testosterone. A two-drink minimum served as an entrance fee, so Cami bought them both a beer. Their host handed them bottles from a red cooler, and they made their way to a love seat in the back of the room.

"Girl, I'm going to have to get lip surgery or something," said a flat-chested woman with dimples. She took a swig of the beer she was balancing on her leg and belched. "It's not natural to smile every day of your life."

A light-skinned woman with copper hair extensions nodded. "I know that's right. Let me tell you what happened to me a few days ago," she said. "This salesgirl saw me standing at the makeup counter, and do you know that heifer kept me waiting for damn near an hour before she brought her blonde butt over to ring up my lipstick?"

"Cracker-ass crackers," someone piped up from a chair next to the love seat. "Just the other day I was –"

But the fair-skinned woman, warming to her tale, refused to cede the floor. "One whole hour!" she repeated. "Now you know a couple of years ago, I would have cussed the bitch out and called her manager to boot, but I just stood there grinning like a fool while she waited on other folks."

"And you know she would have called you an angry black bitch – not to your face, of course."

"I'm still a black bitch. I'm just a happy one now."

Dismayed grunts and knowing sighs sounded around the room, as if the collective dignity of the women had been crushed at the makeup counter. Then Cami chimed in, "Not all of them are cold-hearted."

The two previous speakers glanced at her. Nia nudged her friend in the side, hoping she wouldn't bring down the wrath of this restless tribe. The Anti-Rage law, AR-42b, had fostered a solidarity between black women that Nia hadn't experienced prior to its passage. Before anger became a punishable offense, Nia encountered some truly sullen sisters in her daily travels. There were many solitary black women in Los Angeles. They sprouted up like dark poppies along the side of a highway, their petals drooping from exhaust fumes and years of neglect. Nia passed them on sidewalks and in the malls, at beauty salons and in coffee shops. Sometimes they regarded her hesitant smiles with suspicion or took in her outfit, purse and hair before returning the greeting. They masked their aloneness with sarcasm or attitude.

Their unfriendliness reminded her of the girls she grew up with who laughed at the awkward way she danced at house parties – when she was invited and when she pried herself away from the wall at the beckoning of some sweaty teenage boy – the ones who elbowed each other when it was her turn at the Double Dutch rope. But in the past few years, as soon as stagnant smiles became a way of life for all them, their aloofness gave way to vulnerability. They seemed genuinely relieved to run into other women of color on the street.

Now Cami was about to shatter that unity. She was light-skinned with naturally curly hair, which may have been reason enough for their contempt. Undaunted by the sudden silence, she continued, "Some of them are conscious. A few white women at my school fully own their emotion privilege, and they're lobbying to change the law."

"Lip service," the beer-chugging woman said, and raucous laughter filled the room. "Becky might protest about how the sisters are being treated, but do you see her giving up her right to have a fit in public any time she wants? Nope. See her staging a frown-in or rage-in on our behalf? I didn't think so."

"I'm just saying we need to know who our allies are."

"Y'all are killing my buzz," said a skinny girl standing in the corner, her face swathed in shadows. She seemed to be the only woman not holding a beer or a plastic cup filled with liquor. "I didn't come here to talk about allies or white saviors. I'm mad, and I want to stay that way."

Rage was a current that radiated along the baseboards and crackled up the walls, rivaling the bass of the music. Nia feared a fight would break out, that a woman drunk on thwarted fury would start throwing punches at the nearest target. But someone started clapping to the music. The host cranked up the volume of a Nina Simone song, and several women left their chairs. Nia wasn't familiar with the folk singer's music, but she knew the enlightened thing to do was wiggle in her seat and pretend to sing along. A few others made their way to the middle of the floor to dance with their friends. The seated women raised their arms, urging them on. Then more patrons shimmied on to the dance floor. Cami grabbed Nia's hand, but Nia shook her head, sipping her Corona. She was still terrified to dance in public, the fallout of those failed house parties so many years ago. It occurred to her that as her fellow outlaws swayed and sang under the hot green lights – hooting and laughing as they danced next to each other – they were buoyant, defeating the purpose of the speakeasy.

After several hours of watching the revelers, she and Cami took their leave of the party, which was still in full swing.

"So what did you think of your first speakeasy experience, or speak-harshly, I should say?" Cami asked as they left by the back door of the salon.

"It wasn't as bad as I thought it was going to be. No fights, and I didn't get cussed out."

"I was almost hoping for some drama," Cami said, a smile playing on her thin lips. "My nights are too sterile."

They neared the mouth of the alley and headed down the street. Headlights washed over them. Both women looked up with nervous smiles. But it was only an SUV, reggae blasting as the vehicle sped down the block. They exhaled and continued walking, head down. Night time was a particularly dangerous time to be caught on the streets by the CAPs.

"I don't understand why all black women have to pay for the sins of a few black women," Nia said.

"I don't consider what Sapphire 8 did to be a sin. It was actually an act of bravery, of self-preservation," Cami said.

"Yeah, but if not for their 'bravery,' we wouldn't be penalized for having a temper. And I'm one of the calmest people I know."

Although Nia felt no kinship to that motley group of teachers, students and activists known as Sapphire 8, she was ashamed that she didn't have the courage to stand up for anything she believed in. She just wanted to do her job, collect her paycheck and come home and work on her screenplays. But her basic freedoms were dashed several years ago around the time Sapphire 8 began making headlines. Incensed by what they believed to be a media war against black women – nightly reports on the unmanageability of black women's hair, columns dedicated to professional black women's lack of suitable mates and scientific studies expounding on the unattractiveness of black women – these activists started fighting back.

Adopting the creed: "Real women rage!" Sapphire 8 firebombed news vans from Hollywood to Hawthorne. These anarchists in dreadlocks and afros (and the occasional wig) doused newsstands with fake blood and spray painted Angry Black Woman on the walls of businesses that advertised with their oppressors. For several months, the "Rage Brigade," as they were dubbed by one conservative pundit, was able to evade capture. They might have been able to flee to Cuba and cultivate the next generation of frowning militants, had it not been for Rebecca McGee. A blonde reporter with a penchant for tight sweaters and even tighter smiles, Rebecca had been covering the group's rampages ever since the first C-band dish exploded. During a live broadcast, the newswoman boasted of an exclusive interview with an S8 member, a former ceramics teacher from Watts. But during their on-air chat, the teacher yelled, "Real women rage!" and pulled the detonator on her IED, blasting herself and the intrepid blonde reporter to bits.

Taking a cue from their fallen sister, the remaining seven women of Sapphire 8 sacrificed themselves for the movement. They walked into newspaper offices and TV stations with bombs strapped to their bras. They wanted to leave charred reminders in the very institutions responsible for scorching the collective reputation of black women.

Shortly after the death of S8, copycat groups sprang up in the Midwest, Georgia and New York. Although not as deadly or destructive as their predecessors, these rage brigades shone a national spotlight on the vermin known as black women's anger. Just as September 11 forever branded every keffiyeh-wearing man or burqa-wearing woman as a potential terrorist, after the reign of Sapphire 8, the patriotism of black women was called into question. Black women were frisked as they stepped on to government property and profiled as they pulled their luggage to the curb at the airport. How to deal with this public menace on a wide-scale? Thus, the Anti-Rage laws were born.

"What do you think will happen in the long-term?" Cami asked as they neared the car. Nia disengaged the alarm on her silver Jetta, and they hopped in and locked the doors. "We can't keep our anger bottled up forever. Think we'll see a resurrection of Sapphire 8?"

Nia thought of the smiling corpses in the funeral home. "Every rebellion is squashed eventually," she said, starting the engine.

After dropping Cami off at her apartment in Leimert Park, Nia inserted her Sade CD, crooning along softly with the singer. Certain songs created a soundtrack in her mind. She saw herself dashing through crowded streets, falling into the arms of a laughing lover, all while a silent onlooker applauded. Sometimes she wondered who that onlooker was – Cami? God? Her future self?

Nia signaled for the off-ramp near Universal Studios. "I dream too much," she said, "That's my problem."

She gazed at the billboards on the side of the freeway. Monster flicks and romantic comedies. When she first moved from Pennsylvania to Los Angeles four years ago, she dreamed of becoming a screenwriter and penned four scripts that weren't too shabby. But her hopes of selling them had faded. After the passage of AR-42b, serious roles for African-American women, already paltry to begin with, began vanishing altogether. The actresses who did work regularly were offered parts as buffoons or smiling mammies in low-rent comedies. Cami joked that it was only a matter of time before the studios resorted to blackface again. Biracial actresses, who looked more white than black, could always find work. Nia knew several mixed-race women who passed as white to avoid any confrontation with the Rage Patrol. But not Cami, the daughter of a Mexican lawyer and a black nurse. Although her hair was wavy and her skin the color of hominy grits, Cami was definitely a race woman.

Nia was a few minutes away from her apartment in North Hollywood when she heard the dizzying song of sirens behind her. Her heart raced, though she knew she had done nothing wrong.

"Just stay calm," she said aloud, as if assuring a nervous passenger. She slowed, pulling over to the curb. "Could just be a regular cop car, and they're probably answering another call."

But the cruiser pulled up behind her, its baleful white light illuminating her car. In the rearview mirror, she saw the red hood of the patrol car. Nia reached into the glove compartment for her registration, trying to keep the document from slipping out of her fingers. There were few cars out at 1:00 on a Wednesday morning, but at least she was parked on a main thoroughfare. There was little chance that she would be sexually assaulted in a well-lit residential neighborhood. Or so she hoped.

The officer took his time walking to the car. Nia reminded herself not to look directly into his face, not to speak unless spoken to, not to question, only comply. She had never been stopped by the Rage Patrol before, didn't even have a record.

"Let's see some ID, hon."

Nia was surprised to hear a woman's southern twang. Sexual assault had been averted for now, she hoped. She kept her eyes on the steering wheel as she handed the officer her identification.

Shining a flashlight on the license, the patrolwoman said, "Well, Miss Nia Jones, it's kinda late for you to be out, isn't it?"

Nia's lips quivered, yet she continued to smile. *What's my excuse? That I was dropping off a friend?* But where had they been so late when most bars that allowed black women closed at 11:00? No curfews had been imposed – yet – but CAPs were known for taunting black female motorists to boost the readings on their Rage-dars. Maybe this officer would rig her device as well. Maybe she hadn't met her quota for the month. Nia wanted to confess, "I was at a speakeasy!" so she could accept her punishment and avoid this torment. Instead, she said, "I couldn't sleep, so I was just driving around to get some air."

"Why couldn't you sleep, Miss Nia? Were you upset?"

"No, ma'am. I was too … happy to sleep."

She ventured a glance at the officer to see if she believed her story. A squat redhead with a crooked nose and dull gray eyes, she held her Rage-dar near Nia's face. It was a rectangular black instrument that resembled a paddle, and it emitted a high-pitched noise as numbers aggregated on the digital display. Nia shrank back against the headrest.

"Looks like someone was Driving while Irritated."

"I didn't do anything wrong. I was just singing along to my favorite song. I was … happy."

"Are you calling me a liar?"

"No, ma'am. I'm not."

"The Rage-dar doesn't lie."

The woman went back to her patrol car. Sweat pooled in Nia's bra. In spite of the cool February night, damp hair tickled the back of her neck, and she fanned herself with the car manual. What was taking the officer so long? Maybe she was radioing for backup to help restrain an uppity gal with a piss-poor excuse for being out so late. Maybe the responding officers were going to ask her to step out of the car and drive her down some dark alley …

The redhead returned and was pushing something through the open window. Nia glanced at the red-and-white paper in the woman's hand. A DWI.

"Sign this and get home," the officer said as she tossed Nia's license and registration on the passenger seat. "Better learn to tame your temper. You're in the system now."

Nia signed the ticket, and then stared at her windshield as the patrolwoman walked away. The glaring white light, the physical thing that had invaded her car, reluctantly withdrew. Then the cruiser moved silently down the street.

After a few minutes of gazing at the neon sign of a Mexican restaurant a block ahead, Nia finally started her car. She just wanted to get home so she could shower and wash away the scum of shame from her encounter with the officer. *I'm in the system now. My first DWI.* She looked at the ticket. She had registered a 35 on the Rage-dar, a fine of $350.

I wasn't even angry. But now she had the strong urge to rip up the ticket and feed it to the wind, regardless of who was watching.

"Bitch," she said.

Out of habit, she looked around, even though she was alone in her car. But the word felt good on her tongue. It was the first time she had cursed outside her home in over two years. She had trained herself not to swear, lest she should slip up in public.

"White bitch!"

She drove east on Lankershim toward her apartment, eyes burning. *I wasn't even mad.* Things were only going to get worse now that she had a record. For once, she wished that Sapphire 8 was still around, or any support group that she could vent to. She passed a car dealership a few blocks from her home, the one that always made her smile because of the fake people propped against a railing on the roof, looking down on the fleet. When she first moved to the area, she did a double take, thinking the mannequins were real. Once she figured out they weren't, she laughed when she drove by, remembering how easily fooled she had been. Now tears stung her eyes as she glanced at the pretend audience above her. *They're about as joyful as I am*. Her emotions got all tangled in her head. She smiled when she was miserable, chuckled when she was mad. She just didn't want to go to her grave like the women from her church, with a forced smile on her lips.

"Your hair looks nice today, Nee."

Nia glanced up from her computer. Her coworker, Gennifer, stood in the entrance to her cubicle, gripping a white binder. Nia touched the hair that she had hastily slicked back into a bun. It was in no way a cute style, but it matched the way she felt as she'd gotten dressed for work, nondescript but functional.

"Thanks, Gennifer."

She gave her a quick smile. When she wore updos or intricate braids, her coworkers sized up her new coifs, but said nothing, or asked if they could touch her hair. Only when her tresses were styled in some basic 'do like today, did they comment on the "niceness" of it, as if encouraging her in her pursuit of plainness.

"Anyways, just wanted to let you know Alyssa wants you to rewrite that presentation for the Fletcher campaign. Said it needs to be punched up."

"I'll get right to it." Nia felt her face smiling. Alyssa rarely communicated her displeasure with Nia's work to her; she always asked Gennifer to relay some message, although Nia and Gennifer both held the same position as assistant account executives. She was testing Nia, trying to demolish her calm disposition with each second-hand critique.

God knows she can do whatever she wants and never have to worry about being called out for discrimination. Nia blew dust from her monitor. She didn't blame Gennifer. She knew her portly coworker felt embarrassed being the mediator in Alyssa's games. Nia actually liked Gennifer. They grabbed coffee on their morning breaks or chatted about their interests outside of work. But their friendly repartee stopped short of Gennifer asking about AR-42b. The way they laughed over lattes, onlookers would never think the darker woman in the duo lived in fear of being busted for her attitude.

"What'd you do last night?" Gennifer asked.

Nia turned around, surprised to see her still loitering by her cubicle.

"Typical Tuesday for me. I just went home and chilled with the man beast. The game was on and we –"

"I got a DWI last night – Driving while Irritated," Nia said, interrupting the brunette's chatter. In spite of the bluntness of her reply, she managed a shaky grin.

Gennifer switched the binder to her other arm. Her nails were unpolished but neatly filed.

"That sucks. Were you angry?"

"I was minding my own business, driving back home from … dinner with a friend. There was no reason for the officer to pull me over."

Nia considered Gennifer one of her closest friends at the ad agency. With her, she didn't have to punctuate every sentence with a grin, as she did with her fellow workers. Yet, Nia didn't quite trust her.

Gennifer lowered her voice, as if the blemish were on her record. "I hate that for you, Nee. I really do. I know you're not an angry person, but what can you do?"

"Pay a $350 fine and make sure I don't get pulled over for a second offense."

Gennifer whistled. "Damn, $350? There goes your mocha latte budget for the month."

Although Nia knew her coworker was trying to make light of the situation, her corny jokes didn't make things better. Gennifer wasn't the one who had pulled out a Rage-dar, yet she couldn't help thinking the brown-haired woman was partially responsible.

"No more treats for me." Nia felt her throat tightening. "I'm having withdrawal symptoms already."

Gennifer drew a circle on the carpet with her ballerina slipper. They inhabited a work world of stilettos and strappy sandals, and the fat woman's flats made her nearly as much of an outsider as Nia. "I can always let you borrow a few bucks."

Too bad I can't borrow a new mouth. Nia opened the document containing her inferior presentation. *But I'd never expect you to trade faces with me.*

Over the next few weeks, Nia found herself growing increasingly cranky. It was a new feeling for her, but one she wasn't ready to abandon. Her moodiness was also dangerous, because she sometimes forgot to conceal her attitude in public. She failed to return tepid greetings from cashiers, wouldn't allow other cars to cut her off on the freeway.

She began to despise her female coworkers for their emotion privilege. If Alyssa yelled at her in a meeting, Nia had to grin like an idiot and apologize, even if she wasn't at fault. She hated the casual "That sucks" comments from her redheaded and brunette coworkers after a public drubbing. She didn't want them feeling sorry for her. She envied their ability to hang up on a rude vendor without fear of censure, to openly fume when someone "borrowed" a stapler or tape dispenser from their desk without returning it. Nia was one of two black people in an advertising agency of more than 50, and the other employee of color was a man. She had no one to confide in by the water cooler or in the ladies room.

Black men weren't profiled the way black women were. Although they filled the prisons for armed robbery, drug dealing or murder, those crimes were tame compared to the homegrown terrorism that was a black woman's wrath. Like their white female counterparts, some brothers were sympathetic to AR-42b, but most weren't willing to be inconvenienced. If they happened to be walking with or talking to a black woman and she had a public meltdown – cussed them out for looking at another woman or for being insensitive – they could be considered accessories to a crime. So black couples were on the decline in the Golden State and across the nation as Anti-Rage became the law of the land.

I'd never date a man who didn't have my back, Nia thought one afternoon as she ate lunch on a bench across the street from the business park where she worked. Fluted purple flowers drooped over a hedge enclosing the nearby elementary school. She noticed that more and more schools featured these leafy borders. *To protect their kids from the stares of strangers and make the kiddies think they're playing in some brambly paradise.* Disembodied laughter rang out as she took a bite of her tofu stir fry – last night's leftovers.

Nia thought back to the women she met in that basement stained with green light. Now she had more in common with them than she had when she first walked into the beauty shop. A twisted kinship. She regretted not speaking up that night, if only to curse or scream. She could do those things in her apartment – albeit muffling her voice with a pillow – but how lovely it would be to cuddle her rage and not be ashamed? Even before AR-42b cracked her spirit, Nia never experienced an "angry black woman" moment. She never dressed down a salesgirl for following her around a store, never cussed out a boyfriend for being insensitive or sassed an employer for treating her like a mule in a skirt and heels. She never swiveled her neck, rolled her eyes or snapped her fingers in the face of someone attempting to trample on her humanity, all while making her out to be the animal. She never did any of those things, because she thought she was better than that. She never wanted to be lumped in with that race of sassy black chicks. And what good had it done her? She felt her throat growing hot at the insults she had not hurled, the snappy comebacks she had not uttered. Now, she would never be able to feel that release. She was in the system.

As if summoned by her thoughts, a red-and-black patrol car cruised down the boulevard. Nia choked as she tried to chew her barely-seasoned bean curd and smile at the same time. The vehicle slowed. She picked at the food in the cardboard carton on her lap, would allow her gaze to rise no higher than the tires and gleaming silver rims a few feet from her. She feared that she would not be able to swallow her lunch, that the day-old food and ancient ire would shoot out of her mouth and onto the checkered car idling across from her.

I'm happy. This is the happiest I've ever been in my life.

"Hey, you."

I could die of happiness.

"In the black skirt. You hear me talking to you, girl?"

Nia met the gaze of a red-faced man with a crew cut. Instinctively, she crossed her legs.

"Yes, sir. Were you speaking to me?"

The officer fanned himself with a black device. "Beautiful day to be outside, isn't it? Seems like you'd be much happier living in Southern California, enjoying all this sunshine."

Nia willed her lips to spread. "I love sunny days. I'm definitely happy to be outside, sir."

The man studied her for a few moments and then lowered his Rage-dar. He said something to his Latino partner and they both laughed. Then the patrol car continued down the boulevard.

Asshole.

Something rustled at Nia's feet, and she jumped. A pigeon stood on a dead leaf, scaly pink feet gripping his bounty like the captain of a raft afloat on a concrete sea. Satisfied that Nia was of no threat, he pecked around the bench again, one red eye on the ground, the other regarding her. Nia usually fed birds – the crusts of this or the leavings of that. Even though she could no longer finish the blocks of tofu she'd been nibbling on before the CAPs pulled up, she flung the container at the bird. He squawked, releasing his leaf at last. Dirty feathers drifted to the sidewalk as he took to the sky.

"Hey, Nee. Alyssa's been looking for you."

Gennifer was standing by the sink in the restroom as Nia entered on her way back to her cubicle.

"For what?"

"She said it had to do with the brief you turned in."

"I was at lunch. She knows I usually take a lunch from 1:00 to 2:00."

Gennifer fiddled with her wedding ring, a movement that annoyed Nia. Most white women on her job – no matter how dumpy or trashy or uneducated – had husbands or partners or dated regularly. No man had asked Nia out in over two years. Black men rarely dated black women in L.A., and men of other races never glanced her way. Although she had a degree and considered herself attractive, she was too much of a risk.

"I figured as much. That's what I told her."

"How come she never addresses me directly? She always has to go through you."

"Not always." Gennifer pulled out a tube of gloss and began dabbing her lips. "You feeling okay?"

"It's that time of the month," Nia said, entering a stall. She regretted the lie. She didn't want to have to tamp down her temper in front of Gennifer, hated making an excuse for her growing irritation. They were alone in the bathroom, but she heard voices approaching the door. "I'll go see what she wants in a few minutes."

"Okay. I'll let her know."

"You don't have to be the go-between, you know?" Nia said as a loud current of laughter rushed into the bathroom. "I have a mouth."

She could only imagine Gennifer's face at her tone and the expressions of the coworkers who recently entered. But she didn't care.

Fuck these Beckies. She squatted over the toilet. The outburst in her head helped calm her. Maybe she would call Cami after work and they could drop by the speakeasy again. *I need to let it out,* she said to herself. *Before I get arrested. Or worse.*

As Nia left the restroom, an uneasy feeling settled in her stomach, replacing her new boldness. She always worried when she was summoned by Alyssa. It reminded her of that time in fourth grade when she didn't finish her homework and Miss Summers scolded her in front of the class. Just as she hated that teacher, she hated her boss. Alyssa was a thin redhead with a loud laugh, but her humor was rimmed with menace. Nia felt like a sell out for yukking it up at that silly Valley Girl routine, that she had to pretend to be dumb, less offensive. *I'm not laughing today.* She rounded the corner and approached her boss' open door. *It's criminal to be so peppy all the time.*

Alyssa was on the phone when Nia knocked, and she waved her in without looking up. Nia knew the redhead would finish up her call as Nia sat there, even if it lasted for several minutes. She examined her nails as Alyssa argued with someone from pest control about termites at one of her properties. Finally, the phone was returned to its cradle, and Nia looked up.

"Such a beautiful day today. It totally sucks to be cooped up inside. How about we close the office for the rest of the day and head to the beach?" Alyssa laughed as she stared out her window, which overlooked a park. Nia marveled at how quickly this woman could switch from bratty to benevolent. She didn't trust the sudden sunshine.

"Gennifer said you wanted to see me."

"Yeah, I do. It's about that brief you submitted for the Fletcher campaign."

"What about it?"

Those deep-set green eyes took in her hair and white blouse before saying, "Are you feeling okay, hon? You don't seem yourself."

Nia felt her lips moving upward and she mashed them together. "I'm fine. I just have a lot of work to do." She met Alyssa's gaze. "I was revising a presentation before lunch. I came to see what you wanted so I could get back to work."

"Oh?"

"Yes."

Alyssa loosened the black elastic band on her ponytail, shaking free her hair, which was an unnatural red color, like a withered Roma tomato. She combed her locks with her fingers, and shook her hair out again, as if she were the star of a shampoo commercial. Nia knew the fake grooming was another one of Alyssa's stall tactics – a way of flaunting her authority. But she would not be intimidated. Not today.

"What concerned you about the brief?" Nia repeated.

"You know, Nia. I don't think I like your tone."

"I'm not asking you to like it." She paused, noting the withered gaiety in Alyssa's eyes. "This is the way I spoke when I first started working here."

"Things are way different now." Alyssa gathered her hair, snapping the elastic band around the flimsy ponytail. "You're a smarter girl than that. You know better."

"I'm not a girl, and I never knew you thought I was smart." Now the smile she'd been restraining finally broke free. "Not the way you always complain about my work to Gennifer."

"If I complain about your work to Genn, it's because Genn can run circles around you writing briefs, editing copy, dealing with vendors – everything." Spittle landed on the desk near Alyssa's keyboard. "You are really treading on thin ice here, girlfriend."

"If I'm such a horrible worker, why haven't you fired me?"

Nia felt a prickly feeling in her chest, as if she were witnessing her own stabbing. She also felt a galloping glee at holding her own against her boss. *Wait 'til I tell Cami. Wait until the women at the speakeasy hear this.*

"You black bitch. I understand the law now." Alyssa opened the bag of candy corn that she kept handy near her computer. She sucked on a piece for several moments before adding, "Have to protect decent people from your kind."

"Pity there's no law to protect my 'kind' from you."

The color drained from the redhead's face, and her green eyes looked more sunken than usual. "I'm going to have to report you," she said, picking up the phone. There was a mournful note in her voice, like a cattleman realizing he has to put down a wounded mare at the height of her breeding age. She looked at the wall above Nia's head. "You were one of the good ones. What's got you so riled up? I'd never take you for someone so sassy."

Nia rose, resting her fingertips on the edge of Alyssa's desk. She smiled, as if about to compliment her boss on her outfit. Then, she said, "Real women rage, bitch."

Before the skinny woman had a chance to reply, Nia slammed the door on her way out of the office and quickly moved down the hall, under the curious stares of her coworkers.

Nia awoke in the back seat of her Jetta, an arm draped over her forehead. It was getting dark outside. She heard a trunk slam next to her car. A few minutes later, an engine started.

After talking back to her boss, she fled the ad agency. Now she was hiding out in the parking lot of the Baldwin Center Plaza a few miles from the speakeasy. It was a good thing she still carried her purse after returning from lunch, because she never returned to her cubicle, never shut off her PC, never said goodbye to Gennifer. Alyssa had reported her to the Rage Patrol, especially after Nia uttered the credo, "Real women rage." It was the language of terrorists, of angry women who strapped explosive devices to their bodies, who hurled gasoline bombs at local TV stations.

I can't even call Cami. Nia listened to the hurried footsteps of shoppers with not a thing on their minds but the next sale. *She'll be considered an accessory. I can't have her held accountable for what I did.*

She sat up slowly, peering out the window. It was nearly 8:30, and the mall would be closing soon. She planned on heading to the speakeasy in an hour or so, the same time she and Cami had visited a few weeks before. Someone was sure to be there. Forbidden dens such as theirs encouraged regular rebellion in black women. That was the whole purpose of the meeting place; it provided a safe forum to practice unsafe behavior. She needed to tell someone about her act of bravery. She finally had an uppity moment! *Sapphire 8 would be proud of me.* She climbed over the seat and slid behind the wheel. *I finally acted up.*

Nia cruised around the area to pass time. In Ladera Heights, a neighborhood some of her coworkers referred to as "the black Brentwood," she drove by beautiful homes on a hill overlooking the city. Stately Spanish colonials with terraced yards. Taking in the colorful houses and manicured lawns helped relax her, made her feel like less of a fugitive. An hour later, she drove down the hill, navigating her way to Heliotrope Boulevard. Passing the strip mall that housed the beauty salon, she turned down a side street. As she parked behind a raggedy Buick with a boot on the tire, she felt the same fear she always felt of entering the hood, especially as a woman on her own. *Sitting here is only going to make me more nervous.* Gathering her courage, she opened the door and activated her alarm. Then, pulling her purse up, she made her way down the street.

The stillness of the block was punctuated by her heels clacking on the pavement, a reminder that she still wore the same clothes in which she'd stormed out of the ad agency. She knew she looked a sight in her wrinkled shirt, the powder long since faded from her face.

I can't hide out forever. That's for sure. Nia rapped on the door. Was the password the same, or did they change it after each meeting? Surely, they wouldn't leave any black woman outside in the dark – password or not. *I have to talk to someone.*

She heard feet shuffling to the door, and then a voice called out, "Rainbows or unicorns?"

"Sunshine."

The same host from a few weeks ago opened the door. This time, her head wrap was a faded gold color.

"You by yourself?" she asked. When Nia nodded, the woman said, "You know it's dangerous to be walking alone."

"I really need to vent tonight. It was worth the risk."

As Nia followed her hostess through the salon, she noticed that the mood was more somber. Jazz music wafted from the stereo below, and the green light in the basement had a sickly hue. She bought a beer, taking in her surroundings. There were fewer patrons than before, and the conversation was subdued. Nia swallowed the disappointment in her throat. She'd been hoping for a lively audience to regale with tales of her harrowing afternoon.

"We need to lay low for a few weeks after tonight," the hostess announced to the ten or twelve women who had gathered. "Just need to make sure the CAPs aren't on to our little meeting place."

"Ain't no law against black women getting together to dance and drink beer and shoot the shit." It was the same sober skinny girl from last time. She stood in her same spot against the wall. Her hands were empty. Nia was relieved to see someone she recognized.

"It is if they got an attitude while doing it," said a dark-skinned woman with a short silver afro.

"The CAPs can kiss my entire happy black ass." The speaker's hair was braided into six or seven neat corn rows, making her tiny head look even smaller. "I'm a bitch and proud of it."

"You're a bitch if you do, bitch if you don't." Nia was surprised at herself for uttering those words, but she wanted to feel a kinship with the women.

"True that."

"I should know. Let me tell you what happened to me today." She took a swig of her beer, wanting to take her time telling the tale, reliving the moment. "My boss said she didn't like my tone of voice. So I said, 'That's the way I've always talked to you.' Then she had the nerve to say I'm a bad worker – as hard as I work – so I said, 'Why haven't you fired me?'"

Someone near the back of the room whistled. "No, you didn't."

"I sure did, and I didn't smile either," Nia said, her grin edged with pride. Her speech was freer too, more colloquial. She was sad that Cami wasn't around to witness her speaking up, to cheer for her in this moment. "She called me a black bitch."

"Now see, in the old days, I would have put a foot in my boss's ass if she ever called me out my name," said the silver-haired woman.

The sober girl stared at Nia in awe, and Nia felt her cheeks flush with pride. She was sitting in a basement with other black women, sipping beer and listening to jazz, and she felt like she belonged. Their eyes weren't judging her now, but seeing her as one of their own.

"Then what happened?" the hostess said, leaning forward, her eyes shining. "I know Becky was too through!"

"Trust and believe, she was. Her eyes got all big, and she said, 'Why you so snippy today? I thought you were one of the good ones,' or something like that." Nia paused so her audience could digest the full effect of her next words. "Then I stood up, looked her dead in the eye and said, 'Real women rage, bitch!'"

The room fell silent. A saxophone wailed in the background like the lone mourner at a gravesite.

"You said what?" The awe drained from the sober girl's eyes.

"Real women rage." It took Nia a minute to realize that the women were pulling away from her. She felt their camaraderie retract.

"Tell me you did not say that."

"Why? I did say it. I thought this was a speakeasy." Nia began to feel like that awkward girl at the house party again – the wallflower afraid someone was going to ask her to dance. "I thought this was a safe place to gripe and vent."

"Yeah, about what you *would* do if someone disrespected you, about what you *would* say if someone called you out your name. Those are the rules. But you crossed the line, making terroristic threats. That kind of shit will get this place shut down." The hostess leaned back in her chair, cutting her eyes at Nia. "For all you know, the CAPs could have followed you here."

"No one followed me. I'm alone."

"You got that right. Look, no hard feelings, but you got to go." The hostess rose, straightening her yellow headwrap. "I'm not taking the fall for another woman's meltdown."

Nia fumbled for her keys to avoid making eye contact with anyone. She was getting kicked out of the happy black bitches club. Sapphire 8 would be so disappointed. *Guess they're not so radical after all.* She headed toward the steps. They were all fugitives, they were all outlaws – whether they kept their rage inside or not. She paused on the step.

"No matter how happy you act, you'll always be bitches beneath the smiles."

She walked up the steps and through the ancient salon, the wailing saxophone at her back. As she stepped outside and heard the click of the deadbolt, she realized there was nowhere to go. She no longer had a job; she couldn't contact Cami. She had been rejected by a group of black women who bathed in the sludge of their oppression. Like hogs in a pen they wallowed, rooting up every petty remark or mean-spirited action, fighting each other for the slops. But they accused her of sullying them.

Maybe I should have listened to my mom and gotten myself diagnosed with a mental health disorder. She walked toward the mouth of the alley. Maybe she needed to go home to Pennsylvania and lay low. Loretta Jones would be more than happy to take her in. But the thought of returning to her small hometown saddened her. *I don't want to leave L.A. I built a life here.*

A red-and-black car cruised down the street.

It passed the alleyway, stopped, and then kicked up gravel as it reversed and headed toward her. Nia's mouth went dry. She had gone without smiling for so long today that she almost forgot what was mandated of her. Now, she willed her lips into a grin.

The car parked on an angle, blocking her passage. An officer stuck his head out the window. His features seemed to be crowded in the middle of his long face. He smiled at her.

"Out kinda late," he said. His voice was pleasant, like a stranger asking for directions. As he spoke, he fanned himself with a long black device. "Nice girl like you shouldn't be out in a bad neighborhood like this."

"I was visiting a friend," Nia said. She held her purse in front of her stomach.

"What's your name?" The officer stepped out of the squad car, carrying his instrument with him. His voice still retained its affable twang.

Deja.

Capricia.

Penelope.
Shawnetta.
Prostheta.
Sapphire.
Nia.

"Something wrong with your ears?" The officer's smile slipped, and he brandished his Rage-dar. "I said, what's your name?"

"Nia. Nia Jones."

As the man headed back to his squad car, Nia glanced behind her. There was a dumpster at the end of the alley near the beauty salon, but it looked like a dead end. She could sidle around the police car and take off down Heliotrope, but how far would she get in heels and a skirt, the patrolman in hot pursuit? He would shoot her in the back. She was as sure of it as she was her name. As quickly as he smiled at her, he would pull a gun on her, accuse her of assaulting an officer. Her legs felt boneless, and she pressed back the urge to pee.

After a few minutes, the man returned, his face wiped clean of amusement.

"Got some bad news, Ms. Nia Jones. You're in the system. Looks like you were pulled over a few weeks ago," he said, shaking his head. "Says here you also made terrorist threats to a lady named Alyssa Godfrey. She called it in."

"I didn't threaten anyone." Nia felt her feet moving backwards. "I never even raised my voice."

"You're in a real bad position. Got a lot of things hanging over your head."

If he touches me, I'll stab him with my heel. I'll bite him. I'll gouge his eye out. I'll scream.

The paddle in the man's hand emitted a shrieking noise, and they both looked at it. Red numbers aggregated on the screen, and the officer whistled.

"Fifty-two," he said, with a pleased grin, like a hunter who'd bagged a good-sized doe. "Haven't seen numbers like that since … well, I don't think I've ever seen a number that high. That's enough rage to go around."

"I've never been happier," Nia said, but her lips refused to support the lie.

The officer was close enough that Nia could smell the mousse in his hair – a minty smell that masked something sour.

"I could make this a lot easier for you," he said, a hand on his belt. "Pretend I never even saw you, that you were never on my radar. I know you have to let that anger out in some kind of way."

"I'm not angry," Nia repeated as the officer closed in.

Rent-a-Cracker

As Shawnetta Jones rounded the hallway leading to her apartment, she saw, covering her welcome mat, the plain brown carton containing her White Man. She walked around the package, which was the size of a washing machine. *I can't believe it's really here. Going to be a bitch getting him inside.* **Naturally Nordic Industries** was stamped on one side of a box that was slightly darker than her skin. She waived her signature upon delivery because no one in her building would try to steal so heavy an item. Besides, there was little foot traffic outside her door.

Shawnetta slid her key in the lock and turned the knob. Pushing her purse up on her arm, she rocked the carton from side to side as she pulled it across the doorsill. *It's actually not that heavy.* Hollow squishy sounds met her ears. It was like dragging a sedated child over the threshold. She closed the door, pausing in the foyer to listen. Overhead, her neighbor's bulldog scampered across the floor, nails clicking on the wood. In the kitchen, the refrigerator crackled as it made ice. The carton was still. She was anxious to open the package, but afraid of what she would unleash not only in her one bedroom apartment, but in her life. But the White Man wasn't a threat. The sales rep at Naturally Nordic Industries had boasted that their clones were "100 percent docile and loving. They do whatever you want them to. Just give the order."

Well, I have six months to find out. Shawnetta stepped out of her heels near the back of the leather couch and dropped her purse on a cushion. Once in the kitchen, she retrieved a pair of shears from the wooden storage block by the stove. She returned to the box and sliced the clear sealing tape with one quick motion. As she peeled back the flaps, an odor like rubbing alcohol and burnt eggs escaped from the opening, not the wet fur smell she had anticipated. Her order slip was placed face down on a mound of bubble wrap, and she was tempted to squeeze the air-filled ovals that resembled a mosaic of transparent eyes. Instead, she read her receipt:

Qty: 1 Naturally Nordic Adult Male Companion

Features: Blond hair, blue eyes. 75 inches. Chin cleft. Small scar on neck. Hair and skin are self-cleaning. DO NOT submerge in water!

Name: Answers to Rapsilico. If customer reprograms to different name, please restore to default upon return to NNI.

Rental charge: $3,350. Prepaid. Customer billed $100 late fee each day Companion is held past return date.

Although Shawnetta couldn't see the clone's face, she felt giddy. All that was visible through the plastic wrap was downy yellow hair. But he was hers. Her very own White Man. A companion to play with for the next six months. *I can't lift him out. Should have turned the box on the side before I opened it.* She grabbed one of the flaps and tugged. The box fell to the floor with a dull thud. The bubble wrap popped as she hauled the sleeping form out of its resting place and across the hardwood flooring. She severed the plastic covering with the open blade, and the body sighed as she removed the wrapping. The Man lay on his side, knees pressed against his chest. He was barefoot, clad only in jeans. His hands were tied in front of his legs with a black ribbon.

Probably to prevent too much shifting during delivery. Shawnetta knelt before the clone and untied the ribbon. One hand fell free, the hairless knuckles brushing her leg. She was about to toss the band in the trash but thought she'd need it to tie his hands again when she shipped him back, so she tucked it in the pocket of her cardigan. She stretched the White Man out to his full length, wiping her hand on the leg of her pants when she was finished. It would take some time getting used to the feel of his skin. The flesh was life-like, but warm and greasy, as if they'd oiled him up with Vaseline and left him to bake in the sun for a few hours before packaging. Now he lay facing the ceiling. His milky blue eyes were open. That was one quirk in the duplication process, the NNI sales rep explained. The clone didn't blink. "Makes him seem all the more human that way," the man on the phone said. "Just think of it like this: you'll always be the object of his gaze."

Her White Man – Rapsilico – seemed as real as she did, and part of her expected the thin lips to part as he poked out his tongue or spit in her face.

But his mouth was still. He had arched light-brown eyebrows, separated by a few stray hairs. His nose was thin and slightly tilted to the right, as if a jealous sculptor had given it a final twist. His hair was of medium length, flattened by the bubble wrap. She reached out to fluff the golden locks, but paused midway to his head. She had never touched a white man's hair before. Had never dated or been intimate with anyone but black men. Had never desired to. Now she stared down at the supine figure who would be her boyfriend for the next six months. She blushed, staring at his muscular chest and rippling abs.

"Why you want to rent a cracker?" Claudine asked a month ago when Shawnetta told her of the ad for NNI. They sat on the outdoor patio of a raw foods restaurant in Santa Monica.

Shawnetta bit into a piece of flax seed bread laden with nut cheese and chewed slowly before answering. It was a hassle just getting Claudine to dine with her. Her friend was strictly steak and potatoes and turned up her nose at what she called "white people's food." But Shawnetta had to tell someone of her intentions. She hadn't made many friends since moving to L.A. from Columbia, Maryland five years prior, and the woman sitting across from her with the fuchsia dreadlocks was the one she confided in most.

"Every time I go to dinner, or the movies or the museum, it's with you, or I'm by myself," Shawnetta said. "I'm tired of being alone. Let's just say I'm investing in male companionship."

"But why a cracker?" Claudine frowned at the vegetable wrap placed before her by a skinny redhead. Shawnetta kept her eyes on her plate, hoping the server had not heard the slur. Claudine was the kind of black woman who said "nigga" in mixed company, who asked her white coworkers at the insurance company why their hair smelled like mayonnaise. She had about as much couth as the rolled-up veggie-filled collard green she was sniffing suspiciously, but Shawnetta loved her because she always spoke her mind.

"Me and black men are officially over. Done," Shawnetta said. "They don't look at me. They don't like me. Fine. I'm thirty-one, and I'm not getting any younger. I don't have time to sit around in my apartment waiting for Hakeem or Jamal to decide I'm worthy of their attention."

As she spoke, a blonde woman in a convertible slowed for the stoplight, hip-hop blaring. She wore shades and a wide smile, and she said something to the black man sitting next to her. Shawnetta looked away. She always acted as if she never saw such couples, would stare at the sky or the ground if they walked toward her, as if the act of turning her head somehow caused them to disappear. She dreaded venturing to Santa Monica or Culver City because of the large number of black male/white female pairings. It was one of the reasons she fled Columbia, Maryland, which was an interracial Disneyland. *It would be different if sisters dated outside our race as much as brothers do, to even things up.* She sipped her carrot juice cocktail. But she passed so many single black women in L.A, their ring fingers as empty as their eyes.

"Oh, I see what's up." Claudine watched the couple in the convertible drive off. She was a cherry-brown woman with a smattering of black moles on her cheeks that she called freckles. "Trying to get even with Becky."

"I'm not trying to get even with anyone. I'm just keeping my options open."

"With a robot? And a white one at that." The mother and daughter at the adjacent table glanced over at her loud chuckle.

"The NNI models are not robots, Claudine. They're life-like Adult Companions. You've probably seen them around and didn't know it," Shawnetta said. "One hundred percent docile and loving – guaranteed."

Claudine played with a lock of hot pink hair, amusement shining in her eyes. "If you wanna hook up with a brain-dead somebody who gives you compliments, I can introduce you to a few Negros at the post office around the corner from my place," she said. "They love redbones with hazel eyes like you."

Now Shawnetta leaned over the White Man, recalling her friend's words. She hadn't been truthful with Claudine. She selected the clone solely on the basis of his white skin. While skimming black women empowerment websites, she found the advertisement for Naturally Nordic Industries. The ad featured a dark-skinned woman with an afro smiling into the face of a pale suitor. It read: "Still Looking for Mr. Right? Let a Naturally Nordic Companion Sweep You off Your Feet until Your White Knight Comes

Along!"

Mr. White Now. Her face was a few inches from the clone's, as if she would awaken him from his dreamless coma with a kiss. Instead, she whispered into his ear: "Rapsilico."

The White Man sprang to life, yanked upright by an invisible cord. He stared straight ahead. Shawnetta fell back with a cry, hitting her head against the couch. The clone turned at the sound, and she glimpsed the scar on his neck.

"I'm your new owner," Shawnetta said when she finally found her voice. She stood and backed toward the door, just in case she needed to run. "I mean, your new companion. Shawnetta Jones."

"Whattup, Shawnetta."

"Hi."

"Can I call you Shawnie?" His voice was deep, his speech clipped. She detected a New York accent.

"Sure. That's fine."

"Solid." He grinned, and she almost expected to see a glint of gold, but he displayed strong white teeth.

Now that he was awake, and she was staring at him face to face, Shawnetta decided that Rapsilico was the most handsome white man she had ever seen. Since she had never dated one before, she didn't want to go with the Golfer, Computer Geek or Suave Businessman models featured on the NNI site. She'd specified on her order form that she wanted a clone that resembled the black men she was most attracted to – thugs. Her very own synthetic wigger. Fortunately, the White Man came with a Vernacular Adjustment Module on the back of his ear that she could press to calibrate his slang if it grew too jarring. She could just hear Claudine saying, "Why in the world did you pay over $3,000 for a fake nigga when you could get the real thing for free?" She realized that her choice was hypocritical, that she resented black men for dating white women with big butts and big lips, all wrapped up in the dainty gauze of street life, when they could have had a woman of color.

The clone, sitting amidst discarded wrappings, glanced at her, unblinking. Shawnetta remembered that her White Man would not make a move until she ordered him to. She felt shy but powerful, a little girl who realizes her dolls are not harmless playthings oblivious to her words, but a brawny army that only she commands.

Pulling out a chair at her dinette table, she said, "Take a seat, Rapsilico, until we figure out what we're going to do next."

The White Man hopped to his feet, jeans sagging off his butt. His movements were not jerky and robotic as she had imagined, but feline. She scooped up the bubble wrap where he had lain, a plastic placenta, and was about to toss it into the box when she noticed another package at the bottom. Opening the item, she saw that it contained a pair of black tennis shoes, a white polo shirt and an owner's manual. *Wonder why they sent him half naked ... unless they wanted to show off his body. But I don't even need to worry about that.* As nice-looking as her White Man was, she didn't plan on having sex with a clone – if that was even possible. She might let him sleep in bed with her once she got used to him, if it wasn't too creepy. But she didn't need him to hold her or nuzzle her cheek as a real lover would.

You are strictly eye candy. She sat across from the Companion. He was her antidote to spinsterhood – someone who would make her feel beautiful and desirable, who had been programmed to treasure her blackness. He would set her apart from the platoon of lonely black chicks who roamed the streets of L.A. like foot soldiers of a forgotten war.

Shawnetta thought of the blondes and redheads at the production company where she worked, the ones with pictures of smiling brown babies hanging in their cubicles, the ones who let it be known that they had a thing for brothers, who frequented black nightclubs, spit slang and punctuated their sentences with a drawn-out "Gurrl."

Wait 'til they see what this gurrl has up her sleeve. She smiled at Rapsilico, who reclined in his chair, awaiting his next directive. *Wait until I show up at the holiday party with my White Man.*

A few hours later, Shawnetta sat across from the clone in the food court of the Beverly Square Mall, biting into a vegetable burrito. For their first date, she had decided to take him out to dinner. Nothing fancy. They were still getting to know each other, or rather, she was trying him out. A plate of refried beans and rice sat in front of Rapsilico to make it appear he was eating. She skimmed the owner's manual before leaving her apartment and discovered that her clone was self-sustaining, and it was not recommended for him to take in food.

A gaggle of overly dressed teens walked by wearing thick eyeliner and short skirts. They tipped across the tiles so as not to fall in their high platform shoes. Shawnetta dreaded coming to Beverly Square, but it was the closest mall to her West Hollywood apartment. As soon as she entered the plaza, she felt profiled at an invisible velvet rope. She always felt that she had to wear an expensive outfit and carry a designer bag just to go shopping, as if the mannequins would frown at her casually dressed self. But tonight, she wanted to be seen. Walking with Rapsilico made her feel high end, as if she belonged among the pricey jewelry and couture clothes. Before leaving the apartment, she changed into a slinky black dress with silver stilettos, swept her permed, shoulder-length hair to the side and pinned a rhinestone barrette to the bang. *We look like we just came from the prom.* She wanted to look dazzling as she paraded her Companion around. *So the brothers can see what they're missing.*

"You got grease on your face. Let me get that, girl." The White Man held out a napkin, patting her chin. The skin on the back of his hands was free of lines.

"Thanks, Rapsilico."

She wanted to glance around to see if anyone had noticed his gentle gesture.

"Don't want to mess up that pretty lipstick."

Shawnetta blushed, keeping her eyes on her food. Two years had passed since she'd last been asked on a date, since a man had complimented her on her hair or her perfume. She wondered if the clone had the ability to tell her how nice she looked, if he really found her beautiful, or if even his praise was pre-programmed. But he was manufactured from the cells of a real, living man, wasn't he? He had to have some memories or original thoughts.

"So, what do you like to do, Rapsilico?"

He said, "Oh, I'm down for whatever – shooting hoops, kicking it at the car show, paint ball. Whatever you like to do."

"I like going to the museum. The California African American Museum has an upcoming exhibit on black surfers and skateboarders." Feeling his eyes on her, Shawnetta tucked a lock of hair behind her ear. "Might be fun to go check it out."

"Aight."

She rose, and the clone leaned back to pull out her chair. She gathered their trays, but he shook a finger at her with a smile and took the uneaten food over to the trashcan. She watched him walk away, a slow-moving strut. Her White Man was sexy, and several women turned to stare at him as he shoved the trash – trays, silverware and all – into the metal bin. She knew their eyes would follow him back to their table, back to her.

Had he been a living, breathing white man with those same chiseled looks and sex appeal, he never would have glanced her way. Now he stuck out an elbow, and she threaded her arm though his. She was glad to be able to lean on him, because the strappy shoes were squeezing her bunions. That same egg smell clung to his polo shirt. She wondered how often he self-cleaned. She would walk him through the men's department at Bloomingdales and grab a few cologne samples.

An interracial couple was headed their way – a deep-brown woman wearing a yellow dress walked beside a handsome man with a goatee. When they neared, Shawnetta coughed to catch the woman's eye, and the woman looked over. Her glance included Rapsilico, and she nodded at Shawnetta. Shawnetta nodded back. Some type of unvoiced kinship had passed between them, born of that simple nod. But was the stranger's white man real? So busy was she calling attention to herself, she didn't notice if he blinked or not. How many other black women were walking around with Naturally Nordic Companions?

"You know that chick, Shawnie?"

She stared at the stranger's retreating back. "Maybe."

It was a little after 10:00 when Shawnetta and the clone returned to her apartment. A pang of disappointment thumped in her chest. She had gotten a few curious glances from passing white women and black men as she and Rapsilico went window shopping after their meal, but not the envious daggers she'd been expecting. Some brothers had the nerve to glare at her as they strolled by with Becky on their arm, as if miffed that she had somehow rowed away from the isle of spinsterhood without needing their raft. *Later for those hypocrites.* She sighed as she bent to unfasten her shoe.

Rapsilico said, “Let me get that, girl.”

She started to decline, but then she said, “Sure,” and sat in a dinette chair so the White Man could remove her shoes. He kneeled and placed her foot in his lap. When she realized Rapsilico was about to yank off the stiletto, she said, “Not like that. See the strap? You have to unfasten it.”

“My bad.”

He fumbled with the buckle for a few minutes, finally easing off the shoe. He slid the other one free and placed the pair against the back of the couch – the temporary home for the shoes she discarded as soon as she came in the door.

He’s a quick learner.

“Can I rub your feet?”

Shawnetta faltered. “If you want to,” she said with a shrug.

“I like your toe polish.”

“Thanks.”

His skin was still oily, but the pressure he applied to her instep felt good. She wanted to cry. She was getting aroused by an artificial White Man, by the sight of his long, pale fingers kneading her aching arches. She wouldn’t turn him down if he offered to draw her bath.

But he didn’t. She realized that he’d be down there on his knees for hours, rubbing her feet until the skin flaked away, unless she gave him another order.

“That’s enough, Rapsilico.” She drew her legs in and stood.

“Aight.”

“Thank you. Good night.”

“Night, Shawnie.”

She picked up her shoes and headed toward the bedroom. She paused, her hand on the light switch. The White Man was still in the dining room on his knees in front of the chair, staring at the wall, unblinking. *I can’t leave him there all night.*

“You don’t have to stay like that, Rapsilico. Come here.”

The clone jumped to his feet and headed toward her. Then he turned around and kicked off his tennis shoes, placing them in the spot where her stilettos had lain.

Damn. Why can't he be real?

He followed her into the bedroom, and she turned on the light.

"Stay there."

"Aight."

She opened her walk-in closet and placed her shoes in a wooden rack. She walked past the clone and opened the top drawer of her oak dresser, removing a pair of panties and a pink cotton nightgown. Normally, she'd feel embarrassed about pulling out such intimate items in front of a stranger, but she didn't feel nervous around Rapsilico. She went inside the bathroom and closed the door. She showered before getting dressed for dinner, so she stepped out of the black dress and changed into her nightclothes. She washed off her makeup at the vanity adjacent to the bathroom, staring at the clone in the mirror. He was standing in the doorway where she'd ordered him, facing the wall behind her poster bed. She knew Rapsilico was self-cleaning, and she wondered what would happen if he got wet.

I'll finish reading the owner's manual in the morning. Shawnetta knew to activate the White Man for the first time, she only had to speak his name. To shut him down, she used the phrase, "Time to close your eyes." It was a silly command, since the clone couldn't lower his eyelids all the way. The deactivation phrase reminded her of something she might say to a fussy child refusing to take a nap.

"I like that nightgown on you. That's a real pretty color."

"Thanks, Rapsilico." She gestured to the armless accent chair next to her armoire. She had purchased the chair because the chocolate velvet coordinated well with her bedroom furniture, and she wanted another comfortable place besides her couch to read. But she ended up doing all of her reading in bed. She spent most of her time in bed. Alone. "You can sleep here."

"Solid."

Rapsilico reclined in the chair, his hands on his legs. He didn't have a change of clothes, and there was nothing she could offer him to sleep in – no pajamas or even a tee shirt left behind by a former lover. They would have to go shopping in the morning. She turned off the light and climbed in bed.

"Goodnight, Rapsilico."

"Night, Shawnie."

"Time to close your eyes."

The clone fell silent. Light from the street lamp streamed through her vertical blinds, bisecting his torso. Shadows hid one side of his face, but she still saw his unblinking blue eyes.

Shawnetta drove east on Wilshire on her way to Claudine's house. It was Saturday morning, and she called her friend an hour ago to ask her to accompany her and Rapsilico on their shopping spree. Shawnetta was eager to show off her White Man, even though she knew Claudine only had eyes for men with dark skin. But her clone was so handsome and polite, he could win over the most militant of black women. *She needs to keep her options open.*

Earlier, when Shawnetta arose, she nearly tumbled out of bed at the sight of the upright figure in her accent chair, hands on his legs, lids at half mast. It took her a moment to realize that he was not an intruder. She decided to shower and dress before activating him for the day. While he was still in resting mode, she raked a wide-toothed comb through his hair, patting the yellow tresses into place. She straightened the polo shirt and shook a few drops from a sample cologne vial in his general direction. Then she called his name.

Now they cruised down Crenshaw in her Jetta, the White Man's arm resting on the window ledge.

"I love sunny days. It's so beautiful outside, isn't it, Rapsilico?"

"Word." He turned toward her with a grin. He would look even sexier wearing a pair of designer shades. "Not as beautiful as you, though."

Shawnetta fumbled for a CD in the case attached to her visor. "What kind of music do you like to listen to?"

"Oh, I listen to whatever – Jay-Z. Snoop. Ice Cube. Whatever you like, Shawnie."

"So, you're a hip-hop head?"

"I always have hip-hop in my head."

I wonder how black they made him. Shawnie signaled to get into her left lane. Claudine's street, Adams Boulevard, was a few blocks away. A Latino selling oranges near the freeway on ramp turned to watch as they passed. *Does he only have a superficial hood knowledge, or is there some soul in his DNA?*

She said, "I loved hip-hop growing up, but now most of it is so commercial. Some ugly, tatted up, gold-teeth fool is always bragging about his money and his bitches," she said. "But we had real music back then – Public Enemy, Digable Planets, Salt-N-Pepa, De La Soul."

"Black Sheep. Eric B and Rakim."

Shawnetta curled her lips in disbelief. "What? You don't know about Eric B and Rakim."

"I know Eric B and Rakim."

"Okay. Whatever."

The blond Man smiled. Then nodding his head, he rapped:

"*I came in the door, I said it before*
I never let the mic magnetize me no more
But it's bitin' me, fightin' me, invitin' me to rhyme
I can't hold it back, I'm lookin' for the line ..."

"Wow." Shawnetta shook her head as she inserted her CD. "Color me impressed."

She was silent for a few minutes, digesting the experience. She felt more attracted to him now. They liked the same artists. Or was he only reciting from an extensive catalog of rap music that had been preselected for him? Her White Man continued to nod in rhythm to an imaginary beat, and she turned up the volume on her Elton John song.

A few minutes later, Shawnetta pulled up in front of the pink bungalow Claudine rented. Three or four kids played catch in the middle of the street. They separated to let her car pass, and then continued to toss the ball to each other.

"I'm going to get my friend. Stay here, Rapsilico."

"Aight."

As she opened the gate and headed up the walkway, Claudine poked her head out the front door. She must have been watching from the window. She locked the door, then turned toward Shawnetta with a wide grin.

"If it ain't the Colored Girl and the Clone."

"Good morning to you too, Claudine."

"You know I'm just messing with you, girl." Claudine chuckled, zipping up her sweater jacket. Although September was still considered a summer month in Los Angeles, the morning was chilly. "Can't wait to check out your new man. How's he treating you?"

"He just came in the mail yesterday. But so far so good," Shawnetta said as they walked toward the car. "We went out to dinner last night."

"That's nice. Who paid?"

"He did." That wasn't exactly true. The NNI Companion came equipped with a wallet in his back pocket, but the debit card he used to pay for their Mexican food was pre-loaded with Shawnetta's money. He would continue to "treat" her with the card, but she had to check the balance and deposit more money when the funds ran out.

Claudine whistled, opening the gate. "That's what I'm talking about. I need to get me a White Man. I always heard they don't mind coming out the pocket." She paused, staring at the pale arm hanging from the window of the Jetta.

Shawnetta said, "Come on. He won't bite. He's super polite, and he's into hip-hop."

They approached the passenger side of the car. Rapsilico stared straight ahead at the ball-playing kids who had resumed their rule of the street.

"You know I ain't into white boys, but damn, that nigga is fine." Claudine bent down to get a better look at the clone, and Shawnetta nudged her. "Can he hear me?"

"Yes. He has ears." Shawnetta opened the door. "Rapsilico. This is my friend, Claudine."

The clone hopped out of the car, and Claudine backed up, a mistrustful frown on her face.

"Whattup, Claudine."

"Hey."

"Can I call you Claude?"

"No."

"Aight."

Claudine studied the White Man. "What's your name again?"

"Rapsilico."

"It fits." She turned to Shawnetta. "Let's go, before my neighbors see me out here talking to Frankenwigger."

She reached for her door, but the clone grabbed the handle first. "Let me get that," he said. Claudine climbed into the car and sat back in her seat, impressed. Shawnetta knew it was because most men in L.A. were sorely lacking in manners. They brushed past Shawnetta to enter the elevator first, let doors slam in her face, and on the rare occasions when they asked her on a date, they were at the entrance of the restaurant long before she'd even descended from the car. Now here was this Companion treating them with more respect than most red-blooded men they knew. After he closed Claudine's door, he raced around to the driver's side.

"I got you, Shawnie."

"Thank you."

It would be nice to put everything in his hands, to turn the wheel over to her White Man and let him chauffeur them around town. She knew his wallet contained a license that specified he was a driving-enabled clone, but she didn't want to take the risk. Not yet. Maybe after knowing him for a few weeks, she'd take him somewhere out of the way to test his skills.

As they drove off, Claudine said, "How old are you, Silico?"

"Rapsilico," Shawnetta said.

"Right. *Rap*silico. How old are you?"

"Twenty-seven."

"Got you a young boy." Claudine winked at Shawnetta in the rearview. "Now do they rent you out to white girls too, or are you only leased to sisters?"

"Claudine."

"What? Everybody in here is grown. I'm just getting to know Rasp – your friend here." She reached up to feel the clone's hair. "If I didn't know any better, I'd think this crack – this White Man was the truth!"

Shawnetta glanced over at her Companion. If Claudine's insults bothered him, it didn't register on his face. He still smiled that boyish grin as he stared at the street ahead.

"Back to my question, Rapilico."

"His name is Rapsilico."

"My mistake. Back to my question, Rapsilico. Do they rent you to white girls or only black women?"

"I'm strictly into sisters."

"Good answer," Claudine said.

"I love black skin," he said

Claudine chuckled a good minute before she said, "They trained you well, honey. But those pretty blue eyes must have cataracts, because that sister sitting next to you is far from black. Well, she black, but she as light as they come. What in the world is this country coming to when even light-skinned chicks are hard up for dates?"

Rapsilico put a hand on Shawnetta's cheek. "She's beautiful."

Shawnetta felt her face reddening beneath his oily fingerprints. The clone had been programmed well … or had her features triggered something in him, some memory of loveliness?

Claudine sat back in her seat, watching the passing scenery. A dread-locked man hoisted a toddler onto his shoulders as they crossed the street. The little girl grasped his ears, resting her cheek against his hair.

"Your windows are dirty," she said.

Ten minutes later, they pulled into the parking lot at the Baldwin Center Plaza on La Tijera and Heliotrope. Although it had been renamed by its new owners several years prior, everyone Shawnetta knew still called it Baldwin Center. She rarely shopped at this mall because it was one favored by black folks, and too many black people congregating in one place made her nervous. If she was ashy because she forgot to put on lotion after getting out of the shower, they noticed. If her hair wasn't styled to a T, they noticed. Their unvoiced criticism was harsher than verbalized critiques from the white people she knew. She would definitely stand out with Rapsilico here, but that's what she wanted.

"Now, this is family," Claudine said, as they neared the entrance. She linked arms with Shawnetta. The clone was close on their heels like a puppy vying for attention. Claudine swatted at him with her free hand. "Back up, son."

"He doesn't take orders from you." Shawnetta turned to her White Man. "She meant to say, can you give us a little room, please?"

"Aight."

Claudine was messing up her plan. Shawnetta wanted to make her entrance hugged up with Rapsilico. Now he lagged behind like a reluctant coworker who had gotten roped into joining them.

"He's nice and everything, but I can't wait until his lease is up," Claudine said. "A little plastic is cool every now and then, but I don't see how you can wake up to that every day."

"Why not? He sure is easy on the eyes."

"True, but black love is a beautiful thing." She nodded at a pregnant woman with braids who was stopped at the crosswalk, waiting for an SUV to pass.

Shawnetta said, "I don't believe in black love anymore."

"That's because you need to come south of Wilshire Boulevard," Claudine said. "You're a beautiful woman, Shawnetta. Bourgie, but beautiful. You always get attention when you hit the hood. Plenty of guys was checking for you at that barbecue we went to on Slauson a few months ago."

"Not the attention I'm looking for. They were, like, ten years older than me and divorced, or had baby mamas," Shawnetta said. She finger combed her hair. She usually slicked it back into a ponytail on the weekends, but she had flat ironed it for the occasion. The burnt orange scoop neck dress she wore accentuated her hazel eyes. "Why should I settle? I have a degree. I have a good job in accounting at a top production company. I'm still young, and I don't have any kids."

"And you never will with Rap hanging around. Girl, it's a conspiracy."

"What is?"

"These clones. What if all the lonely, pitiful, black-man-hating, feeling-sorry-for-themselves sisters just up and got a cracker for hire?" Her chuckle had a bitter edge. "They'd be cuddling with clones every night, never taking time to get to know a real somebody – if that's what they wanted."

Shawnetta sighed. Claudine was so old school. And for all her "black love" talk, she hadn't been on a date in years either.

"Claudine, black women are dying out. We have to keep our options open," Shawnetta said. They walked through the automatic doors of a department store, and she glanced around for men's clothing. "Besides, I'm only going to be with Rapsilico for six months. The Naturally Nordic sales rep said that being with a clone helps attract real white men. It makes them less intimidated because they see you're open to interracial relationships."

Claudine sucked her teeth. "Honey, a real white man wouldn't touch you with a ten-foot-pole. You too close to Becky," she said. "You ain't dark enough, your hair ain't nappy enough, you ain't got enough ass, and you ain't got them strong Nubian features most crackers are looking for when they get their stroll on through the jungle."

"Whatever."

Shawnetta paused by a row of men's suit jackets. She crooked a finger at Rapsilico. "Come try this on, sweetie. We need to find you something hot for the holiday party."

Shawnetta held out a pinstriped black jacket and the clone slipped into it, but it hugged his biceps too tightly. She looked around. A tall dark-skinned salesman rang up a customer at a nearby register. As he handed the woman her bag, Shawnetta waved at him. He jogged over with a smile, which slipped when he saw the White Man standing by her side. She noticed the diminished cheer in his eyes, the same siphoning of joy that echoed in hers when she saw what appeared to be an available black man later joined by a white woman.

"Good morning. Need some help, ma'am?" His nametag read Xerxes.

"My boyfriend is buying a new suit," Shawnetta said. Behind her, Claudine snorted. "Can you help us with some sizes?"

"My pleasure." Xerxes gave Rapsilico the once-over. "You're a 38, right?"

"That sounds about right," Shawnetta said. The black man turned away from her, rifling through the clothes. He handed the White Man a jacket.

"Here you go, sir. I'll get you a size 32 pants."

"Thanks, son," Rapsilico said.

Xerxes paused, his hand gripping the rack. Claudine touched his shoulder. "Don't mind him," she said, nodding toward the clone. "He's on work release, and it's taking him some time to get used to real people again."

"Claudine!"

"What? Black men ain't the only ones on lock down, you know," she said, smiling at Xerxes. "We'll take these pants to the dressing room ourselves, thank you. Save you from seeing all those gangsta tattoos."

The black man chuckled as he walked away. Shawnetta turned to her friend, scowling.

"Don't insult Rapsilico," she said, grabbing the pants. "He has feelings."

"Does he now?" Claudine turned to the Companion. "You have feelings, Rapsilico?"

The White Man looked at Shawnetta, a smile playing on his thin lips. What would she do if he said no?

"Well, do you have feelings?" Claudine repeated. "Speak up."

"Hell yeah, I got feelings," the clone said. "Shawnie's the prettiest woman I've ever seen."

Rapsilico went to the fitting room to try on clothes, and Claudine stepped away to answer a call on her cell phone. Shawnetta was alone with Xerxes. Wire hangers scraped against the chrome rolling rack as the black man sifted through a selection of pastel button-down shirts. He was cute, someone she would be attracted to, with smooth, dark-brown skin and a short haircut edged up neatly at the temples. He smelled good too, a strong rich scent like oakwood and lavender. Pity, she never saw any handsome brothers when she was single.

"Here's another dress shirt in his size, ma'am."

Once Xerxes realized Rapsilico was with her, he'd directed all of his attention to the White Man, refusing to meet her gaze.

Now he held out a button-down light blue shirt.

"Thanks. I'll take it back to my boyfriend."

"You do that," the salesman said beneath his breath. "Sell out."

"Excuse me?" Shawnetta said.

"Just an observation."

Shawnetta frowned at him. All of his attractiveness drained away with that comment. Typical Negro. Acting all unprofessional and familiar just because they were both black, and she was a woman. She'd never run into such a clown working at Beverly Square.

"What observation is that?"

"You look just like the type of sister a white man would have on his arm – light-skinned, long-hair, pretty eyes." His voice was pleasant and conversational, as if displaying a good quality garment for her inspection. "I don't ever see them hugged up with no busted-looking black chicks. Always taking our women."

"Sorry to inform you, but I'm not your woman. I don't belong to you." Shawnetta gave him a dismissive wave. In spite of her anger, she felt triumphant. "You have a lot of nerve worrying about who I'm with. Brothers date Becky all day long."

"Not me," Xerxes said. The polite friction in his voice deepened. Shawnetta lowered her eyes, staring at the mole on his collarbone. "I'm strictly into sisters."

"Yo, Shawnie." She turned around as Rapsilico approached. She heard the black man moving away. "This look aight?"

The clone grabbed the lapel of his new suit and turned to the side. A price tag dangled from one sleeve.

Shawnetta sighed, running a hand down the polyester fabric. "It fits," she said.

It was a little after noon when Shawnetta dropped Claudine off at her house. They had only spent two hours at the mall, not the all-day excursion she planned. Not only had she grown weary of Claudine's wise-cracking, but the confrontation with Xerxes was still on her mind. He was hurt to see her out with her White Man, and even though it felt good to know she was the cause of his anger, those two words "not me" nearly shattered her desire for the clone.

On the drive back from Baldwin Center, she blasted her Elton John

CD, refusing to speak. Claudine continued to make jokes at Rapsilico's expense during the ride. Shawnetta wondered if their friendship could withstand her relationship with the White Man. They met four years ago at an open mic in Leimert Park, back when Shawnetta was dating a Kangol-wearing poet named Kai who channeled Gil Scott-Heron and R. Kelly. Claudine was the emcee for the evening, and after Kai's performance, she quipped, "I don't know whether to throw my fist in the air or throw my panties on the stage." Shawnetta loved her for that comment and vowed to befriend her after the show, even though she was shy about interacting with other black women. The militant and his revolutionary sex poems left Shawnetta's life a few months after the reading, but she and Claudine remained friends.

In spite of Claudine's insults, the White Man jumped down from the car as soon as it stopped and opened the door for her.

"Peace, Claudine," he said, as she stepped down from the car.

"Peace, Rap."

Claudine leaned on the passenger's side window, staring at Shawnetta. "Don't act all hurt, Shawnie. You know you my nigga." She flashed the peace sign. "Black love, baby. Don't forget it. It's a beautiful thing."

"Then why don't you have any?"

Claudine brushed a flaming pink dreadlock out of her eyes. She winked. "I have some every day," she said, walking toward her gate.

Shawnetta waited for the clone to climb back in the car. The kids were no longer playing ball in the middle of the street, but congregated on a front porch, listening to hip-hop and watching her. As soon as Rapsilico closed his door, she took off down the block.

Back in the foyer of her building, Shawnetta pressed the button for the elevator. Naturally, none of her neighbors were around to see her when she was looking cute. It was only when she wore a scarf as she took a basket of clothes down to the laundry room that they materialized outside the elevator doors. Rapsilico stood beside her, carrying four bags. She wanted to get him upstairs to her bedroom so he could model his new clothes for her. Shawnetta had bought her White Man two suits, six pairs of jeans, a pair of khakis, ten shirts, twelve pairs of briefs, pajamas, a robe, several pairs of dress and tube socks and two pairs of designer sunglasses. Her purchases cost half as much as it did to lease the clone. She had taken her things to another register to avoid Xerxes.

Once in her apartment, they both kicked off their shoes at the couch, and Shawnetta dropped her purse on a cushion.

"Let's take a look at your things, Rapsilico, to make sure they fit."

"Aight."

He followed her back to the bedroom, standing in the doorway obediently. She took the bags from him and shook out the contents on the bed. She wouldn't pack these clothes in the box when she shipped him back to NNI. *No other woman is going to benefit from my generosity.* When he left, she would donate his things to Goodwill. She settled into her armless accent chair and waited for him to undress.

"What do you want to try on first?" she said.

"Whatever you want, Shawnie."

"Let's see how the gray suit looks."

He held up the suit jacket and pants for her approval.

"Looks good, now let's see how it looks on you."

He tossed the clothes back on the bed, and pulled off his polo shirt. She saw again the scar on his neck, the size of a mosquito bite. He let the shirt fall to the floor. It was the second time she had seen him naked from the waist up, but this time, she wondered how it would feel to run her hand across his chest. His near-nakedness took away the sting of Xerxes' comment. The clone unzipped his jeans and stepped out of them, standing before her in white boxers. Rapsilico's hips were slim, but his legs were strong and toned. She fidgeted in her accent chair. It was too early in the day to drink – at least for her – but she needed a glass of wine.

"Rapsilico, can you get something for me from the kitchen? If you go in my refrigerator, there's a bottle of wine in the door. Riesling. R-I-E-S-L-I-N-G. Can you get that for me, please?"

"Aight."

"On your way back, grab a wine glass out of my cabinet next to the fridge, please. In the silverware drawer below, there's a red thing called a wine opener. It has a black screw. Bring that back too. Got it?"

"Got it."

He left the room, and she heard him bustling about in the kitchen. She did not trust him to open the wine on his own, but she would teach him in time. She would teach him to cook, to fold her laundry, to take her car to get it washed since he could not wash it himself. Again, she wondered what would happen if he got wet. Maybe some inner intelligence unit would fizzle out. No need to worry about that. She would take care of him. She sighed, crossing her legs. *This is how it feels to have a live-in partner.* A significant other. It felt good to be waited on.

Her White Man returned after a few minutes, the bottle of Riesling under his arm. He had brought back a champagne glass, but that was close enough. She took the corkscrew from him, and sat the bottle and glass on her dresser.

"Watch, Rapsilico," she said, as she inserted the screw into the cork. "I might need you to open a bottle for me some time. It looks like fun, right?"

"Word."

He watched as the cork slid out of the mouth of the bottle with a pop, and a few drops of white wine splashed the oak. She wiped it away with her hand, saddened that he could not drink with her.

The clone stood before her, silent, as she sipped her wine. When she finished one glass, and he poured her another, she said, "Let's see how that gray suit looks."

Three hours later, the White Man was pulling on his last item of clothes, a brown satin pajama set. Shawnetta didn't own such fancy sleepwear, preferring to settle beneath the covers in cotton nightgowns and floral pajamas, or even the gray short set emblazoned with the name of her alma mater, Hampton University.

"Looks good, Rapsilico. Everything looks great," Shawnetta said, trying not to slur her words. It was getting dark outside, and she reached behind her to close the venetian blinds. During her private fashion show, she had downed a bottle and a half of wine. "Come here. Let me take off the tags."

When the clone was within reach, she grabbed the waistband of his pajamas and snatched away the tag. "Let me have the shirt so I can take that tag off too," she said.

He obeyed, and she snapped off the price tag, dropping the pajama top to the floor. Shawnetta patted the velvety cushion next to her.

"Sit with me for a minute, Rapsilico."

"Aight."

The accent chair wasn't big enough for both of them, so Shawnetta turned on her side to make room for the clone. Once he was seated, she rolled over, pressing her chest to his. He didn't smell as sour as before, just the normal sweat of a man who had been donning and removing clothes for several hours. His skin was warm with a faint sheen, not the greasiness that cloaked him the day before. She ran her fingers through his hair.

"How many owners have you had before me, Rapsilico?"

"I'on know."

"Do you think I'm beautiful?"

"Word."

She snuggled closer to him, running her hand over his chest.

"What do you like most about me?"

"I like your hair."

"That's it?"

He craned his neck, as if to sear her features on his retina. "I like your eyes. You got real pretty eyes."

She nuzzled his neck to hide the blush creeping into her cheeks. Her eyes were her best feature – brownish gold tinged with green. Rapsilico had a brain. He had a mind of his own. He couldn't have been programmed to say those things – could he?

"Thank you, Rapsilico. You have pretty eyes too."

Here she was, flirting with a clone, a White Man who had been en route to her apartment in a box the day before, who had emerged on her living room floor from plastic bubble wrap. Now she wanted to kiss him. Instead, she touched the scar on his neck.

"What happened to you?"

He regarded her with unblinking blue eyes. "What?"

"This scar on your neck." Taking his hand, she pressed his finger to the wound. "Feel that?"

"I'on know what that is." He toyed with a hank of her hair, and she was glad she had flat ironed it that morning. "Pretty."

"You're sweeter than any guy I've dated. I wish I didn't have to give you back."

Shawnetta fell asleep like that, with a hand on her White Man's chest, as it rose and fell. Rose and fell. He put his arms around her.

The next day at work, she bumped into her boss, Heidi, in the break room. The blonde woman unpacked the contents of her lunch bucket and stacked the containers in the refrigerator.

"Mornin', Shawnetta. How's it going?"

"Good morning, Heidi. Everything's great. Did you have a good weekend?"

"Really good. We took the kids to the park, and then my youngest had a birthday party to go to." She closed the door of the fridge, appraising Shawnetta's outfit. "Gurrl, that color looks good on you! Is that blouse new?"

"This old thing? No, you've seen it before."

The blonde woman studied her face. "Oh, it looks new. You just look different, I guess," she said as she walked away. Heidi was a senior accountant at the production company. She was one of a handful of white women at the job who had black husbands. Women like Heidi loved to bring their biracial kids in on "Take Your Child to Work Day," not to inspire the kiddies or provide an educational environment for them, but so the other workers could "ooh" and "aah" over the golden-brown complexions, could fondle the soft ringlets.

I'm going to start hanging up pictures of my White Man in my cubicle.

Shawnetta knew Heidi and the rest of her coworkers noticed a change in her. She couldn't hide it. She glowed, and she greeted them in the mornings with an easy grin like a woman used to getting great sex on a regular basis. Except she wasn't. She hadn't even kissed her White Man, and he'd been living with her for nearly a month. She allowed Rapsilico to lay in bed with her now and hold her as she fell asleep. Sometimes, she would awaken in the middle of the night to see his ice-blue eyes trained on her face. "Time to close your eyes, Rapsilico," she would say groggily, and she felt the rumble of stillness that signaled he was shutting down. Every day when she returned home from work, she called him out of his resting mode, and he appeared in the doorway of her bedroom with a grin. He removed her shoes at the door and gave her a foot rub for a half hour. She taught him to make simple dishes – stir fry veggies with rice or spaghetti with soy ground round. He learned how to pour wine, and he never splashed droplets as he removed the cork.

He's such a good learner, she would say as she observed the clone folding her clothes or running a mop across her hardwood floors.

"Who knew white men were such good maids? I need to get me one," Claudine said when Shawnetta invited her over for drinks the following night. Shawnetta had gone three weeks without speaking to her friend, but she couldn't stay mad at her forever. Besides, it was natural for a woman to feel envious when she saw her girlfriend blossoming while she wilted in her own clod of dirt.

Shawnetta laughed. "He has a good teacher."

Claudine watched as the blond Man ran a chamois over the white leather sofa. "I bet you make him clean in his drawers when you're alone."

Shawnetta regarded Claudine over the rim of her glass, saying nothing.

"Well, whatever floats your boat, Shawnie. I like him. He's cool peeps. What have the Beckies at the job said about your boy?"

"They haven't met him yet." Shawnetta squeezed a wedge of lime and then dropped it into her mojito. "The holiday party is in a few months. That's when I'll make my big reveal."

"Good thing you don't have family in Cali. What would your mama say if you showed up on her doorstep with a big ole strapping clone?"

Shawnetta tittered. "Emma Lou Jones used to say, 'If he can't use your comb, don't bring him home,' so you know Rapsilico would be a double shock to her."

"True that." Claudine glanced at the figure polishing behind her. "But I guess more and more black mamas better get ready for their daughters with their robo-boyfriends and a future free of grandkids."

Shawnetta lowered her eyes, tracing the rim of her glass with her finger. "I still want kids. I'm going to have them one day too."

"I know you will, Sis. If you hadn't pissed off dude at the department store, you could have been on a couple of dates by now. He was fine, and he was checking for you, too. You saw how he ran over until he peeped your rent-a-cracker."

"He wasn't checking for me."

Shawnetta pulled a sprig of mint from her glass and sucked on it, trying to put the argument with Xerxes out of her mind. Even when Rapsilico's lease expired, and she boxed him up and mailed him back to NNI, she wouldn't go back to black men. She was moving on, as many of them had.

"Shawnetta, are you living in your head again?" Claudine's voice tilted her out of her reverie. "You better call Rap over there before he rubs a hole in your cushions."

Shawnetta looked over at her White Man. He'd been polishing her sofa for the last thirty minutes. "Good job, Rapsilico. You can stop now."

"Aight."

"Can you heat up the sauce that I made earlier?"

"What's for dinner?" Claudine said, watching the White Man's back as he headed toward the fridge. "Please tell me it's not white people's food."

"Spaghetti and ground round."

"White people's food. I love you, Sis, but I ain't in the mood for no fake meat. A sista is starving. Let's order a pizza or something."

Shawnetta shrugged. "Fine. You're a guest. We can order pizza. I'll just get mine without any meat."

Claudine smiled at her. "I won't even touch that one," she said, downing the last of her liquor.

The smell of burning hair hit Shawnetta in the face as she opened the door to Sexy Shearz beauty salon. She'd been with her stylist, Myaisha, for the past three years, maintaining her every-two-weeks Saturday appointments. Although she would not admit it, Shawnetta felt proud getting her hair done in a salon with a Beverly Hills address. Growing up in a small town in Pennsylvania, there was one storefront beauty shop where Shawnetta and the other black girls on her block went to get their hair done. The owner was a gap-toothed woman named Miss Shirley who gave all of her clients the same cap-of-a-mushroom style.

"Hey, chica." Myaisha looked up from the hair she was applying relaxer to. She was a pretty brown-skinned woman with a permed red-violet mohawk and deep dimples. She had the tattoo of an open pair of scissors on the inside of her wrist. The only flaw Shawnetta noticed was a wandering left eye that made the other stylists dub her "Eye-isha" behind her back.

"Good morning, Myaisha. I know I'm a little early."

"That's cool. I got a few heads ahead of you, so have a seat."

The main thing Shawnetta disliked about getting her hair done on a Saturday was the excruciating three or four hours she spent in the salon, especially on a sunny and brisk October morning like today. She took a seat by a bank of dryers and pulled a chick lit novel from her purse. Nothing too serious. She didn't want the other women, who held open magazines on their laps or played games on their cell phones, to think she was stuck up. Myaisha was a single mom, so she always triple and quadruple booked her clients so she would have plenty of heads in rotation on Saturday, her biggest pay day.

Shawnetta was parked down the block from the salon on Melrose, and her White Man waited for her in the car. Her appointment was scheduled for 8:30, and she figured she'd be in the stylist's chair at least until noon. She had instructed Rapsilico to enter Sexy Shearz and look for her around 11:30. She placed one hundred dollars in his wallet to pay for her hair. *Going to be interesting to see what happens when he walks in.* With the exception of delivery men and Marq, a tall stylist with a glistening bald head who specialized in extensions, no men ever came into the salon. It was the unspoken territory of women.

Shawnetta glanced around the salon. *Most black women are embarrassed to let a man see them getting their hair done.* It felt intimate and shameful. The clients having their kinky hair blow dried straight didn't like to sit near the window, where passersby could see the metamorphosis of naps. Someone was always trekking through a brittle trail of hair on the floor and the air smelled green with chemicals.

Myaisha tapped her shoulder. "I'll be with you in ten, chica. Just going to eat my breakfast wrap," she said. "Put your smock on, and meet me in my chair."

That was something else about the salon that Shawnetta loved: There were no oversized, plain black uniforms to don before getting one's hair done. Each client got to select their very own rose-colored, back-belted European smock. So chic!

Ten minutes of sitting in the stylist's chair turned into thirty. Just as Shawnetta's neck itched with irritation, Myaisha took her back to a row of shampoo bowls to wash her hair. As spray from the nozzle soaked Shawnetta's tresses, the beautician asked, "So how's work?"

"It pays the bills, and it allows me to get my hair done every two weeks."

"Well, then we're thankful for it." Myaisha laughed as she scrubbed Shawnetta's scalp. The open scissors on her wrist pulsed, as if they were about to slice her vein. "And how's that white guy you were telling me about?"

"Good, thanks for asking." She hid a smile, leaning back into the sink. "He's going to drop by when I'm done. He said he would pay for me to get my hair done."

"Must be nice. I know it's no problem for them to come out the pocket."

Shawnetta had never had a boyfriend in the four years that she'd been coming to the stylist. She didn't count Kai, who mainly dropped by when she was horny. Over the years, she heard other clients brag about getting a new cut or color to look good for their men, or wanting to spruce up their styles for date night. Shawnetta always listened to their plans with a heavy heart. Of course, she wanted to look good for herself, and she always kept up her straightened styles, even on the weeks when she didn't go to Sexy Shearz. But the idea of getting something special done to her hair to please a mate was something she hadn't thought of in a long time.

"You know I'm an independent woman," Shawnetta said, as a stream of water splashed in her eye. "But I like to be treated too."

"What does he say about your hair?" Now Myaisha slathered on conditioner. It felt cold on Shawnetta's scalp. "Like, does he trip when you get out the shower and it's all fro'ed out?"

Shawnetta's White Man had never seen her hair wet, because she placed him in resting mode during the times that she washed and styled it. He did see her going to bed at night wearing a scarf, but if he found it repulsive that she wrapped up her hair to protect her tresses, he never mentioned it. He always told her she was beautiful.

"He's a good guy. He's conscious," Shawnetta said. "I would never date a white man who made me feel bad about my hair."

Myaisha wrapped Shawnetta's hair in a plastic cap and led her back onto the main floor. She placed Shawnetta beneath a hooded dryer with leave-in conditioner that she hadn't asked for. Her beautician had all kinds of tricks to keep her clients rotating, but to make them feel as if they were the only one she attended to.

Well, she does have a little boy. Shawnetta tried to concentrate on her novel, but her eyes felt heavy. She always had the urge to doze once the hot air enclosed her head. She awakened to Myaisha raising the hood, beckoning her to follow her back to the sink.

By 11:30, the blow dryer whirred as Myaisha raked it through Shawnetta's hair. She needed a trim, but her hair was getting long – a few inches past her shoulders, and she didn't want to lose the length. As Myaisha parted her hair and combed the attachment through another row of wet locks, Shawnetta glanced out the bay window onto Melrose. A woman walked by carrying a little dog in the crook of her arm. A man in a business suit passed her going in the opposite direction. He spoke on a cell phone, looking lost. Then the White Man strolled into her field of vision. He looked down at the paper in his hand and up at the awning of the salon. Shawnetta bit her lip, patting her foot against a rung of the chair. Rapsilico looked so handsome wearing his shades and a new mustard yellow leather jacket, that she forgot he belonged to her.

"Who is that Brad Pitt-looking nigga?" Marq craned his neck to get a look at the clone.

"Sure is a cutie pie," said a woman with pink perm rods in her hair. "And I'm not even attracted to white guys."

Myaisha tapped Shawnetta on the shoulder with her rat-tail comb, and Shawnetta hit her back. She felt giddy again, the same way she felt when she first opened the carton and gazed down at the plastic-wrapped form. There was someone waiting for her.

"I think someone in here knows him," Myaisha said.

The women turned toward Shawnetta. Before she had a chance to process what she was feeling, the bell over the door jingled.

"Yo," she heard the White Man say to the receptionist, "I'm here for Shawnie."

"Shawnie?" Myaisha said with a giggle. "Aww. Your boo has a nickname for you."

She turned off the blow dryer, and swiveled the chair around. Shawnetta faced the mirror. Her hair was parted down the middle. One half lay long and straight, caressing her collarbone. The other half was a spongy globe of naps. As she regarded the contrasting textures, the White Man approached Myaisha's station.

"I'm looking for Shawnie."

The stylist tilted a rat-tail comb in Shawnetta's direction. Was it her imagination, or did the clone pause, unsure? *Rapsilico, it's me.* Her stomach muscles tightened. Would the White Man embarrass her and leave her in the salon amidst the green air and discarded locks? Would he say her hair was ugly and nappy in front of the twenty or so women with similar textures?

"Almost didn't recognize you, yo." He lifted a hank of straightened hair and let it fall back against the designer smock. "Your hair looks nice."

Behind her, Marq snickered. "Girl, you trained this one well." He resumed threading a weft of blonde highlights into a braid on his client's scalp, and the woman laughed with him.

Myaisha held up her blow dryer. Woolly strands collected in the teeth. "She's going to be another hour. You can wait out in the reception area, if you want."

The clone raised his shades, locking eyes with Shawnetta. "Should I stay here or in the car?"

Shawnetta shook her head. "You can wait for me by reception. I'll come check on you in a minute."

"Aight." The White Man turned on his heel, crushing wisps of hair underfoot.

Shawnetta began to feel adventurous in the White Man's presence. Not since college, when she strolled along the canals of Amsterdam with several girlfriends her senior year, sucking on a cannabis lollipop, had she felt so daring. She dined at new restaurants, visited new museums and traveled to new parts of town with Rapsilico that she would have never experienced on her own. Before he arrived on her doorstep, she felt scrunched up in her own life, boxed in by her job, her hatred of happy couples, her lack of a mate and of purpose in life. But while holding the White Man's arm as they strolled through the Museum of Tolerance, or as he sat across from her in a Vietnamese restaurant as she tried Pho for the first time, she felt a limb unfolding, a hand stretching out.

After awhile, Shawnetta realized she was no longer competing with white women. She could walk toward them on the street while they were hugged up with their black beaus and not look away. She knew that black women would always be the last chosen, considered the ugliest, the fattest, the angriest, the least intelligent. But she did not look away.

A few weeks before the holiday party, Shawnetta stood before her bedroom mirror trying on a new cocktail dress. It was an off-the-shoulder number with a straight skirt that was gathered at the left hip. The deep lavender color accentuated her eyes. Her four-day-a-week routine at the gym was paying off, and she was proud to see the definition in her arms. She felt flirty and feminine as she twirled in front of her dresser mirror.

The White Man lay on the bed, wearing his pajama bottoms. He was propped up on two satin pillows, watching her. She still had not been intimate with her Companion, but she liked modeling for him. She liked to think her smile or her movements triggered something deep within him, imprinted a memory of her on his irises.

"How do I look, Rapsilico?"

"Beautiful, Shawnie."

The phone on her nightstand rang. She sat on the edge of her bed and picked it up. When she announced herself, the man at the other end said, "This is Operator PA077 from NNI Industries. Hope I didn't catch you at a bad time, ma'am."

"No, I was just talking to my Companion."

"That's perfect. They're just great, aren't they?" the operator said. Without waiting for her response, he continued. "That's actually the purpose of my call this evening. You're at the midway point in your rental agreement, and we just wanted to give a quick courtesy call to see how things are working out for you."

"Everything's great." She looked over her shoulder at Rapsilico, who was staring at his reflection in the dresser mirror. "He's more than a man. More than I had hoped for."

"Excellent, excellent. I'll note that in your files for your sales rep. For being such a valued customer, you get a twenty percent discount toward your next rental."

Shawnetta paused. She had not thought about what she would do in March when she had to ship her White Man back to the manufacturer. *I'm not ready to let him go.* When she first leased him, her goal was to meet a real live white man while she was out with the artificial one, that his presence would somehow make her a more desirable catch. But another rental hadn't even crossed her mind.

"Can I rent Rapsilico again?"

"We've had that request before, but per our terms of service, that's not a possibility, unfortunately. Our Companions are merely temporary mates until the real thing comes along."

What if he doesn't come along in the next three months?

"I've updated your file. I'll let you get back to your Companion. Have a nice night."

"Wait. I have another question." Shawnetta rolled over and touched the White Man's throat. "Rapsilico has a scar on his neck. It looks like a mosquito bite. Did he get hurt or something by a previous owner?"

The man laughed, a wet robotic sound. "No, ma'am. That's just his flush port. All Companions are equipped with them."

Shawnetta gripped her cordless. "A flush port? What is that?"

"Our Companions will be rented many times over their life spans. It's just a process to help them give each and every woman 100 percent of their attention," he said. "They can't be 100 percent loveable and docile with Shaniqua if they're confusing her with Ranae."

Shawnetta hung up on the operator's words, feeling sick. She flopped on her stomach, wrinkling the cocktail dress. In three months, NNI would rinse clean all memories of her from the White Man's data banks – her hair, her smile, her toenail polish.

"Do you think I'm pretty, Rapsilico?" She toyed with the White Man's hair.

"Word. The prettiest woman I've ever seen."

She turned on her back, facing the ceiling as he did. "Do you love me?"

He touched her cheek. "You're beautiful," he said.

At Beverly Square, shoppers strolled past Shawnetta, their bags rustling, as she reclined in the makeup artist's chair. The woman brushed on eye shadow the same lavender shade as Shawnetta's cocktail dress. Her eyes would be dramatic, her lips nude. Since her dress was off the shoulder, she wore her hair up, with a few tendrils hanging down to her lobes, which sparkled with dangling rhinestone earrings.

The White Man stood a few feet behind her, his hands clasped in front of his suit jacket. He wore shades, although it was nighttime and he was indoors. He looked like a Secret Serviceman who had been booted from the job for being too debonair. *So what. It's L.A, and the cool peeps wear their shades inside.* The holiday party started in an hour, and they would be fashionably late. Shawnetta had decided to get her makeup professionally done for the occasion. She wanted this night to be special. In spite of what the NNI operator said, she knew Rapsilico was different. She was looking forward to spending Christmas with him. She and the White Man set up a three-foot high artificial tree in the living room by the patio door and hung red and green ornaments from the stiff branches. They strung flashing lights across the valance of her vertical blinds. In the evenings, they sat on the couch in the dark – she with a glass of wine in hand, he with his arm draped over her shoulder – watching the multicolored twinkling.

"Your boyfriend doesn't talk much." The makeup artist's name was Greta, and the spearmint gum she chewed didn't mask her smoky breath. She was a blonde with pockmarked skin and a German accent. Shawnetta noticed that the girls at the makeup counter either had flawless skin or a bad case of acne. There never seemed to be any in between.

"He's the shy handsome type," Shawnetta said.

"Nothing wrong with that."

Shawnetta wiggled her fingers. "Rapsilico, come here." Her eyes were closed, but she felt him moving closer to her. "How does my makeup look?"

"You look amazing, Shawnetta. That color looks wonderful on you."

"Thanks, babe."

Earlier, before they walked out the door on their way to the mall, Shawnetta pressed the Vernacular Adjustment Module behind his ear. It was a little knob that felt like a hardened cyst. She rubbed it a few times until his speech was free of "aights" and "solids." Although she found her White Man's slang sexy, she decided to tone it down for the party. In real life, she didn't think she could date such a proper man. They bored her. Even though she was a professional woman, she didn't need a man who golfed or played tennis or talked business deals with his pals at the country club. She would take Rap over Biff any day.

Now Shawnetta felt something wet and cold on her closed lid near her fake lashes. The makeup artist painted on a thin streak of liner. She said, "How long you guys been dating?"

"Three months," Shawnetta said.

"Ah. Seems like you've been a couple longer than that."

"It does."

"One thing is for sure," she said, as she drew the liner pen across the other lid. "You guys would make great-looking babies."

Twenty minutes later, Shawnetta paid for her makeup and squeezed the bag into her clutch. It was a sparkly silver purse that matched the rhinestones on her shoes. Then, linking arms with Rapsilico, they headed out of the boutique and into the mall. Was it only three months ago since she paraded the White Man through this very plaza in the hopes of attracting the angry stares of black men and white women. Now that she considered Rapsilico as something akin to a lover, she felt bad for using him.

"It's our three-month anniversary, Rapsilico. Time flies."

"No doubt about it. Happy anniversary."

Shawnetta took small, delicate steps so she wouldn't slip on the tiles.

The clone slowed his pace so as not to pull her along. Again, she saw a picture of them in her mind as prom kids. They were an aging King and Queen who had not yet realized the ceremony ended years prior. Rapsilico looked dashing in his three-button black pinstripe suit and attracted veiled stares from passing women – white and black. The diamond stud she bought glittered from his left lobe with false promise.

She handed the White Man her keychain as they headed toward the yellow terminals to pre-pay for parking. Over the past month, she had taken him out to drive late at night to test his skills. They cruised through the deserted parking lots of malls and home improvement stores. When she felt confident with the clone behind the wheel, they took the 118 Freeway toward Ventura. She never traveled to the more rural areas of L.A., had only driven that far west once for a job interview when she first got to town. Before Rapsilico, she lived her life within twenty square blocks, rarely driving south of Wilshire or north of Hollywood Boulevard.

"You're going to make a left when we get out of this parking lot, onto La Cienega. You have to insert the ticket and wait until that arm lifts before you go. Remember?"

"Yes. I remember."

Shawnetta leaned back in her seat, taking in the Christmas decorations strung from the awnings of businesses they passed. The season never felt as festive to her as it had in Maryland. Maybe because the streets were devoid of snow and kinship.

A line of cars snaked past the valet stand as they neared the nightclub where the holiday party was held. A few of her coworkers milled about the arched bamboo entry gate. Everyone looked underfed and glittery. She sighed. The functions were so superficial, but she had to put on her game face and hobnob with the women she worked with. They were always extra friendly when they saw her outside the production company, throwing their arms around her as if welcoming home a long-lost friend. But she had never been inside any of their homes, and they had never walked inside her door either. In past years, she had taken Claudine as her date, and they sat in the corner drinking all night, laughing at the rigid forms flailing on the dance floor.

"Stop here, Rapsilico, and put the car in park. But leave your keys in the ignition." Shawnetta checked her makeup in the mirror on her visor. Her nose was already shiny, and she blotted the sheen with the sponge from her compact. "That man is going to hand you a ticket and move the car for us. We'll get it back when we leave."

A dark-skinned Latino wearing a blue jacket opened the door for Rapsilico. Her White Man was so tall, she was always amazed when he unfolded himself from the car and stood up. She noticed how service people bowed a little when interacting with him, the kind of deference she never received.

"Good evening, sir." The attendant handed Rapsilico a stub.

Rapsilico said, "Good evening."

"Enjoy the club."

"Thank you. Have a good night."

The attendant opened her door. He composed his face before saying, "Good evening, ma'am. You look nice tonight."

"Thank you." She handed him a camera. "Can you take our picture?"

She waved Rapsilico over and put her arm around his waist. He smelled good tonight, a hint of melon and sandalwood. They could have been models promoting a new L.A. hotspot – especially with her flashy rhinestone earrings and Rapsilico's shades. She thanked the valet and returned the camera to her clutch. Then taking the White Man's arm, they headed toward the front door.

Club Citi-ZEN had recently opened its doors, yet another Japanese-inspired restaurant that doubled as a hangout for the pretty people. To get to the main entrance, partygoers crossed a modern wood walkway where fat, multi-colored Koi swam lazily in the pond below. Twenty-something women shivered in spaghetti strap dresses as they smoked and chatted beneath the lattice patio cover. Shawnetta glanced up at the snatches of dark-blue sky visible through the crossbars.

The club was packed and sweaty, the kind of funky heat that would wilt her hair before the night ended. She looked around for familiar faces. There were a few male production assistants standing regally by the bar, their hair moussed, their button-down shirts freshly pressed. They gestured with self-importance, as if their days did not consist of making script copies and delivering them on a cart. As an accountant, Shawnetta held a higher position and was far removed from their clerical world, yet when she passed them in the halls, it always seemed as if she were the one in the junior position.

A server approached with hors d'oeuvres, and she plucked a mini croissant sandwich from the tray. She still felt ashamed eating in front of her clone, like a mother enjoying a chocolate bar while her child starved nearby.

He dabbed her mouth with his index finger. "Just wanted to remove that crumb sticking to your lipstick, Shawnetta."

"Call me Shawnie."

"Shawnie."

It was a little after nine, but she was ready to go home. She missed their quiet nights on the couch. She sidled through a pack of moist bodies, trying not to muss her dress. The music was so loud, she felt the bass vibrating in her chest. The tendrils from her upsweep were limp. Everyone was so friendly and carefree, loosened by the free booze and throbbing hip-hop.

Across the room, she spotted Sarah, one of her coworkers from payroll. The redhead wore an unflattering green dress that emphasized her stomach rolls. Sarah went about her duties with a surly air, and she never smiled or laughed, unless it was at someone else's misfortune. In spite of her ugliness and lack of professionalism, she had found someone to marry her. Her husband Bernard stood beside her, a tall balding man with the same cranky air. No matter how trashy or uneducated her coworkers were, they were never without partners. She gripped her White Man's arm more tightly.

Shawnetta said, "Hey, Sarah. Having fun?"

"Yeah."

"Looks like it. Hey Bernard. How's it going?"

"Great."

They were silent for a minute, watching Rapsilico. She didn't want to introduce him, didn't want Sarah rolling his name around on her tongue. Instead, she said, "Have you seen Heidi?"

"She was here earlier with her husband. Said she could only stay for a few minutes." The redhead spoke to Shawnetta but kept her eyes on the White Man's face. "Her husband's company is having a Christmas party too, and she left to go to his."

Shawnetta opened her clutch and pulled out her camera again. Handing it to Sarah, she said, "Can you take a picture of me and my boyfriend?"

"Sure. Does he have a name?"

"Biff."

As soon as Sarah snapped the picture, Shawnetta retrieved her camera. "Thanks, lady. Gotta run," she said. "Nice seeing you again, Bernard."

Shawnetta grabbed the clone's arm and walked away before they could ask questions. She didn't belong here. The hair at the back of her neck was damp and beginning to curl. Her stomach felt queasy. She just wanted to charge through the writing maze of artifice in front of her, retrieve her car from valet and go home to watch her twinkling Christmas lights.

"Are you feeling okay, Shawnetta?"

"Shawnie."

"Shawnie. Can I get you something?"

"Let's just go home, Rapsilico. Do you mind? I'm tired."

"Okay."

As they headed toward the door, a black woman in a red dress stood in the entrance talking with one of the higher-ups. She was a new attorney for the production company, a dark-skinned woman in her forties with a neat mound of kinky hair that she kept trimmed short. When Shawnetta passed her in the hall or in the bathroom, the lawyer acknowledged her with a curt nod. Now she said her goodbyes to the executives and stepped all the way inside the door, a white man on her arm. Her date was tall, his blond tresses wavy. He turned to the attorney and smiled, and Shawnetta glimpsed the cleft in his chin. She dropped Rapsilico's hand, walking ahead of him on her way to the exit. As the gap between the couples closed, the woman faced her. Shawnetta nodded, and the lawyer gave her a wide smile. Shawnetta did not smile back, glancing instead at the face of the black woman's date as she brushed past. The white man grinned at her, a joy that did not quite reach his unblinking blue eyes.

"Shawnetta, what's the rush? Don't leave me."

So quick was Shawnetta to get away from the couple that she didn't realize she had left her White Man behind. Now Rapsilico stumbled toward her, trying to navigate the night through his designer shades. His foot slipped, and she gave a little cry. He toppled over the walkway into the Koi pond. It seemed that she heard the splash before he even hit the water, and several partygoers cried out in unison. She covered her mouth with her hand as two burly bouncers reached down to hoist Rapsilico from the pond. Shawnetta wanted to leave the White Man there, amidst the swelling crowd. She was fearful of what she would see when he was pulled to safety. Would his skin bubble and peel, revealing computerized innards beneath? Would he short circuit all together, lying face up on the high-end wooden deck with a mute smile?

Instead, he sputtered as he was heaved out of the water, removing the soaking suit jacket. His sunglasses were gone, but the chiseled good looks Shawnetta had grown to love were whole – intact.

"My bad, ya'll. Thanks for the help out."

He gave the bouncers the brotherhood shake, a complex intertwining of hands, and then headed her way, his new Italian leather shoes squeaking.

"You see that, Shawnie? Yo, that was bananas."

She put her arm around the White Man's waist, his shirt soaking her dress. Apparently, the unexpected bath had only affected his Vernacular Adjustment Module. She knew she would be the laughing stock of the holiday party, but she didn't care. Her Companion was safe. *Thank God, hiatus begins on Monday.*

"I'm just glad you're okay. Are you hurt?"

"Nah, I'm good. I'm good."

"Let's go home," she said, as they headed toward valet. "We need to dry off."

"Word."

Back at her apartment, she changed out of her wet cocktail dress in her bedroom closet as Rapsilico slipped out of his clothes in the bathroom. She had given him four fluffy towels to dry off with, and she heard him humming as he changed. Now he stood at the door of the closet in his bathrobe. She pulled her nightgown on, startled.

"You scared me, Rapsilico."

"My bad."

"Can you pour me a glass of wine while I wash my makeup off?"

He smirked. "You drink too much, Shawnie."

"Excuse me?"

"You need to lay off the Riesling."

She stared at him, puzzled. "Just pour me a glass, please. I need it now."

"Aight."

When she heard him moving around in the kitchen, she headed toward the vanity. So much for "100 percent loving and docile." Her clone was talking back to her. *Maybe this is the danger they warned about when he gets submerged in water.* Were the effects temporary or permanent? Would NNI charge her for ruining their model? Would they have to discard the clone and start from scratch with the cells of another white man?

"Shawnie, your wine out here."

"Coming," she said, peeling off a fake lash. Without the makeup and glamorous upsweep, she felt plain. She looked like every other light-skinned, long-haired black woman in L.A., as if she herself were a clone and did not know it. She sighed and went to join her White Man.

He was lounging on the couch, his feet up. The multicolored Christmas lights dappled his fuzzy white robe. "There it go," he said, pointing to her wine on the coffee table as if she could not see the glass. In spite of his hoodness, he was still sexy to her, much more so than his tepid proper-speaking self.

"Thank you, Rapsilico." She sat beside him on the couch, nuzzling his neck. His skin was cold.

"Why you always up on me, Shawnie? Acting so thirsty." Although he smiled, his blue eyes were hard.

"I'm not acting thirsty." She pushed away from him. "What's wrong? We always cuddle at night."

"You cuddle."

She stared at him. In his designer robe, he looked like some inmate she had brought home to pamper. "So you're saying you never wanted to hold me?"

"Your hair be scratching my face sometimes."

Shawnetta held up her hand. "Stop lying, Rapsilico. I rarely go to bed without wrapping my hair in a scarf – "

"It be slipping off in the middle of the night."

"How would you know?" She wanted to add "cracker." But she said, "You're in resting mode."

"My eyes are always open."

"Whatever." She grabbed her wine, about to rise. She would not let the White Man see her tears.

"Hold up. Hold up. I'm just messing with you, Shawnie." He pulled her back onto the couch, pried the wineglass from her hands and placed it back on the coffee table.

"You hurt my feeling, Rapsilico."

"My bad." He pressed his chest to hers, playing with a lock of her hair.

Beneath her nightgown, her nipples hardened. She was getting aroused again by her clone. But she didn't want to kiss him or have sex with him. She just wanted to be desired by him.

"Rapsilico, do you think I'm beautiful?"

"Here we go again."

"What's that supposed to mean? You always tell me you think I'm beautiful."

"Then why you asking?"

She brushed her knuckles against a jaw line where no hair ever grew. "Because that's the way you tell me you love me."

She reached for the White Man, and he allowed her to pull him close, like a mother embracing the petulant child who has just smacked her face. "Do you love me?"

His breath was a gust of wind blowing across a frozen sea. "Shawnie, you know you my nigga."

She held him there for a few minutes, listening to the quiet hum of his body. She brushed his golden tresses, which were sticky with her tears.

"Time to close your eyes, Rapsilico," she said. The white skin beneath the bathrobe pulsed itself into silence. Tomorrow, she would bind his hands with black ribbon, cocoon his body with bubble wrap and fold him back into his plain brown box. But for now she held her White Man, as the Christmas lights flickered, casting colored shadows across their legs.

The Death of Common Women

It was a deadly time to be common, black and a woman. All across the country these homely outlaws were being killed. They yanked them from their cars in Chicago, ambushed them at supermarkets in Philly and lay in wait for them outside of beauty salons in Los Angeles.

Deja Jones knew she wasn't common, but every night that she made it safely inside her Miracle Mile apartment, she slid home the deadbolt and pressed her back against the door, knees barely able to sustain her weight. *I have pretty eyes,* she reminded herself. And they were lovely – brownish-green flecked with gold. She had long legs, good teeth and straightened soft-brown hair that brushed the back of her shoulders. In spite of her looks, which once drew catcalls and sly stares from passing men, she still didn't feel safe, so she limited the time spent outside her small one-bedroom home.

Before the purges, when plain-featured women of color weren't hunted, when even the ugliest among them could walk the streets without fear, Deja spent most of her time out of doors. Every morning, she went jogging in her neighborhood, past the condos and luxury homes, past the turrets and bay windows, past the women walking little dogs on rhinestone leashes. She loved when the Jacaranda trees were in bloom. When they spilled their purple flowers on the sidewalk, she felt as if she were trampling through a dream.

She grew up in a small Pennsylvania coal-mining town, and there wasn't much beauty to be found outside her row home. Most days after school, she climbed the uneven front steps, let herself inside with a key that hung from her neck and headed straight to her bedroom to read. The worst part of being alone in that closet-like room was the laughter that reached her ears through the screen as the other kids played Double Dutch or practiced the latest dance moves on their stoop. *Here I am, twenty-nine and back in that closet again.*

Late last year, there were rumblings about the removals. As Deja sat in

Sexy Shearz beauty salon on Melrose, she heard several patrons discussing the purges. Her stylist Myaisha pulled a flat iron through her hair, and Deja craned her neck to listen.

"How do they know who to pick?" asked a light-skinned woman with a long nose who sat in a salon chair across from Deja. The woman's stylist parted a section of hair and smoothed on a smelly layer of lye. "Because there are a couple of chicks in my acting class who should have been gone by now."

Nervous titters filled the shop. A woman with green curlers in her hair and an open magazine on her lap spoke up. "Maybe they're just missing." Her rosy brown complexion was free of blemishes, and her voice had a southern lilt. "I can't believe ugly women are being killed on purpose."

"Why not? Women get killed every day," the fair-skinned lady said. Her eyes began to water from the chemicals being applied to her long locks, and she wiped the moisture away. "Maybe it's some type of population control."

"Just don't let 'em breed. That'll fix the problem," another voice chimed in, and the salon erupted in uneasy laughter again.

"I don't think the police would allow it," the woman with the green curlers said.

A stylist dismissed the speaker with a wave of her rat-tail comb. Her hot pink hair was the same color as her smock. "Girl, please. As if they care when we disappear." She pulled strands of hair from the teeth of her comb and dropped the kinky ball to the floor. "Wouldn't surprise me if the po-po was behind it."

"Looks like everyone in here is safe," said Marq, the salon's only male stylist. His bald head glistened with sweat as he sewed a wavy weft of extensions to the hair of the woman in his chair. "At least all of my clients."

Laughter rivaled the blare of blow dryers and piped in hip-hop music. Once the rose-colored smocks were removed, hairstyles assessed in mirrors and credit cards swiped, the women returned to their cars feeling sorry for the hunted, but assured of their own future. But as time passed, several regulars began to miss their standing appointments, among them the woman with green curlers in her hair.

Deja often compared herself to other black women. There were two who worked in the payroll department at her job with questionable looks. One was a nut-brown woman with big nostrils and a flat behind. Her other coworker was a few shades darker with thick lips and small wide-spaced teeth set in purple gums. Any day, the black-hooded attackers could spill out of the elevator of the stock brokerage and fall on those women. She felt angry that their commonness would somehow alert the death squad and bring destruction right to her cubicle. During those times, fear was a hammer in her chest.

One morning, Deja saw it happen. It was not yet 6:30, and she was driving south on La Brea to an early service at her mega church in Inglewood. She felt safest on Sunday. There were few cars on the road, and she believed God's hand was shielding her Jetta as she made her way down the hill to Grimes African Methodist Episcopal.

"He who dwells in the secret place of the Most High shall abide under the shadow of the Almighty," Deja recited softly. The psalm comforted her, made her feel grateful for a kind of holy invisibility. As she idled at the light on Pico, she heard a scream. Her first instinct was to make sure her doors were locked. When she confirmed that they were, she peeked out the passenger side window. A black-hooded figure wrestled with a woman near the bus stop. As he whipped an arm around the woman's throat, his sleeve fell back to reveal white skin emblazoned with a black tattoo, a dark rose. The woman's purse dropped in the scuffle. Pennies and nickels jangled on the sidewalk, and several coins rolled into the gutter. The victim's mouth was an arc of pain, and she continued to shriek, but weaker than before. Deja locked eyes with the dying stranger. There was nothing beautiful about that face contorted in fear – plain brown eyes, big nose and thick lips smeared with blood. Pleasure tickled her stomach as the woman fell to the ground. Then the light changed, and she drove off.

For the duration of the twenty-minute ride to church, she wondered about the dead woman. *Why in the world was she out by herself so early in the morning? Was she a prostitute? No, she didn't have the looks for that.* Deja turned up the volume on her gospel song to dispel the threads of worry collecting in her stomach. She felt ashamed for relishing in the assault, but that lady made herself an easy target. Maybe she thought she was immune somehow, free. *She had to see her face in the mirror each morning and know there was no protection.*

After service, Deja stopped by the organic market around the corner from her house. It was nearly 10:00. As she parked in the underground garage, some of the fear that clogged her throat daily began to dissolve. While at Grimes, surrounded by thousands of other women, in their fancy hats and tailored suits, her spirits lifted. Standing there beneath the stadium lights, hands raised in worship, she felt renewed. Pastor Lidell opened his sermon with a prayer for slain members, then remarked to his dwindling congregation – which was largely black and female – "Watch and pray, saints. Watch and pray. Ask God to search your heart and cast out anything that does not look like Him. Bind that spirit of commonness."

Now Deja lifted a red shopping basket with a chrome handle from a stack in front of the store and headed inside. "I am made in His image," she murmured to herself as she roamed the tight aisles. She placed a jar of coconut oil in the basket. She would also buy hemp seeds and witch hazel to make a facial scrub. One good thing that came out of the purges – if there could be anything good about the death of common women – was that Deja took better care of herself. Once she considered herself a laid-back beauty, preferring to pull her hair into a ponytail and dab on berry-colored gloss before going about her day. Now she rose an hour early each morning to curl her hair, line her lips and glue on fake lashes. The paunch she'd fretted over was gone, and she now fit into size 6 dresses, like the black number she wore to church. The year before, she would have never strolled into the sanctuary in something so slinky. *But a girl has to look out for herself.* Deja headed toward the bulk food bins at the back of the store.

As she walked down the center aisle, she thought she saw something dark and shadowy out the corner of her eye, over by the frozen section. But when she glanced to her left, there was nothing there. *Probably just my reflection in the freezer door.* She quickened her steps, her heels clacking on the tiles. Now there was movement by the produce section, some blackness lurking behind the mound of seedless watermelons. Deja spun around, holding the red basket in front of her as she rushed toward the exit.

"Miss?"

A young Latino kneeled by a shelf, stocking pasta boxes. Downy hair brushed the collar of his blue shirt. "Can I help you find something?"

Deja glanced over her shoulder at the section she'd fled. A blonde woman placed two bagged grapefruit on a scale, then reached for a green twist tie. There was no one else around. Deja sat the plastic basket on the floor next to the stock boy.

She said, "I left my wallet in the car. Can you watch this for me?"

He nodded, and she tried to smile, but her face felt tight. She hurried away.

"Miss?"

Deja glanced back. Maybe the kid was going to turn her in. Maybe he mistook her for some common lady. But he said, "If you're scared of what I think you're scared of, you got nothing to worry about."

Then, whistling, he returned to his boxes of pasta.

Safely back in her apartment, Deja kicked off her shoes at the front door and ran to her bedroom, throwing herself on the comforter. *I can't live like this,* she mumbled into the pillowcase. She could move back to the East Coast where she had family, but black women were targeted all over the country, especially in pockets of the inner city. She'd heard from her mom that several of her female cousins vanished. The news saddened her, but she wasn't too close to the women, hadn't seen them since they'd all played tag in her grandmother's backyard when she was ten. Deja worried about her mother's safety, but Vanessa Jones was in her sixties. *Mom has lived a full life.* Besides, her mother's golden-brown skin was still radiant, her features beatific. *Best to stay where I am right now until the end of the purges.*

She turned on her side, reaching for the leather-bound Bible on her nightstand. She owned two – this one and a monogrammed King James Version that she kept on the backseat of her car. "Search your heart," Pastor Lidell had said, "and cast out anything that does not look like Him."

I am good. I tithe, I pray and I go to work every day. Pay my bills on time too. She lay on her back, staring at the stucco ceiling. Overhead, she heard nails clicking as her neighbor's poodle chased some doggy toy across the hardwood floor. *Just like that boy at the market said, I have nothing to worry about. So why do I still feel so afraid?*

She was the only black woman in her 32-unit apartment building. Although she rarely reflected on that detail, now she felt lonely. She missed the presence of other women of color. At Sexy Shearz salon, she felt snatches of camaraderie, but she wasn't able to sustain that feeling of belonging once she walked out the door. Deja didn't have many black female friends, had never chatted with her two plain-featured coworkers or invited them to lunch. *It's hard for me to get close to people.* She cradled the Bible to her chest. In high school, the other kids teased her for having light skin and long hair – even though some of her tormenters had light skin and long hair as well – had mocked her proper speech, her love of reading and playing the piano. As an adult, she sensed that same jealousy from other "sisters" she passed on the street – felt it in their stares, the brusque greetings they returned.

What'll happen if they kill off all the ugly black women in the world? Whose features were safe? Were dark-skinned women targeted and those with big noses? Were big-lipped women a threat and those with nappy hair? What if, after the purges, all that remained was a race of slim-featured, milky-skinned, long-haired beauties? God Himself had rinsed the earth of common folk and repopulated the new world with people who resembled Him. She had been spared. *Maybe there's some divine purpose for all of this.* The hammer of fear that pinned her heart now lifted. *Everything happens for a reason. Maybe God saved me because He has plans.*

She replaced her Bible on the nightstand, feeling lighter than she had in a long time. Humming, she stepped out of her dress, her mind already focused on the organic stone-ground grits and eggs she would cook for breakfast.

Deja's new confidence lasted for nearly three weeks. It withered away as she witnessed something horrifying while driving home from work. Three young ladies crossed in front of her Jetta as she paused at the stop sign. Their silky extensions, longer than Deja's real hair, blew in the April breeze as they chatted with one another. Their complexion – a creamy brown – was fairer than her own, but whether the result of makeup or skin lighteners, she couldn't tell. They had stately noses, thin lips, and slim, high behinds that fit just right in their jeans. Most of all, they were laughing – a self-assured, feminine sound. That laughter caused the hammer to slam against her chest, pulping her fearlessness. She withered in the wake of their loveliness.

A horn blared behind her, jolting her out of her reverie. She turned left onto La Brea, heading home, feeling defeated, feeling common.

Over the next several days, she noticed more beautiful black women – at the post office on Wilshire, at the dry cleaners, at the market – and one had even been sitting in the reception area at her job, waiting to be interviewed. Where had they come from – this crush of golden women? Had they been living here all along, like daisies bordering a garden, revealed at last when the weeds were rooted up?

I won't survive, Deja said to herself one morning as she drove into work. She was running late, the first time in nearly six years of working at the brokerage. She would have to find some ugly women to hang out with for protection. She was an open target in the Miracle Mile District. *Maybe I'll move to Inglewood, closer to the church.* She took the elevator up to her office. On streets named Crenshaw and Slauson and Heliotrope, her beauty would bloom again. She'd be safe.

Deja made a left at the reception area, heading toward the payroll department. She would invite her coworkers to lunch. What were their names? Aileen and Tricia? Yeah, that was it. But which one was Aileen and which was Tricia? *I'll just swing by their office and say, "Hey ladies. I've been meaning to come by and say hello." Then we'll chat for a while, and I'll invite them to eat with me at the café.*

As she formulated her plan, the nervousness ebbed. It would be good for her to make new friends, at least associates. Someone to talk to over coffee about the panic she felt. As women more hunted than she, Deja longed to know how her coworkers dealt with the fear, the threat of being sluiced away in this genocide of homely girls.

She forced her lips into a grin as she neared the payroll office. She rarely came over to this side of the building, and she wondered if Aileen and Tricia would think it odd to see her standing in the doorway. A woman looked up at her knock, and Deja's smile faded.

"Can I help you?"

It was the woman she noticed in reception a few weeks ago, interviewing for a position. Her smile was wide and happy, her long curly hair brushing the edge of her desk.

"Good morning. I'm looking for Aileen and Tricia."

"Those names don't sound familiar, but I just started today."

"They work in payroll." Deja's mouth was dry and she forced out the words. "This is their office."

"I'm the new director of payroll. Cecilia Rose. This is my office now." The woman's lavender blouse was unbuttoned at the collar, and a small silver cross dangled from her neck. "Maybe they were transferred to another branch."

The woman went back to her paperwork, signaling the end of the conversation. Deja was hesitant to leave the office. The smell of burned coffee wafted to her from the kitchen. Around the corner, the Xerox machine hummed, churning out warm new copies. *I'm alone now.* She headed back to the village of cubicles. She didn't even have an office, a door to close and lock. Her heel snagged on the carpet as she rushed back to her station.

As she reached the bank of elevators in the lobby, the doors slid open. Deja whimpered as a black-cloaked form emerged, an inky rose tattoo seared on his arm.

Scotoma

Keturah Jones lived a decent but predictable life, according to her coworkers and friends at Grimes African Methodist Episcopal, but that was before a thirteen-year-old Colombian porn star took up residence in her left eye.

But before all that, before the haunting which led to her bloody suicide in the closet of her North Hollywood apartment, Keturah was a celibate churchgoing woman who masturbated nightly to Internet porn. Since God hadn't provided a husband as He promised, she wore the widow's weeds of self-pity, mourning the loss of a lover whose touch she had never known. Watching free X-rated video snippets was less of a sin than outright fornication. *At least I'm not buying flicks from Bed Behavior*, Keturah told herself often. She wouldn't pay for smut, because that solidified her addiction. God's mercy was easier to obtain as long as no money changed hands.

Each night when she came home from her job at the public relations firm, she hung her keys on the fish-shaped brass hook in her kitchen, stepped out of her pumps and returned them to the wooden rack in her closet and booted up her laptop. As the machine whined to life, Keturah hung up her skirt and blouse and tossed her panties in the hamper. Then she slipped beneath the covers with her computer. Although she lived alone, she locked the bedroom door and plugged in her headphones, lest her neighbors hear the actors' groans and inane dialogue through the thin walls. She didn't want anyone to think her a freak, or worse, a lonely freak. As she came, she muffled her moans with a satin pillowcase that smelled of coconut hair oil and pulled the plugs from her ears. Then she pushed the machine to the side of the bed like an impotent lover, climbed out of bed and dropped to her knees, naked and trembling.

Sometimes the bodies of the porn stars thrashed against Keturah's closed eyelids for hours afterwards. Like frisky ghosts, they roiled on the dark expanse of membrane, even after she reached for the Bible on her night stand and shook her head as if to physically expel them. A few years ago, when she was only watching an hour or two of porn a night, the specters faded as soon as she powered off her laptop, rinsing out of her mind and down her cheeks. But lately, the men and women that she climaxed to seemed to break free of the screen like refugee children, tumbling through time and space across the hazel border of her iris.

If God loved me, He would have provided a man a long time ago so I wouldn't have to masturbate. There were no eligible would-be husbands at Grimes A.M.E. Hordes of handsome men attended the weekly service either by themselves or in the company of other women, but they never looked her way. The ones who smiled at her or marveled at her eye color – greenish-brown rimmed with gold – were ushers with pot bellies, graying hair and missing teeth. At thirty-seven, Keturah had some belly flab, and the flesh under her arms wiggled when she raised her hands in worship, but she wasn't fat. She had strong teeth and smooth skin the color of the waxen calla lilies arranged in a vase on her dining room table. She was well-groomed and a believer but alone. So she fingered her widow's weeds and waited for Pastor Lidell's sermon to end so she could rush back home.

During one of her late-night sessions, she noticed a trend in several videos. Some adult actresses dressed in bobby socks and pigtails to appear much younger than they were. "School girl" was a popular search term on the sites that she frequented, along with "dad fucks daughter" and "teen fuck." But some of the performers, their legs folded over the hairy back of a sweating man, looked much younger than eighteen.

Never could understand why a grown man would be interested in the hoo-hah of a girl his daughter's age. That's just nasty. Keturah gazed at the gaunt bodies of those nymphs. One such porn star was named Little Lourdes. Judging by the number of times her video snippets had been viewed, she had a following, unlike the nameless blondes and redheads bouncing atop an equally anonymous lover.

Little Lourdes, "the Colombian cunt fantasy," wore ribbons in her two pigtails, one white, the other red. A jagged bang draped her forehead, nearly masking her bored brown eyes. She had shapeless hips and her breasts jutted like tiny mountaintops that had never known the protective grace of snow.

Unlike the other performers who actually had sex in the three- and four-minute previews of longer videos, Little Lourdes was a tease. She reclined on a couch, legs spread. Her hand groped beneath the elastic of her white cotton panties, but whether to pleasure herself or to protect her vulva, Keturah couldn't tell. Right before the clip ended, a naked man emerged from the bedroom and squatted between the girl's thighs. Then the video faded to black.

On all the Web sites Keturah searched, she couldn't find a single free clip of Little Lourdes that showed penetration. You had to pay to watch. She was embarrassed to be hunting for what was likely child pornography, because the girl couldn't have been more than thirteen. But lust overpowered those feelings of guilt. Lust overpowered everything.

When I was her age, I didn't even know I had a clit, Keturah said to herself one night after an unfruitful search for the teen porn star. The laptop was warm on her naked belly. When she was thirteen, she thought most boys in her North Philadelphia neighborhood were too surly or smelly for love. That year, nineteen-year-old Darnell Gibson wrested a kiss from her (her first) in the alley behind Antonello's Pizza. The son of a drug dealer, Darnell thought he was a catch with his tight Jordache jeans and gaudy gold chains; most of the girls Keturah walked to school with agreed. But his sloping haircut and fleshy lips never appealed to her. She preferred to read *Mad* magazine in her bedroom than sit on the front stoop with the other girls on her block, giggling about crushes. Darnell finally cornered her one night while she was walking home from the pizza parlor, a cup of blueberry water ice in her hand.

"What, you too good to give me a chance, redbone?" he asked, backing her against the side of the building. She hated the term. Redbone. Back then, most fair-skinned girls were called that, a name shouted from the doors of pool halls and liquor stores; it was both a slur and a compliment.

"I'm not allowed to have a boyfriend," she answered, trying to break free of his thick fingers.

"You ain't no princess, girl. I know where you live."

By the time her mountain of blue ice dissolved to a watery hill, she stopped fighting him. His tongue was sticky from the Now and Laters eternally lodged in his cheek, and she shut her eyes to block out his wide face. He crushed his pelvis against her knickers, driving her further into the wall. Keturah thought she would be repulsed by the feel of his wet lips, so she was shocked when her newly budding breasts began to tingle beneath the Hershey Park T-shirt she wore. When Darnell finally released his grip on her waist, she tossed her drink to the ground and ran home.

Keturah had never been kissed by anyone who loved her. The five men she'd dated in the eighteen years since losing her virginity were nice enough, but they all just seemed to be marking time until the real thing came along. Since her daily route between work and home never wavered, any matchmaking would have to be providential. She didn't hang out in clubs or bars, and thought she'd look too desperate signing up for an online dating service. So every morning, she kneeled by her bed and prayed for an imaginary mate: "Father, I hope my husband is having a good day today. I pray he's a leader on his job and in life. I thank you for his beautiful smile, his smooth brown skin and muscular chest. I hope he surrounds himself with godly friends and puts You first in his life …" She felt silly asking God to watch over a would-be lover and then deliver him to her at the divinely appointed time, but she knew of several Christian women who prayed their spouses into existence this way.

How would her future godly husband feel, knowing his libido would be compared to men with names like Peter Sins and Dick Diablo? Although Keturah would never admit that she had an addiction, she rehearsed sex scenes in her mind throughout the day. As she sat beneath the stadium lights in her Inglewood mega church, her monogrammed King James Bible balanced on her knees as she tried to focus on the sermon, her nipples hardened in remembrance of the previous night's marathon. Images of open mouths and dirty feet appeared in her head. Then she'd squirm in the hard stadium chairs and fan herself with a program. She'd open her Bible, but meditation was useless during those times. Jesus' image was invariably mingled with those humping bodies in her head, powerless to extricate Himself from the mural of flesh.

More than physical release, the videos provided a backdrop to her blues. There was a joylessness in the sex that stank through her computer screen.

She didn't like to see other people happy, because their bliss magnified her sunless life. So she chuckled at the bodies being pummeled, the slurs masquerading as foreplay, the greasy-haired women who looked as if they smelled like spoiled ham. Laughter was a wedge that blocked the revulsion in her throat. She always cried at the point of orgasm, like a woman ashamed for enjoying the rapist's thrusts. She thought this secret sin would bring her closer to God, that He would take pity on her and raise her from the well of self-destruction. But the deity was like a director in her skin flicks, off-screen and silent except for the occasional stage direction tossed with perverse indifference.

One Sunday morning, Keturah looked up from her monitor, surprised to see the pink tongue of dawn probing beneath her venetian blinds. She glanced at the clock on her nightstand. 6:15. She'd spent nine hours searching for new positions, new faces – something to excite her. *Have to get ready soon.* She removed her earphones and slid her laptop onto the comforter. The machine sat open like a hungry mouth. Most nights, she fell asleep with the computer on, the way some people doze to the comforting white noise of a television. She curled on her side, facing the bedroom window. *Hope God really speaks to Pastor Lidell this morning, because I need a touch from Him.* She closed her eyes. She hoped the little leaf-brown preacher could tell her how to make sense of her life, preferably within an hour and with four or five bullet points that she could turn into a To-Do list and clip to her refrigerator. She would be forty in less than three years, and she didn't want to wake up on that day with one hand between her legs, the other wiping her eyes. Mocking her fears, two pale bodies rutted against her closed lids.

The alarm buzzed a few hours later. Keturah opened her eyes.

A pair of flat brown ones stared back at her.

Keturah pushed away from the bed, spilling over the side. She landed against the baseboard, her legs tangled in the sheets. Her laptop hit the nightstand, then clattered to the floor beside her. The battery cover skittered across the hardwood tiles like a giant beetle, coming to rest beneath the bed. The cracked monitor was a dull blue eye that dissolved to a bruised black. As she lay there, she felt the vibrations of the automatic garage door opening one floor below, the rusted pulleys belching in protest. After a few minutes, she placed her hands on the mattress to steady them and slowly rose.

A girl lay on the bed.

She was naked from the waist up, her fingers snaking inside her cotton bloomers. The other hand toyed with a plaited pigtail that hung to her breast.

"Jesus," Keturah said, slapping her palms against her eyelids. When she removed her hands, the girl was still there, on the right side of a queen-sized mattress that no other body had indented in six years. She made no depression either; she seemed to be rising from the bed rather than sinking into it. Although her scrawny torso was solid enough that the headboard and yellow walls weren't visible through her skin, she had a dewy look about her, as if her flesh were weeping.

Little Lourdes.

"Get out!"

The girl stared at her. She removed the hand from her underwear and pinched her flaccid nipples. Keturah realized that she was naked as well, her heaving body close to the bare body of this stranger, and she dropped to her knees, glaring at the intruder from the edge of the mattress.

"Get out, before I call the cops."

As soon as Keturah voiced that threat, she realized how ridiculous it sounded. How would she explain to the authorities the presence of an underage porn queen in her bedroom? They would confiscate her computer hard drive and discover the electronic trail from hundreds of X-rated websites that she had visited over the years, some of which contained videos of children having sex. Unsure of what to do, she hurled a pillow at the girl and ran into the bathroom.

Keturah locked the door and turned the shower on as hot as she could stand it, trying to rinse away the slime of the past nine hours. As the water battered her belly and thighs, she thought about the child in her bed.

"The enemy is playing tricks on me, trying to make me think I'm losing my mind," she murmured.

She emerged from the shower, wrapped in a towel, and peered around the alcove that separated the toilet from the bedroom. Little Lourdes was gone.

"Thank you, Jesus!" Keturah said, shaking a fist at the ceiling. It was only an illusion. She had only dreamed about the last thing she saw before falling asleep. Then her joy soured. She kneeled next to her overturned laptop, closing the cracked display panel. She carried the machine in her arms like a dying lamb she had rescued from the slaughter. In the closet, she zippered the laptop inside a leather case and placed it behind the hamper. Maybe the broken machine was a sign from above. She would take her time getting it fixed. Now that she could no longer watch X-rated videos, God would be forced to provide her with a long-awaited husband. If He loved her.

Keturah yanked a black crepe dress from a hanger, her ire rising. *It's not fair. Why do I have to beg for a nice Christian man to start a family with?* There were plenty of nonbelievers at the public relations firm who had mates. The atheist she passed each morning at the water cooler wore a wedding ring. The agnostic two cubicles over who ate a smelly tuna melt sandwich for lunch every day had a live-in boyfriend. Even the closeted Scientologist account executive, who left pamphlets on upcoming Dianetics workshops in the bathroom by the soap dispenser, was on her second husband. *Why am I always alone?* Keturah thought as she left her apartment. *I'm the faithful one.*

The heels of her black pumps echoed on the pavement of the underground parking garage as she made her way to her car. Even though she was in a funk, she wouldn't dream of skipping service. She had been a member of Grimes for six years, ever since she relocated from Philly to accept the job at the firm. After her strange morning, she needed to surround herself with other people of faith.

She disengaged the alarm on her Jetta, opened the door and tossed her Bible on the passenger seat, where it slid to the floor mat. She bent to retrieve the leather-bound book and then strapped herself in. As the engine hummed to life, she stared at the windshield in astonishment.

Little Lourdes leaned on the hood of the car like a monstrous ornament, pressing her torso to the glass.

"You devil," Keturah said, glaring at the nipples on her windshield. A hiss sounded from beneath the hood, and blue fluid shot into the child's face. Keturah turned her wipers on at the highest speed, and the blades whisked across Little Lourdes' chest like frenzied black hands.

Keturah gunned her engine and sped through the garage, her tires squealing on the grease-stained concrete. She honked her horn impatiently as the automatic gate took its time to rise. Once she emerged into the September sunlight, she stuck her head out the window as she drove. At several minutes past nine on a Sunday morning, the North Hollywood neighborhood was quiet. A woman stood by an oak tree as her sweatered poodle squatted in the grass. Several joggers ran laps in the park at the end of her block. Glass bottles tinkled in the cart of a homeless man who muttered to himself as he crossed the street in front of the Jetta. And a teenage porn queen wiped methanol from her cheeks, still clinging to the car's windshield.

The mouth of the 101 Freeway was less than a mile from Keturah's apartment. She headed there now, fishtailing her car in an attempt to knock the girl from her field of vision. Even as Keturah signaled for the entrance ramp and zipped down the highway, Little Lourdes hung on, her arms outstretched like an angel poised for flight. The wind blew her bangs back to reveal a clear brown forehead, and her red and white ribbons bandied about in the breeze.

"I rebuke you," Keturah said through the glass. She braked suddenly, a maneuver she remembered from several car-chase movies, and then stepped on the gas. Her Bible thudded to the floor mat again, and she glanced over at it. When she looked back at the windshield, the girl was gone.

Thank you, Lord, for protecting me. Keturah drove the speed limit for the remainder of her forty-minute ride to church, reflecting on the imp's intrusive presence. There were so many other horny viewers to choose from. *Why is she haunting me?*

"I don't even pay for it," Keturah said aloud, as if to remind her Maker that she hadn't yet crossed the threshold into true addiction and sin. But the girl had chosen to incarnate in her bedroom, and then atop the hood of her car, for a reason. Keturah was more confused than frightened. One thing that years of Christian living had instilled in her was a belief in the supernatural. Stranger things had happened to the men and women of the Bible.

Serpents spoke with honeyed tongues, color bloomed in the cheeks of dead girls, women fleeing debauchery looked back and turned to brine. If a carpenter from Nazareth could erect Himself from the granite embrace of death, surely a thirteen-year-old porn star from Colombia could hurl her spirit through time and space to inhabit Keturah's gaze. *Maybe this is an astral projection.* She drove up the freeway off-ramp and turned left on Heliotrope Boulevard. The church was less than a mile away. *But why did she choose me?*

Keturah pulled into the parking lot of the stadium, early as usual for the ten o'clock service. There were only about a hundred cars in the lot, but by the time the pastor took his place on the dais, that number would swell to several thousand. She grabbed her purse and Bible and alighted from the Jetta, smoothing down her dress. A red piece of fabric hung from the car's antenna. With a sigh, Keturah uncoiled the ribbon and flung it to the ground. The material was warm and scaly, as she imagined the molted skin of a python would feel. *The enemy is busy.* She spit on her fingers and rubbed them on the hem of her dress. Then she headed toward the ramp that led to the entrance of the church.

The girl waited for Keturah at the curb.

A deflated pigtail hung to her breast. Her panties were stained a grayish brown as if she had been frolicking in the sandbox at the playground. Keturah glared at the girl, but decided to ignore her. Yet, as she walked on the opposite side of the incline, Little Lourdes walked ahead, a magnet that Keturah was forced to follow. She stopped when Keturah stopped, and her bare feet skipped along the pavement when Keturah's heels clicked up the ramp.

"Cunt," Keturah said under her breath. She had never uttered that word to anyone, let alone on church grounds and to someone of her own sex, but it made her feel in control. It occurred to her that the half-naked nymph a few feet away might be visible to other churchgoers, might be mistaken for someone who belonged to her. She stopped short, pressing her behind against the wall as a silver-haired woman and two sullen teens in jeans and suit jackets approached. They glanced at her, and she tried to read their expressions. She felt like the woman in the Gospel of Luke who had menstruated continuously for twelve years. Wan from the flow of a renegade womb no cloth or prayer could staunch, she felt their judgment, saw their noses wrinkling at the coppery scent of her secret shame.

"Morning," the old woman said as she passed, her feathered hat tilted at a jaunty angle. "Have a blessed day."

Keturah's mouth was so dry, she couldn't return the greeting.

Little Lourdes watched as the trio made their way toward the open doors of the arena, oblivious to her presence. Then she followed them, trailing her fingertips along the stone wall. Keturah wished she'd walk that way forever, up and up and around the bend of her sclera, disappearing back into her carnal cosmos. But the girl turned around and stared at her.

"What do you want?" Keturah said. The child stretched out her hand. Her fingernails were long and dirty. "Get away from me. I don't have anything for you."

The girl took a step to the side, as if daring her to pass.

I wonder if she can walk through me. Keturah kept her eyes on Little Lourdes's brown ones. Or worse. Maybe the girl would get stuck inside of her and try to take over her body. She shook her head at the thought of that rape, then hurried to the door of the church without looking back.

Once inside the stadium, Keturah searched for Doreen, who was a greeter on alternating Sundays. Doreen didn't look like the type of person who'd welcome people to service. Her unkempt brows were united in an arc of bewilderment, and her bottom lip stiffened when she smiled. They met a year ago at a single women's seminar sponsored by the church and exchanged phone numbers. Doreen had been fired from three jobs for proselytizing to her coworkers, a fact she proudly recited during the event as proof that she was "totally sold out for Jesus." Keturah had applauded Doreen's testimony as the other participants did; women in their mid- to late-thirties who had been dateless for years, but being that "sold out" made her uncomfortable. Everyone had to be dedicated to something, but she didn't think she could be that committed.

Keturah spotted Doreen chatting with the grandmother who passed her outside. She didn't consider the greeter a true friend, someone she'd ask to the movies or to lunch: every paragraph she spoke was laced with scripture, every conversation a sermon waiting to unfold. But today she needed a "warrior in the Word," as she called Doreen and her ilk, to help rid her of the ghastly presence.

She stood on one side of the door waiting for Doreen to finish her conversation. Little Lourdes leaned on the other side, crossing her legs as if she had to pee.

Doreen nodded when she noticed Keturah, sweat already ringing the armpits of her lilac dress. They hugged briefly, and Keturah pulled her to the side.

"I know we haven't talked in a while, and I apologize for not calling you sooner, but I hope you're free this afternoon, because I could really use a friend," she blurted out as she watched the girl from the corner of her eye.

Doreen raised her unibrow, unaware of the porn star who crouched on the other side of her, wiping her legs. She had a tolerant air about her like a woman accustomed to carrying the burdens of others and liking it. "I can make time before the evening service. I can't talk right now, but just know that whatever you're going through, God sees it all," the greeter said. "He is our refuge and strength, a very present help in time of –"

"I'll call you later," Keturah said, thankful that the throng of parishioners had welled up behind her, threatening to cascade down the steep steps of the stadium.

"Be blessed."

Keturah selected a seat at the end of the aisle in the blue section of the arena, with an unobstructed view of the altar. She didn't like sitting too close to the pulpit, because other congregants shot sharp stares at those who walked out before the close of Pastor Lidell's message. She always left a few minutes before the benediction to avoid the snarl of traffic in the parking lot.

Little Lourdes flopped down a few feet from her on the concrete walkway that separated the aisles. Keturah thought the porn star would be petrified in the presence of so much holiness: the flag bearers standing in the balcony twirling their purple banners, the old women in white by the altar raising their hands in praise, the teen organist, eyes closed, tongue protruding, pressing sorrow from his keys. But the girl looked around with interest, as if the worship ceremony were a spectacle put on for her benefit.

A fat usher wearing white gloves made his way up the stairs, passing out programs. He handed a few copies to a bald man and a woman with blonde dreadlocks sitting one row ahead of Keturah. She held her breath. The usher smiled at her, oblivious to the open thighs he stood between. If Little Lourdes bent forward, she could lick the pleat in his trousers. His shiny wingtip shoes were inches from the child's crotch, and Keturah winced as if her own clitoris were about to be crushed. The porn star stared up at him blandly, then slipped her hand inside her panties.

"Stop that!" Keturah said.

The child blinked, but her wrist still moved beneath the elastic band of her underwear. The couple glanced back, the man's shaven head sweating under the stadium lights. The usher looked stunned, as if he'd been caught jacking off behind an unfolded program. Keturah stammered out an apology, but the man moved on, his knees disappearing through Little Lourdes' head as he waddled up the walkway to more receptive worshippers.

Cheeks burning, Keturah opened the Bible resting on her lap. The book was a nest for old bulletins announcing workshops and church concerts that she meant to attend but could never find the time. She flipped through to the New Testament, and the wispy pages were made even more transparent by her tears.

She was Paul on Damascus Road, about to be knocked from her horse into the dust. But instead of rendering her sightless by the heat of His holiness, the Savior had cursed her with a blind spot, a scotoma that wiggled in her field of vision. How much more evil would she have to look upon before the scales fell from her eyes?

Lord, I really need a touch from you. Keturah rubbed her damp lashes. She glanced at her tormentor. The girl picked at her toenails, the unraveled braid caressing her leg. Bent over like that, her naked back exposed like a wound, she looked vulnerable, less obscene than she appeared in her video advertisements. Despite the innocent gesture and the dewiness of her skin, Keturah wanted to crush her.

"I can't stay for too long. I have to head back before 5:00 service."

"That's fine. I'm just grateful you came," Keturah said, taking Doreen's jacket. The woman still wore the sweaty dress she had on during the morning service. Keturah glanced at the clock on her stove. It was 3:15. She wondered if an exorcism could be performed in an hour.

She brought two steaming cups of chamomile tea to the dining room table and sat across from Doreen. Doreen didn't even comment on the niceness of the apartment – the granite countertops and blue denim couch, the gold-framed Monet print hanging on the wall. She pulled a Bible and a small bottle of oil from her purse, setting them on the placemat in front of her.

"Sounded like you were really troubled, so I just wanted to be prepared," she said.

Little Lourdes sat cross-legged in the corner, beside a vase of sunflowers. Her underwear had grown darker since the morning's escapades. The material was now a pungent brown, like drying blood.

"You want me to pray first?" Doreen said. She was always ready to get down to business, and Keturah envied her for that. Doreen was at least ten years younger, but she seemed much more mature. Keturah should have been the wiser Christian woman, more anchored in her faith, mentoring the younger believer. Instead, she was like a lamb teetering on newly discovered legs.

"Don't you need to know what the problem is?" she asked.

She was hesitant to reveal the hours she spent watching online sex. Not that Doreen would judge her, but naturally she felt embarrassed admitting her obsession, and she wasn't sure if she was ready to give it up entirely.

"God'll reveal it. Let's pray."

They lowered their heads. Doreen took Keturah's hands in her own, her fingers as coarse as the bamboo placemat. Keturah closed her eyes as Doreen beseeched the Almighty to purge them both of "sins of commission and omission, of the lust of the flesh, and the lust of the eyes and the boastful pride of life."

Keturah squinted during the prayer, watching the porn star's reaction. She was disappointed that the girl hadn't curled up into herself and dissolved into a puddle under the powerful petition. Instead, Little Lourdes raked her fingers through hair which hung down in dirty waves. Keturah examined the pouty lips, which were fuller than her own, the skin reddish-brown like the chewing tobacco her great-grandmother Reena used to press against her gums, the bare mountain peaks of her breasts, and wondered what it was about the child that drew her in. She wondered how she became an Internet prostitute in the first place, how she earned the title of "Colombian cunt fantasy."

"– speak to your heart during that prayer?"

Keturah stared at Doreen. "Come again? I was still meditating."

"I said, did the Lord speak to your heart while I was praying?" She still wore that look of weary acceptance.

Keturah faltered. If she didn't come clean with Doreen, she might be stuck with the girl forever. "You said something about lust earlier, and I guess God did speak to me. I have something to confess," she said. "Sometimes I watch bad movies."

"Like what? Occult stuff?"

"No. Internet porn."

"Oh."

Doreen's lip twitched, then she placed both hands on her forehead, consulting her spiritual index on how to proceed.

Might as well put it all on the table. "It's beyond just flipping through a porn site or two. Sometimes I watch for hours. Even when I turn it off, I still see people fornicating."

"Have you prayed about it?"

"Yes," Keturah said. "I pray for a husband too so I won't need to watch dirty videos."

"Do you want to stop watching pornos?"

"It's over," Keturah said, thinking of the broken monitor in the back of her closet. "But there's something else I haven't told you, something demonic."

Doreen snapped her fingers, and Little Lourdes looked up. "I knew something wasn't right when I walked in the door. I sensed it."

"There's this one … performer. I can't get her out of my head."

"Her?" Doreen frowned as if this admission were more disturbing than a porn addiction.

"Doreen, you know I'm strictly into men," Keturah assured her. "But this performer – I watched her once or twice. Now her spirit follows me everywhere."

"Like a ghost," Doreen offered, glancing around the apartment. She looked over at the sunflowers, locking eyes with a presence she couldn't see.

"Exactly." But "ghost" wasn't really the word for the lewd visitation. *How can Little Lourdes be a ghost if she's still turning tricks somewhere in the world?* Keturah wanted to mention her theory of astral projection, but thought it would go over Doreen's head. Or worse, it would make Doreen think she was dabbling in the occult as well as sexual sin.

"Well, there's only one ghost in the world, and that's the Holy Ghost," Doreen said. She glanced at her watch. "I have to leave in ten minutes. Do you want me to pray for you again?"

"Help me, Doreen. What can I do to get rid of this thing?"

"You invited her into your life by watching smut. You have to command her to get out. The Word says, 'Everyone who looks at a woman with lust has already committed adultery with her in his heart.'"

Yeah, me and about 70,000 other people, one big online orgy. Keturah said, "I told her to get out this morning, but she's still hanging around."

She motioned to the corner, and Doreen followed her gaze. "She even followed me to service this morning and played with herself during Pastor Lidell's sermon."

"That snake," Doreen said, opening a bottle of olive oil. "Not surprised she followed you into the house of the Lord to act up. There are fallen angels everywhere."

She rose from her chair and splattered several droplets against the wall by the sunflowers.

"Wait. My landlord just painted in here this summer," Keturah said.

"Do you want clean walls, or do you want the demon out of here?"

"I want both," Keturah murmured to herself. Doreen walked over to her. Dipping her finger in the bottle, she painted two tiny crucifixes on Keturah's closed lids.

"Now," the greeter said, proud of her work, "your eyes belong to God again."

For good measure, she drew a slick cross on the dining room wall by the light switch. Keturah hurried around the table to the hall closet, handing Doreen her coat.

"I don't think that imp will be haunting your apartment after tonight," Doreen said, heading to the foyer. "You need to get down on your knees before you get in bed and thank Him for deliverance."

"I'm always on my knees," Keturah said, opening the front door. Then to herself: *But I never feel anything from Him.* Once she heard Doreen's flats squeaking down the corridor, she peered around the wall of the dining room.

Little Lourdes sat among the drooping yellow sunflowers. She rubbed the sheen on her already moist skin. Oil dotted her cheeks like tears.

On Monday morning, the day after Doreen's greasy exorcism, Keturah opened her eyes and discovered that she was alone in her bed. She threw back the covers and sat up, pinching her arm to make sure she wasn't still asleep. When she confirmed that she was solidly in the world, she went from room to room, opening closets and cabinets, looking in the storage shed of her patio, and even in her refrigerator. Little Lourdes was gone, banished to her cyber brothel. Prayer really did work.

Keturah hummed along to a gospel CD as she drove to work, the first time in months that she listened to a non-secular song in her car. But she had a lot to be thankful for, and she wanted to show God that she was truly changing. It was hard to believe that just the day before she was hurtling down the 101 Freeway with an underage porn queen clinging to the hood of her Jetta. But the memory of her shame was fading fast.

At work, she was able to pass the cubicles of her coworkers and not envy the silver wedding frames on their desks or feel a pang of sorrow at the pictures of cross-eyed babies tacked to their bulletin boards. She could finally pack away her widow's weeds. *My husband's on the way*, she said to herself. *I can feel it.*

By the end of the day, her hopes darkened. She wasn't going to make it. She had watched porn for more than 1,400 nights in a row, and her lust returned with a vengeance. She caught herself masturbating at her computer while uploading an electronic press kit for a client. It started as an itch between her thighs, the pleasantly annoying sensation she felt sometimes when she held her urine for too long. Then she rubbed her legs together beneath her desk to maintain that wonderful friction as she fantasized. Closing her eyes, she saw bodies rutting against her lids. She pictured herself there in the darkness, bucking beneath the last lover she had known. Although she couldn't quite recall the man's features, she saw her own with clarity – the hazel eyes slit in desire, the pouty lips, the hair hanging down in dirty waves, the reddish-brown skin the color of snuff.

She opened her eyes.

Keturah pushed away from the desk, almost toppling over in her swivel chair, and hurried to the toilet. She saw the girl's face clearly now, although her lashes were damp with tears. But the porn star wasn't skipping beside her or straddling the hood of her car. Keturah rushed into the restroom to confirm her discovery, nearly colliding with the pregnant receptionist who was on her way out. She leaned over the sink, as close to the mirror as she could get, and raised her left eyelid. There, in the hazel whorl of her iris, a miniature figure floated, arms outstretched.

She bit back a scream as the bathroom door opened. Her coworker, Cynda, walked in. The smile she always wore faded as she glanced at Keturah.

"Hey, lady. You look a little pale. Are you feeling okay?"

"I'll be fine. Rough day."

"Rough today. Tomorrow will be easier," Cynda said, staring at herself in the mirror. The biracial woman floated through the office in a state of bliss, as if she conferred with God's free-spirited half-sister each morning before coming to work. Keturah didn't know what her religious background was. She didn't think Cynda was a Christian, because she was much too joyous. As Cynda ran her fingers through her silken afro, Keturah glimpsed the glint of a diamond with her good eye.

"Congratulations," she said.

Cynda glanced at the engagement ring, as if surprised to see it. "Oh, this? Thanks, girl. Xerxes proposed this weekend." Her laugh was low and sweet. "I had been intentioning a proposal a year ago when I got back on the dating scene. Then yesterday, I got one."

Keturah forced a smile, barely hearing her coworker's words. She rubbed her left eyelid, feeling the knotted mass beneath her fingertips.

"Do you believe in prayer?" she asked.

"Absolutely." Cynda pulled a tube of lipstick from her purse. "And visualization too. I couldn't live without my dream board. What you focus on manifests eventually."

"Even abstract things? How can you put love on a dream board?"

Cynda dabbed a wine-red color on her thin lips. "I like to look at people in love. Holding hands, walking on the beach, that sort of thing. It reminds me of what my soul is seeking," she said. "So I cut out pictures of happy couples from magazines and tack them to my vision board. Whatever I'm intentioning shows up in my life eventually."

Keturah blew her nose with a stiff paper towel. Her eye felt irritated, as it did when a stray lash swam beneath her lid.

"What if something you didn't put on your vision board manifests?" she said.

"Then more blessings for me."

"What if it's not a blessing? What if it's something you don't want?"

"Like what?"

"Like – a toxic friendship."

"Some things just resolve themselves, you know? That's my theory anyway," Cynda said. Her gray eyes shone. With her indigo necklace and flowered skirt, she reminded Keturah of some Valley Girl guru. "But if the friendship is going sour, just send that person some love, and bless her and let her go."

Keturah watched as the door closed behind her. She rubbed her eyelid as if the motion would dislodge the offensive object from her socket. But it felt as if she were embedding it deeper.

How can I love her when God doesn't even love me?

By the time multicolored lights and tinsel hung throughout her office, and shaggy wreaths materialized on her neighbors' doors, Keturah had stopped attending service at Grimes. Before she used to replay sex scenes in her head while pretending to focus on Pastor Lidell's words. But when she started paying attention to the sermon in earnest, blotting out the wailing babies behind her and ignoring the cute new visitors who squeezed past her knees in search of seats, the spread-eagle figure in her eye began to stir.

Keturah barely glanced at herself in the mirror as she got ready for work, was no longer proud of her gold-rimmed eyes. The left side of her face had begun to sag under the weight of her wanton eye. Right before she dropped out of church, she avoided Doreen, sneaking into the opposite side of the stadium from where the greeter was stationed. She didn't want to be asked if the demon had disappeared, because one glance would reveal that her face was still haunted.

On the last night of her life, Keturah huddled on her couch, staring at the ceiling as she groped between her thighs. She hadn't watched porn in several months, had no desire to repair her shattered laptop. As she toyed with her graying pubic hair, she recalled Doreen's prayer about the lust of the flesh and the lust of the eyes. If simply watching Little Lourdes' video snippets amounted to adultery with the porn queen, as Doreen believed it did, did that mean that Keturah and the child were lovers? And adultery implied marriage, so were they wedded as well?

You never even answered my prayers for a husband, she said to the silent stucco. Was the specter in her eye God's vulgar idea of providing a "mate" for her?

What do you want? Keturah asked, or rather she directed that thought at the child.

Little Lourdes glided through the greenish-brown channels of Keturah's iris, a mosquito flitting across a pond. Keturah pressed a hand to her lid to see her nemesis more clearly, and she felt a ripple against her palm. The girl was completely naked now. Her bony legs were no longer hindered by the soiled underwear, and Keturah noticed the bald innocence of her vagina. The other plait had escaped its white ribbon, and her locks, finally freed, trailed behind her like a veil. She was beautiful.

I'm sorry, Little Lourdes. Keturah removed her hand and folded her arm across her chest. *I'm sorry for wanting to see men hurt you.*

The girl drifted in the darkness, like an obscene genie come to grant one final wish. Her body swelled, larger and larger, until Keturah feared her eye would no longer be able to contain her, until she ruptured the whisper thin sac of conjunctiva, spilling out of her socket and down her cheek.

The hems of skirts and dresses brushed against Keturah's nape as she knelt in her closet. She unzipped the black computer case, slicing her finger on the fragmented LCD screen. With a muted crunch, she ripped a chunk of glass free from the hard plastic border of the monitor. *I only wanted to be touched by someone who loved me.*

When the shard punctured her eye, there was a jolt of light in her left temple then wet blackness. She fell back against the wooden shoe rack, fingers groping the air as if to receive the caress she'd been searching for. She felt as the apostle Paul must have felt, writhing in the dirt of Damascus, blinded by the Almighty's face as well as by His piercing love.

There, on the floor of the unlit closet, she felt the hum of the automatic garage door opening below her. Blood tickled her ear, pooling beneath her neck. The last thing Keturah saw was the girl bending over her, and something warm and scaly pressed against her cheek. Then she drifted deeper into darkness.

The Healing Room

Montserrat Jones was too excited about the purchase of her new home to dwell on the fact that she had just moved into an exclusive community for neurotic women. She'd worry about that later. But for now, she walked through the living room, touching the tan sofa that had been delivered a few days ago, running a finger across the soft leather for dust. There was none. The house was designed for single women, the realtor said, with a lifetime self-cleaning functionality, an anti-insect system, a de-aging sauna and a healing room that kept the blues at bay.

Never thought mine would be the sole name on a deed. She straightened a painting above the fireplace. The brown lady within the frame sat in a wicker chair on a veranda. Curly hair tumbled to her shoulders, and she held a tea cup in her lap as she gazed into the woods. Montserrat owned five pieces by the same artist, a Creole woman named Mignon. She lost herself in the pastoral settings – genteel women reclining on the terraces of woodsy cottages and lakefront houses, or strolling through meadows, parasols at their sides. She glimpsed her reflection in the glass. Several braids had escaped her bun, and she gathered the wiry locks, pinning them in place. She used to believe that she would move straight from her apartment in The Valley to her future husband's house, but when twenty-five passed and then thirty, and that fantasy never materialized, she decided that she wasn't going to tread those 800-square feet of rental property for the rest of her life. She wanted something that belonged to her.

When Montserrat pulled up outside the gates of the housing community in the Miracle Mile District more than a month ago, the real estate agent, E'lann, buzzed her in, his green eyes shining as he regarded her silver BMW. He helped her out of her car, and then threaded his thin arm through hers as if she were an invalid regaining the use of her legs.

"Not another community like ours. Finest healing rooms in L.A. County," he said with a grin as they walked toward the model home. He was a circus barker, trying to coax her to see a magic show. His skin was sun-worn, darker than her own, and spicy cigar smoke lingered on his blue button-down shirt.

"So I've heard," Montserrat said, taking in the two-story Spanish colonial. She had been house hunting for three months when she saw the ad for Heather Hollows. In it, a beautiful smiling woman, eyes closed in bliss, leaned back in a rocking chair. Sunlight sliced the woman's torso as it streamed into the small but elegant room. The headline read: "You don't have to dream of Paradise. Hearth, home and healing awaits you at Heather Hollows!"

It sounded so appealing. A few days later, she stood inside the model home. Like the healing room in the ad, this one featured a rocking chair in the middle of a bright compact room. It didn't feel any different from her own bedroom. Noticing her disappointment, the agent led her to a back office. "Our healing rooms are custom built to fit your needs. We like happy customers," he said. He pressed a square yellow button on his desk, and a large-screen television monitor on the wall blinked to life. The picture dissolved to the image of a sunny room with a rocking chair in the center. Then another room. And another. They were all filled with rocking chairs of varying sizes. There were healing rooms for depressed women and those coping with bipolar disorder. There were rooms for women with OCD and those with multiple personalities. "Designed by a woman psychologist too. We call them Built-in Blues Busters," E'lann said with a wink.

"So you've had a good success rate?" she asked.

"One hundred per, Ms. Jones. No complaints, no malfunctions yet."

Montserrat wanted to have the anxiety room installed in her new house, but she settled on a general healing room. She didn't want E'lann, or anyone else, to know exactly what was wrong with her. She rarely spoke of the heart palpitations, leg tremors and chest pain that had ailed her for the past year, that had brought her to the emergency room more than a dozen times.

"Girl, that's a white woman's disease," her friend and stylist Myaisha called it when she confided in her. "You're stronger than that, Monie." But she hadn't felt strong in a long time. She felt like those old ladies at the nursing home where her great-grandmother lived out the last months of her life, frail women who smiled as they puttered around in slippers and torn bathrobes, unaware that they had lost their mind. She hadn't lost hers. Yet. It would be good to have a therapeutic place in her very own home, instead of dealing with the embarrassment of a psychiatrist's chair, the pain of having to rely on meds. She reached in her purse for a pen as E'lann brought over a folder of paperwork to fill out.

Now she walked down the upstairs hallway of her new place, heels clicking on the hardwood flooring. The air smelled of fresh paint. There were no bothersome balls of dust along the baseboard; no silken spider web brushing her face. She had hung several Mignon paintings on the wall, and she touched the silver frames as she walked past those solitary women.

She stopped outside a closed door. Her healing room. The placard above the doorknob featured a woman seated in a yoga pose, hands clasped in front of her breasts. Montserrat had been living at 6 Felicity Lane for over a week, but she hadn't used her healing room. No bouts of panic had stricken her, no worrisome thoughts had caused her to climb the stairs. *I'm not super anxious, but I just want to try it out, in case*, she said to herself, as she turned the knob. *To be prepared.*

A rocking chair stood in the middle of the room, facing a gold accented wall. Sunlight streamed across the seat, pooling on the floor. The rays weren't coming from outside, but from a silver nozzle in the ceiling. Montserrat stepped out of her shoes, entered the temple, and closed the door.

Kind of steep at $5,500 a month, she thought, settling into the chair, *but if it works, it will be worth it.* Although her job as a makeup artist more than paid the bills, she wasn't one to splurge. No designer shoes or expensive purses filled her closet. She hated to pay $300 an hour for a session with Dr. Guntsworth, but the day her hand shook so badly that she nearly jabbed a client in the eye with a liquid liner pen, she knew she had to get help. That was nearly a year ago, and she still felt nervous whenever she tied a black smock around her waist. Now she could cancel her Thursday appointment with the psychologist, and the thought cheered her. She'd just tell Dr. G. that she was working things out on her own.

She pressed a switch on the arm of the chair and closed her eyes. The room came with no user manual, but she knew how to turn it on. She knew that much. E'lann explained that there was a sensor in the chair that could discern the user's emotions. Unlike traditional talking therapy, the healing room had a unique way of influencing free association. "What way?" Montserrat asked, and the agent had grinned, shaking a finger at her. "Wouldn't our competitors like to know?" he said by way of an answer.

Now she rocked in the chair, the sunlight strangely cold on her skin. Something within the house shuddered. Her arms and upper body began to shake as if she were sitting in one of those automated massage chairs at the nail salon. Montserrat opened her eyes. The chair (or was it the room?) rocked harder. She felt a ticklish vibration beneath her bare feet, and her toes curled. She closed her eyes again. After a few minutes, she heard another faint noise beneath the shuddering. A child's laughter? Why did that tinkling, merry sound cause gooseflesh to rise on her arms?

She felt for the switch, and the rocker grew still. She felt that same pang of disappointment that she did when walking through the healing room at the model home. *Maybe I really need to be anxious for it to work.* She collected her shoes. Her stomach growled. It was nearly one o'clock and she hadn't eaten breakfast yet.

Downstairs, she opened the fridge, trying to decide on what to eat. The food reminded her that she needed to plan some type of gathering to celebrate buying her first home. She wasn't sure if she would have a housewarming party, if she would invite the paternal relatives that she'd only visited a half dozen times since moving to Los Angeles from Philly seven years ago. Her father's family had traveled west from Georgia during the Second Great Migration of the 1940s, lured by the prospect of lucrative jobs in the California shipyards and aircraft factories. But unlike many black migrants, Montserrat's paternal relatives didn't put away money to open their own businesses – funeral homes or barbershops. The women didn't collect quarters for pressing hair in their kitchens, or stack up dollar bills in mason jars from selling peach cobbler or fried catfish out the back door of their homes. They were content laboring in oil refineries, cleaning houses or trudging home from the steel mills, smoke from the blast furnace still lingering in their hair.

Common. Montserrat stood at the kitchen counter, coaxing hummus onto a plate with a wedge of pita. This younger generation of Joneses (except her) lacked drive as well. Her father's relatives were bus drivers and postal workers, lumbermen and secretaries. They called her bourgie when she bought a BMW (a used one, but still a luxury car) and moved from North Hollywood to Studio City. She'd never hear the end of it if they knew her current address.

Finished with her food, she returned the hummus to the refrigerator and stacked her plate in the dishwasher. With that movement, green liquid welled in the dispenser. Water flowed as she closed the door. E'lann promised that she would never have to buy another box of detergent. *So far, so good.* When she rose, she noticed that the constellation of pita crumbs had vanished from the counter, and the black marble shone as if recently polished. The steady hum of the dishwasher followed her out of the kitchen.

She needed air. It was Friday, and she had taken the day off to meet with the new gardener, Estancio. Earlier, they discussed installing a flower border of Mediterranean perennials in her backyard to bloom next spring – geraniums, hollyhock and thistle. The beautiful June afternoon beckoned, and she felt guilty for wasting the day inside. Grabbing her key, she headed out to the bank of silver mailboxes a few yards from her front door. One of her neighbors was already there sorting bills, wispy black hair tickling the collar of her blouse. As Montserrat approached, the woman turned, a ready smile on her lips.

"Hey there. I'm Elza. I live down at 10 Felicity." She shifted her mail to the crook of her arm and shook Montserrat's hand. Her palm was dry and cracked.

"Montserrat. Nice to meet you."

Elza's smile grew even wider, revealing small, crowded teeth. She repeated the name, pronouncing it perfectly. "That's really pretty."

Montserrat smiled with her. At the Beverly Hills cosmetics counter where she worked, white customers were charmed by the black girl with the regal name. Some had even visited the monastery in Spain which housed the black Madonna, for whom she'd been named, and could attest to the wooden beauty of the Virgin. Black folks blinked when she introduced herself. They never fixed their lips to say her name right. They called her Monie and left it at that.

Elza said, "I've been here for three months, and I'm so happy. Don't you just love your room?"

"I love my house. This is a nice community." Montserrat unlocked her mailbox, flipping through a few circulars and an envelope bearing the previous occupant's name. Becky Claymont. Had she been healed? Montserrat hoped her neighbor would notice that she was preoccupied and leave her alone, but she felt those quick grey eyes on the side of her face.

"You know I used to wash my hands all the time, every time I walked into a kitchen or a bathroom. Germs everywhere." Elza rubbed the skin on the back of her hand as if wiping away an imaginary lather.

How did one respond to a confession like that? "Oh, I know the feeling." White women in L.A. were always so forthcoming with their dysfunction.

"It's so nice to never have to worry about cleaning again," Elza said.

"Sure is, and you just reminded me, I have to unload the dishwasher. Nice chatting with you."

Montserrat nodded, leaving Elza to contend with her soap-stained hands.

Glad I'm not that kind of crazy. Montserrat closed the front door behind her. *She probably wonders what's wrong with me though.* Again, she was reminded that she wasn't supposed to be this fragile. She sniffed the newness of the house, its untainted white walls. Elza loved her healing room. Maybe she hadn't given hers a chance. She needed to know that it wasn't some high-priced gimmick, that she could actually be well one day.

She passed the women in the paintings and once more stood before the door of the healing room. Stepping out of her heels, she walked inside. The overhead sunlight still streamed onto the rocking chair, and she eased beneath its chilly beam. Fingering the switch, she felt a groaning beneath the floorboards and closed her eyes. Outside a car alarm beeped as it was disengaged, and she heard a door slam down the block. Her bare feet slid forward and back, her toes tracing the lines in the distressed oak. Her breathing slowed. She leaned back, arms resting on the chair. In the blackness, she saw her mother's mother kneading rags of dough for apple pie. She smelled the slick sweetness of sugar and cinnamon being stirred into a pan of melting butter. Her lips parted, tasting the crust. Her hand closed on the flaky dough. It was hers. She didn't have to share with her sister or cousins.

Now the shuddering subsided to a soft tilting motion. Montserrat felt herself pitching forward and back, as if she were lying in the white glider on Nana's front porch in Germantown. Something orange thumped against the side of the house. A basketball from the Catholic school across the street had bounced into the yard, crushing Nana's hydrangeas. Through the open living room window adults laughed and gossiped as they played Pinochle, and she heard coins jangling as they were thrown on the living room table. "You came here with all that money, but you gonna leave a porpoise." That was Papa. A bricklayer with an eighth grade education, her grandfather created his own language, substituting "porpoise" for "pauper" or "zink" for "sink."

Montserrat smiled as she rocked in the creaky metal bassinet. Her grandparents' Philadelphia home was a way station for family who blew in and out of the living room like autumn leaves. The sounds and smells were a part of her. She was home. She saw sneakers and penny loafers and other shoes lined up against the baseboard inside the front door. Nana wouldn't allow company to track dirt in her house. Her own home was just as spotless as the ones she cleaned across town. Then the front door slammed. Heavy work boots squeaked as their owner moved toward the glider.

Montserrat rose, nearly ripping the pocket of her gray slacks on the arm of the rocking chair. She looked back at the chair as if it were a living thing that had tried to restrain her. The floor boards still vibrated, and she leaned forward, turning off the switch. The laughter dissolved like a pat of butter in a hot pan. The oily perfume of fresh paint replaced the burning smell of sugar and cinnamon, and she opened the window, inhaling.

What the hell was that? Sure didn't feel like healing.

The houses across the street were identical to hers, two-story Spanish colonials with horseshoe arches and iron trellises. A crow perched on the red-tiled roof of one house. He cawed several times, a lonesome plaintive sound, and birds she could not see cawed back. Satisfied with the response, he flew off, black wings flapping. A thin woman with long yellow hair alighted from a two-seater, carrying a bag of groceries. She raised a hand as another neighbor, a brunette wearing sunglasses, shook her bangled arm out the window of her Porsche. *I just moved to Beckyville.* In several homes, the upstairs windows glowed with impossibly sunny light. Montserrat wasn't sure if she wanted to meet the rest of her neighbors, although the women seemed friendly enough with each other. She didn't fancy chatting about former therapists or the pounds of antidepressants they no longer had to swallow. Twenty homes. Twenty single, unwell women. She stood in the doorway of the healing room, unsure if she wanted to sit in the chair again. How long had it been since she'd returned to the home of her childhood, to the row houses and cobblestone streets of Germantown? Twenty years? She knew the house had been put up for sale after Nana's death during her freshman year of college. The new owner had accepted it as is, with the peeling green paint and the cracked cement of the front porch. But had he kept the glider?

This must all be a part of the healing process, Montserrat thought as she opened the door. She blinked. After the light of the healing room, her eyes had to adjust to the shadowy hallway. She felt more embarrassed now than frightened by the experience. The women who raised her would scoff at the idea of her needing sheetrock and artificial light to heal her. She felt their spirits converging in the hallway, judging her: her great-grandmother Hattie who packed snuff and a pugnacious wit tightly in her jaw, and who once protected her property from the Klan with a nine-shooter Winchester rifle ("Ole Bessie," she used to say, cradling an imaginary pistol. "She ain't stopped smokin yet!") Nana, who believed her homemade remedies could cure any ailment – the thick, smelly salve rubbed on an inflamed chest and then covered with flannel, the mason jar that sat in the kitchen window, filled with a grayish-brown stew of rock candy, onion and corn liquor, guaranteed to quiet a phlegm-packed cough with one sip.

Montserrat slunk past those sacred shadows, opening the door of her bedroom. The blue and gold comforter was turned down on her four-poster bed, and a mahogany armoire stood in the corner. That was the extent of her bedroom furniture. She couldn't stand a cluttered house. "Less is more," her grandmother used to say. Montserrat dropped her shoes by the bed and fell across the comforter, not bothering to peel back the covers. All that shifting and rocking had exhausted her. She drifted off to sleep.

A bell clanged in her head – faint but urgent. Montserrat swatted at her face as if trying to brush away a fly. Then she opened her eyes. It was just the doorbell. Wiping sleep from her lashes, she glanced at the clock. 7:04. Damn. She had "napped" for more than five hours. At the window, she peered out at the fading sunlight, at the rosy clouds unraveling across the sky. When she lived in The Valley, her friends never dropped by her apartment without calling first. They knew she was funny that way about her space. A red Mustang was parked in the driveway behind her car. Fentisha.

What is she doing here? Montserrat headed downstairs. Although she and the redhead sometimes grabbed a sandwich on their lunch break, their interaction ended at Shimmer, the Beverly Hills makeup counter where they both worked. She masked her irritation as she opened the door.

"Hey, Fentisha," she said, forcing her voice to be upbeat as she greeted the grinning white woman on her front step. "Guess you couldn't wait until Monday to see me."

"You know it. Just 'cause you took the day off from work didn't mean you took the day off from me," Fentisha said, pulling up the strap on her yellow sundress. Her giggle was high and horsey.

"How did you get in?"

"Sorry to break it to you, Sis, but these gated communities ain't foolproof. I drove in behind one of your neighbors."

Montserrat stepped aside, letting her in. That whinnying laugh and the street talk Fentisha was so proud of annoyed her. It seemed that the more proper Montserrat's speech, the more sprinkled with slang her coworker's became. Montserrat knew that, as a child, Fentisha hung out with mostly black kids in her Arlington Heights neighborhood. She often laughed that she could braid hair and jump Double Dutch better than most of the girls on her block.

"I ain't going to keep you long. Just dropped by to check out your new spot," Fentisha said as she walked through the foyer. She ran her eyes over the leather furniture in the living room, the crystal vase in the corner by the fireplace. Montserrat frowned. Fentisha's platforms left dirty prints on the floor, but as soon as she lifted her foot, the grime evaporated, as if erasing all traces of her.

"How did you know where I lived?"

"I heard you on the phone at work giving the address to some moving company. Heather Hollows is only ten minutes from my place in K-Town. We're practically neighbors."

Montserrat would have been embarrassed if Myaisha or Lorraine had shown up on her doorstep, but for some reason, she didn't feel ashamed that the redhead knew about her community – that it was exclusive to loons. Maybe because Fentisha was nutty in her own way. She expected most white women in L.A. to be crazy. Even before she moved to California, she'd heard it was the land of Prozac and palm trees. None of the black women she knew in Philly took medication. If they were in pain, they kept it to themselves.

"Anyways," Fentisha said, "I drove around the complex and saw your Beamer in the driveway." She dropped onto the chaise lounge. Rummaging in her Gucci tote bag, she pulled out an oblong box with a bow on top. "Just a little housewarming gift."

"You shouldn't have," Montserrat said, unwrapping a green and brown striped candle. It smelled like a rotting pear and would match absolutely nothing in her home. "So sweet of you." She placed the candle on the mantel above the fireplace. Once Fentisha was gone, she would hide it in an upstairs closet. Maybe re-gift it to one of her cousins for Kwanzaa.

"I knew you'd like it," Fentisha said, easing out of her shoes. "It reminded me of you – earthy and calm, you know?"

Thinking of her night tremors, Montserrat stifled a laugh. *If you only knew.* She started to offer Fentisha something to drink or eat, but thought better of it. *Don't want her hanging around all night.*

"I been researching Heather Hollows. I wanted to buy a home here, but this joint is way out of my range. So can I get a tour?"

"I haven't really straightened up."

"I don't see no boxes, no dirt. I'm hip to the self-cleaning feature. Just a quick peek, Sis. I won't stay long."

With a sigh, Montserrat led her into the kitchen. Fentisha hadn't mentioned the healing room, had no need of one apparently, and she felt angry that the slang-spitting white woman was stronger than she was. Fentisha whistled at the hand-painted tile backsplash above the stove, at the granite center island, where oranges were stacked neatly in a white bowl. Montserrat never left fruit or any food sitting out in her old place, too afraid that the scent would draw gnats. She was afraid of all flying things, no matter how tiny, which was another reason she had been drawn to this house, for the anti-insect feature.

"We're still working out the technology. The microsensors don't know the difference between a bird and a flying roach," E'lann had confided to her. "One customer's canary got nuked, so we don't recommend the dBugn System for households with pets less than three pounds."

That was fine with Montserrat, who hadn't owned a pet since she was seven, when her mother bought her a chocolate lab. Mr. Hershey was the perfect companion with his sad hazel eyes and floppy ears. He followed her up and down the stairs of their small row home, his hoarse bark giving voice to everything she couldn't put into words. But the puppy developed heartworm disease and died before he was a year old. Montserrat found him slumped on his side in the converted doll carriage that she had fashioned into a bed. His hazel eyes were still. The floppy ear felt as stiff as the flap on her penny loafers.

"This kitchen is insane, but let's finish the tour." Fentisha toyed with her red beads. She wore the necklace every day, regardless of the outfit. "Red, like me. Hot blooded," she always joked. Her nails were painted a moldy blue, the new $30 summer color their boutique was featuring. "I know about the anti-aging sauna too. I have to see it."

Now the real reason for her visit comes out, Montserrat thought as they walked out of the kitchen. The hardwood flooring gleamed as they made their way to the back patio. At her old place, she hated to clean because it was such hard work. She could barely find the strength to get out of bed, sometimes going a month or more without changing her sheets. Her dirty apartment was one of the reasons that she discouraged her friends from dropping by. It was a relief to no longer have to worry about that.

At the far end of the patio, a narrow room was walled off by glass. Inside the sauna, several mounds of Himalayan salt were shaped into benches, and the pink and yellow chips glittered. There were two recessed shelves in the clay walls. Montserrat had placed a white candle in one and a glass dish filled with lavender bath beads in the other. The place reminded her of some ancient catacombs, and, in the growing darkness, she half expected to see a black-robed figure creeping toward her with a torch. As she neared the sauna, a light blinked on.

"This is way cool," Fentisha said, forgetting herself and slipping into a Valley Girl twang. She tugged at her sundress. "Have you tried it yet?"

"Not yet. I've only been here for a week."

"If I had an anti-aging sauna, I'd be up in here every day. Not that I need it, ha, ha," she said. "If I were you, I'd advertise this at Shimmer. Five hundred dollars for fifteen minutes. Get that loot. You could pay the house off in a couple of months."

"I didn't buy it for that," Montserrat said, her annoyance returning. "Besides, those ladies who come into the boutique can afford several saunas like this."

A wooden placard on the wall outside the sauna read: Not Recommended for Women under Age Twenty-Five.

"Guess I can't go in then." Fentisha stared up at her with that dopey grin. Unlike Montserrat, who, at thirty-two, was often mistaken for someone in her early twenties, Fentisha had not aged well. Although she was in her early thirties, she had deep lines beneath her eyes and around her mouth, and the skin on her neck sagged. The caked foundation she wore gave her a gummy look. A good hard rain might wash her features away.

"Too bad you didn't bring a bathing suit."

"Girl, if you don't mind seeing me butt naked, I'll strip right now."

Montserrat did mind. She had no desire to see someone she worked with naked; it was too intimate an experience, like seeing your teacher in church. But she suddenly felt sorry for her. *Thank God, good black don't crack.* She pushed a square green button on the wall. That was Nana's favorite saying, her pride in the seemingly ageless skin of black women.

There was a hissing sound from behind the glass, and a fine mist began to spray. Fentisha clapped her hands like a little girl who had been promised a piece of candy. As she lifted the hem of her dress, Montserrat turned away.

"Be back in a second. I'm going to go change."

She walked back through the house. At the foot of the stairs, she paused, listening. With all the hissing, shuddering and humming, the house reminded her of a person, a nervous child not used to adults. She glanced up the staircase. It was only technology; with a switch or a button, the tremors could be controlled. *I'm paying good money to live here. I work hard, and I deserve to enjoy it.*

In the bedroom, she slipped out of her blue blouse and slacks. She pulled a yellow swimsuit from her dresser drawer, snapping off the price tag. Her body embarrassed her – the squishy stomach and stretch marks on her upper legs. In the past year, she had lost fifty pounds, and she knew she needed to tone up, but it was so hard to drag herself to the gym. After tying the straps around her neck, she pulled her braids atop her head, securing them with a clip. She grabbed two towels from the hall closet and headed back to the sauna.

Fentisha was sprawled on one of the salt benches, eyes closed. Even though she wasn't that attractive, her stomach was taut, and her legs were shapely. Montserrat felt a twinge of envy as she tossed her a towel. Spreading out her own towel, she lay face down on the other bench.

"Why you hiding your face, Sis? You're going to miss out on all of these de-aging rays."

I'm not the one who needs them. Aloud, she said, "Doesn't matter where I lay. The manual said there's some hyaluronic acid or something in the clay walls, and light refraction – "

"Spare me the physics lesson. Just let it work its magic," Fentisha said, her voice heavy with sleep. Montserrat grew worried, hoping she wouldn't be too tired to drive home.

"You are so lucky, Montserrat," Fentisha murmured. "Wish I had a plush house like this."

"You said you were looking. How's that going?"

Her coworker snorted. "It's not. Girl, I don't save like you do. We never had much growing up, so as soon as I get some cheddar, I spend it. In my twenties, when I realized I could make money doing makeup, I was too busy buying clothes for the club and $300 designer shoes. Shoot. I'll be thirty-three next year, and I only got about $2,000 in the bank."

Montserrat was glad her face was hidden so Fentisha couldn't see her shock. With her investments and money market accounts, she had close to a hundred times that amount. Her grandmother taught her the value of saving from an early age. Every other week, the old woman would open the clasp on her faded blue purse and hand Montserrat a few dollars. Her sister, Monifa, spent her money on lollipops and comic books, but not Montserrat. She stashed her earnings in a secret place beneath the front porch. She was good at hiding things. She saved those folded bills from age four until she turned seven. When she, Monifa and Mom moved out of Nana's house for good, she had close to three hundred dollars packed into a jelly jar buried beneath the front porch.

Montserrat's left arm twitched. In spite of the hot mist, her skin felt clammy. She raised her head. Her coworker was turned away from her, faded rose nipples pointed toward the ceiling. Her toenails were painted that same moldy blue, and her feet were turned inward, the bunions on her big toes kissing. As if feeling Montserrat's stare, she turned to her.

"So how do I look? Stop me when I get to twenty-five." That same horsey laugh again.

Montserrat wasn't sure but already she thought Fentisha did look more youthful. Her thinning yam-colored hair seemed fuller and more lustrous. Her face was rosy, as if she had scrubbed it with pebbles, and the skin around her mouth and beneath her eyes was smoother. She could pass for a twenty-nine-year-old. Twenty-eight, maybe.

"I definitely see a change," Montserrat said. "A few more sessions, and you'll be getting carded again."

As soon as the words left her lips, she regretted them. It sounded like an invitation for future visits. But maybe it was time to stop fighting the presence of other people in her personal space. Company every now and then could be a good thing, even visits from skinny redheads who acted like black girls from the projects.

"We should get out now. It's been almost a half hour," Montserrat said.

Fentisha swung her legs around, dabbing her damp skin with the towel. "I feel different," she said. "Better watch out. I might show up at work on Monday in a halter and miniskirt."

"I thought you said you felt different."

They both laughed, then Fentisha said, "You look good too, girl. Like you have new skin. But you're beautiful anyways. Wish I had that cinnamon complexion and pouty lips."

She's not so bad. Montserrat covered herself with the towel. Fentisha stepped into her sundress, smoothing out the wrinkles. As they walked back inside, Montserrat realized that Fentisha wasn't wearing panties. *That's so trashy.* She watched her behind jiggle through the thin material.

Fentisha opened the door of the powder room by the patio, and the light flicked on as she stepped inside. Peering at her face in the mirror, she grinned. "Damn, I look good! I better call up some of my exes, so they can check me out now."

Montserrat laughed with her. What Fentisha lacked in class, she made up for in humor. "You can come back in a few weeks, if you want," she said. "I have some champagne that I need to open."

Fentisha hoisted her tote bag onto her shoulder and slipped into her platforms. "That's a bet. But don't tell anyone at the boutique about our little secret," she said, as they walked to the front door. "Let them keep thinking that $150 anti-aging cream I bought is finally paying off."

She made her way down the drive to her little red car, braying laughter, and Montserrat closed the door behind her. She was anxious to see her own face. As she jogged up the stairs, the lights glowed softly down the hallway, a bright path. The women on the wall seemed different in that light, more alive. She regarded herself in the master bathroom. Her face felt tight, and her skin was slightly red, as red as deep brown skin could get. What was that Fentisha had said? It looked like she had new skin. She touched her cheek. It didn't feel that different.

It didn't matter anyway, since it was all temporary. The manual explained that users of the sauna could expect two, maybe three good weeks of "You-thfulness," and then the effects would fade. Poor Fentisha. She'd been so excited about turning back the clock.

Montserrat stood in the door of her bedroom, glancing down the hallway at the healing room. A thread of light was visible beneath the closed door. E'lann explained that the room had a darkness sensor and was programmed to be sunny – when night fell or on cloudy days. The theory was that if a woman awakened in the middle of the night, gripped by panic, sorrow or whatever else ailed her, she could open the door of the healing room, and she would be bathed in brightness as she stood in the doorway, which would cause her sadness to abate.

The Built-in Blues Buster. She shut the door and returned to her bedroom. The sheets she'd slept on earlier were now free of wrinkles, as if ironed with a giant hand. She shimmied out of the bathing suit, tossing it into the hamper. Naked, she snuggled beneath the covers. The light adjusted itself as she closed her eyes. This room was comforting, more maternal than the healing room, and she felt safe in its wooden bosom. On the cusp of sleep, she felt, rather than heard, a soft hum.

The next morning, Montserrat sunned herself in the backyard. Plump grapefruit hung from the tree behind her, and bees droned around the fruit that had fallen to the ground. Red roses bloomed along the back wall of her garden, and the air was heavy with their cloying sweetness. She sat in a hand-woven rattan chair the color of coffee beans, legs folded beneath her, writing in her journal. It was an activity left over from her sessions with Dr. G. More so than documenting her daily thoughts, the leather-bound book was a source of unintentional humor as she read over the silliness of her earlier entries: *May 5: Hair thinning at my temples. Bruises on my legs and not sure why. Dear god, I hope it's not lupus or multiple sclerosis. June 8: I cried when the paramedics came, barefoot at the dining room table, couldn't breathe. One nice man went into my closet (I felt so embarrassed. It's so dirty!) and brought out my sneakers. He put them on my feet for me. August 19: The ER doctor gave me valium. He said I had to learn to "control myself." If I could do that, I wouldn't keep driving myself to St. Joe's once a week …*

Montserrat chewed on the tip of her pen, thinking of how far she'd come from those tremor-filled days. Yet, she still didn't feel whole. A bug landed on her leg, and she brushed it away, rubbing the spot on her skin with her knuckles. She'd left the screen door open to air the house out. No pesky black flies would buzz their way through the opening to infiltrate her space. Recalling E'Lann's story of the nuked canary, she hoped no hummingbird would fall victim to those invisible rays.

It's so peaceful out here. She watched a black bird chasing its mate in and out of the branches of her avocado tree. It would be nice to have a guy over for a glass of wine. She'd only dated two men since moving to Los Angeles. Neither of her ex-boyfriends ever called to say hello or see how she was doing. Her relationships didn't end badly – there were no hurt feelings over missed dinner dates, no blowups over unfamiliar phone numbers on a bill. The men had simply moved on with their lives, and she wasn't a part of the journey. She didn't feel rejected; she just assumed that her life would always be like this – brief romances punctuated by years of solitude.

Through the open door, she saw the Mignon painting in the living room. Montserrat felt as serenely lonesome as the woman in the frame who sat on the veranda in the woods, forever balancing a white teacup on her lap, a painted figure come to life but trapped in a bucolic setting. Yet around her, car doors slammed and garbage bins rolled down driveways. A dog yipped as its owner led it down the sidewalk. Twenty single neurotic women were going about their lives within their gated community, each trying to eke out some semblance of sanity.

"Why are you always so anxious?" Lorraine asked a few months back as they drove out of the parking lot of the movie theater. Montserrat rolled her window down to get some air and to let her friend's anger escape. When Lorraine was mad, the fine hair over her lip seemed to darken.

"I don't know."

Twenty minutes into the movie, Montserrat felt a rapid pulsing in her neck and knew she was going to pass out in the darkened theater. After squirming in her seat, trying to will the panic away, she ran out to the lobby. Lorraine joined her a few minutes later, scowling. Montserrat was glad she wouldn't have to see the remainder of the film, some soulless romantic comedy. With tears in her eyes, she asked her friend to drive her to the hospital.

"Everyone gets anxious," Lorraine said, as the familiar white-and-red emergency room sign came into view. "Everyone's chest hurts sometimes."

"Not like mine," Montserrat mumbled to herself.

"You have to be stronger than this, Monie. Your name ain't Becky," Lorraine said, but her voice had lost its scolding tone. "You can't let L.A. break you."

It didn't break me, Montserrat thought as she rose, tucking the journal beneath her arm. She slid the screen door shut and headed upstairs, where cold sunshine awaited her.

Montserrat lined up lipstick on the counter at Shimmer. The tubes stood at attention. It had been nearly a month since she moved into Heather Hollows, and the unconventional treatment was working. Now she used the healing room every other day, and the heart palpitations began to vanish. She didn't feel so anxious in crowds now. As she greeted clients at the boutique, she felt a sense of renewal.

Montserrat loved being in the cosmetics store. When she turned on the stereo upstairs and the showroom was awash with music, when she descended the spiral staircase and caught sight of herself in the mirrored wall at the back of the boutique, when Jorge, the black-smocked Latino with the spiky cornrows and pierced lip, glanced up and said, "Hey, Miss Honey," she felt as though she belonged. She was the empress of the makeup counter. She enjoyed dabbing concealer on an acne-scarred chin, plumping up puckered lips with a pencil and gloss, pressing false lashes over thinning ones. She was one of the most sought after makeup artists in the boutique, and even boasted a few C-list celebrities as clients.

Before heading to the post office on her lunch hour, Montserrat sat on the denim chaise lounge reapplying her lipstick in the mirror. Her fingers were still. She imagined herself running into Elza at the mailbox, holding her hand out to show how steady it was. Then her neighbor would raise her own hands, the skin no longer cracked from repetitive washing. She almost laughed out loud, smearing her lipstick, at the thought of them, one in braids, the other with silky hair, communicating their pain and healing through some primitive sign language.

Finished with her makeup, Montserrat glanced around the store. Stoic ladies, having dined at the posh vegan restaurant a few doors down, vied for the attention of a pouty salesgirl. Weary blondes parked designer carriages against the counter, folding belly fat into $200 jeans. They wielded makeup brushes and eyelash curlers as amulets against the baby blues.

"Girl, that color is hot. Makes your undertones pop."

"Thanks, Fentisha. It's mauve."

"Good for summer."

Fentisha stood at her side, and their eyes met in the mirror. Already, a few lines had returned to the skin beneath her eyes, and the sheen had been siphoned from her red hair. She twirled her beads around a finger.

"Got plans tomorrow?" Fentisha asked.

"No. What's up?"

"I was just wondering."

"You're welcome to come over," Montserrat said, replacing the cap on her lipstick. She rose, smoothing down her gauze skirt.

"You sure? I don't want to disturb you. I know you like your privacy."

"It's cool, Fentisha. I don't mind company. I'll probably take a book out to the backyard to get some sun, but I'll leave the front door unlocked. I'll send you the gate code. Does two o'clock work?"

"I'll be there." Fentisha regarded Montserrat's face. "Have you been using the sauna?"

"Not since you were over."

"You look the same," she said glumly.

"You say it like it's a bad thing," Montserrat said. "I forgot to mention it, but the results aren't permanent."

"So I noticed. But damn, I feel older than I did when I went in."

"You still look the same too," Montserrat lied. She studied her coworker's face. Did she look even older now? Her skin was faded and clammy, but Fentisha smeared on layers of liquid foundation every morning. "We'll talk when I get back."

Montserrat felt uneasy as she drove her BMW south on Robertson toward the post office. She'd read the re-You-thing manual three times before ever turning it on. She didn't recall seeing anything about women looking older after usage, just that the effects would wear off after a few weeks. But what if that was some trick of the manufacturer, to actually age the customer so she had to use the machine more frequently? She stared at herself in the rearview mirror. Had tiny lines formed beneath her eyes? She had good genes. Her mother was sixty-three, and except for dark circles under her eyes from years of smoking, her skin was lineless. She gazed at herself again, longer this time, until a blaring horn interrupted her scrutiny.

The post office was hot and crowded. Ahead of her, people waved envelopes as fans, wiped damp foreheads with the back of an arm. Every so often they moved in unison toward the clerk's window, like cattle driven forward by an invisible prod. Montserrat stood at the end of a line of about ten customers. No matter how crowded this particular post office was, there never seemed to be more than two clerks on duty, usually a man and a woman who worked with an unhurried air as they scanned packages, as they pushed change beneath the bulletproof glass. Her neck itched in irritation as she waited, and she fanned herself with the oblong box she carried. It was her mother's birthday gift, a sterling silver butterfly pendant with purple-tinted topaz gemstones. She wasn't really sure of her mother's tastes nowadays. Zelda Jones' birthstone was ruby, not topaz, but the pendant was something Montserrat would wear for herself, so she thought it made a good gift.

An old lady shuffled to the male clerk's window, her twisted back causing her paisley dress to rise. In spite of her deformity, she had pretty, dainty hands. Zelda would be retiring soon, but unlike this lady, she was spry. She loved to entertain guests and go to dinner with the women from her book club. She had such a calm ordered life.

Probably won't come to see my new house anytime soon. Her mom didn't even know where she worked. She'd been furious when Montserrat quit her job at the bank in Philly to pursue a career as a makeup artist in Hollywood. Montserrat secretly believed her mother's anger was jealousy in disguise. She was jealous that Montserrat sold her belongings, packed everything she owned into two suitcases and hopped a Greyhound Bus for the West Coast to follow her dreams. In the seven years that she lived in L.A., her mother had only visited once, when Montserrat's uncle Jake got married in San

Francisco several years ago, and she wanted to make a vacation out of it.

The oblong box began to shake. Montserrat realized her fingers were trembling, and she shoved her hand in her purse. Her mouth went dry, and she wondered if anyone noticed her behavior. She heard impatient sighs and shuffling feet behind her. *It's happening again.* She used her free hand to massage her carotid artery. It was a trick her doctor taught her to calm the palpitations, along with exhaling forcefully with her mouth closed. There were now three people ahead of her in line, but she didn't think she would make it to the counter. She pressed her legs together, as if to stem the stream of urine she was certain would run down her legs, pooling around her heels.

A hand tapped her shoulder, and she jumped. "You can move forward now," the redhead behind her said, her lips stretched in polite annoyance. Montserrat brushed past her, trying not to run as she pushed open the double doors and headed down the steps to the parking lot.

By the time the automated gate of her housing community swung open, her left arm was leaden. A year ago, she would have thought she was having a heart attack. She remembered that self-righteous clerk in the emergency room at St. Joseph's, beehive hairdo caked with dandruff, telling her she needed to "Let go and let God." Even though the doctor assured her that her heart was fine, she couldn't shake the feeling that she was going to die.

As soon as Montserrat stepped across the threshold, her bladder released. Piss flowed down her legs and splattered on the marble floor as she ran for the stairs. As she took the steps two at a time, the droplets disappeared. The house was a frantic mother sponging up after a toddler who has forgotten how to use the potty. Even the sour smell of urine was stripped from the air.

The light beneath the door of the healing room beckoned. Montserrat slipped into the rocking chair, her wet panties soaking the seat. She pressed the switch. As her body began to shake, she closed her eyes. "Peace," she said. "Peace, be still." That's what Nana would have said, her favorite scripture. There was a familiar groaning, as if the floorboards were about to open up and swallow her, chair and all. Then a tinkle of laughter floated up toward the ceiling, chipping away at her panic. Her facial muscles, clenched so tightly in the car, began to relax.

The smell of cinnamon and hot butter filled the room, and she saw herself biting down into an apple, felt the juice on her lip. Nana's strong hands scooped out a lump of lard from the blue can that sat on the back of the stove. Montserrat watched as she folded the grease into a bowl of flour, salted the mixture and kneaded the dough. Those bent fingers of a laundress were so rough, yet gentle as she wiped tears from Montserrat's cheek. Montserrat touched her own face now, as the floorboards vibrated beneath her bare feet. Grinding and humming, now humming and rocking, the room was like a child soothing itself.

"Mother didn't believe," she murmured, feeling the wetness on her face. The words were caught up in a spiral of giggles that bounced off the gold wall. The room rocked her, and its brightness pressed against her closed lids like a secret. Who was she hiding from? Herself? She was only six. She felt herself pitching forward and back, as if she were resting in the glider on her grandparents' porch again, that Spring of bouncing balls from the Catholic school and adult laughter. No one even noticed when her uncle Jake slipped away from the Pinochle table. She saw those work boots tipping across the cement porch.

No longer cool, the artificial sunlight was a hot hand covering her face, threatening to choke her. She began to sweat. Montserrat gripped the arm of the chair, finally finding the switch. The splashes of laughter dissipated, and the room grinded to a stop. The floorboards pulsed lightly under her feet. She stayed in the rocking chair until her neck stopped throbbing.

Mother didn't believe me. But Nana knew.

It wasn't her fault. He was the guilty one. All those years, she'd blocked out her uncle's hands beneath her Mickey Mouse T-shirt, that slow smile, and with it, feelings of shame and confusion. She felt as if someone had chipped away the sheetrock from her heart. Finally she rose, feeling lighter than she had when she sat down. She was safe here, in her new house. There were no squeaky work boots here, three thousand miles away from Germantown. She walked down the hallway, and climbed into bed, fully clothed. The light adjusted itself as she pulled the covers up to her neck and closed her eyes. The floorboards droned a soft melody as she fell asleep.

Montserrat slapped at her neck, rolling over in bed. She thought she had imagined silken legs tickling her skin, but now she sat up, unsure. As she rubbed her eyes, she noticed a black dot on the wall by her bed. The dot began to move. She swatted at it, and it flitted away. A gnat. But how? The dBugn System – Something buzzed by her ear, and she threw off the covers, running from the room.

At the bottom of the stairs, she stopped. Black footprints darkened the white marble of the foyer. Was someone in the house? She jiggled the door knob. Locked. Peering around the staircase, she saw more dirty prints – some larger than her own; some as small as a toddler's. The grimy outline from Fentisha's platform shoes reappeared. She stood in the kitchen doorway, feeling faint, staring at the white bowl on the center island. She replaced the pyramid of oranges with gala apples that were only a week or so old, but had started to go brown. As she reached for the dull red fruit, black gnats swarmed up toward the ceiling. She snatched her hand back as if stung. Leaning over the sink, she raised the window so the insects could escape. Her throat felt tight. She removed a corkscrew from the silverware drawer and opened a bottle of Merlot that lay in the wine rack on the counter. She read somewhere that you could set traps for gnats by pouring wine into bowls and covering them loosely with plastic wrap. Drawn by the fermented sweetness, the bugs would get trapped inside the bowl and drown. It seemed like a crazy theory, but it was worth a try.

After setting several liquid traps throughout the kitchen, dining room and on the living room table, Montserrat dumped the apples into a trash bag and sat it outside the back door. "This is unacceptable," she said aloud, as if berating the house. E'lann would have to send a technician out. Today. She washed her hands in the kitchen sink then grabbed her purse off the counter, reaching for the phone. As she dialed the realtor's number, she realized that she didn't own a broom, a mop or any cleanser. She wasn't ready to return to that world.

"Morning, Ms. Jones. Thought I recognized your number."

"There's nothing good about my morning, E'lann. There are bugs in my kitchen and dirt on the floor."

"Oh my. That's not good. Are you sure?"

"Yes, I'm sure. There are gnats everywhere."

"Well, I was going to say it sounds like dBugn is on the blink, but if you notice dirt as well, it's probably a multi-system malfunction."

"Only three weeks in?" Cradling the phone on her shoulder, Montserrat grabbed a napkin from the glass holder on the counter. She kneeled, trying to rub out a footprint. The tile gleamed white for a moment, then the bony outline reappeared. It was as if some graveyard waltz had taken place while she slept. "You said the self-cleaning unit was guaranteed for a lifetime."

She heard the shrug in his voice. "That's what the manufacturer says, Ms. Jones, but some lifetimes are shorter than others," he said. "It's Saturday. Don't know if I'll be able to get a technician out on such short notice, but if it's really inconveniencing you, I can put you up in a hotel for a few days."

Montserrat considered his offer. It was tempting to just beat it out of here, leave the house to the gnats and grime. But she'd dealt with worse things in her old place – silver fish and spiders. Even roaches. Although she hated to smash those little bodies, scoop up the lifeless smudges with a paper towel, she did it. There was no one else around to. No, running away from the house she just bought because of a few irritating gnats would erase the progress she had made last night, dissolve her healing.

"That's not necessary, E'lann. Just make sure you get someone out here first thing on Monday."

She hung up on his reply, tossing her phone back into her purse. She needed to go to the store for cleaning supplies. *Damn.* As she'd packed up her old apartment, she had thrown out a box filled with rags, furniture polish, disinfectant and other cleaning products. Now she had to start over.

Montserrat ran upstairs. E'lann said the problem sounded like a multi-system failure. She toyed with the knob of the healing room, and then opened the door. Sunlight streamed into the room. Not the synthetic kind. It was nearly eleven o'clock and the blinds were drawn. Just another beautiful July morning in Los Angeles. Montserrat lowered herself into the rocking chair, as if it were a fragile woman she didn't want to bruise. She pressed the switch, and an empty clicking sounded in the room. Her own rocking sounded just as hollow. She shook the chair, as if that motion would activate some mechanism within the bowels of the house. But the chair and the room were still. As she searched the walls for a switch, a fuse box, a bypass valve, she noticed a small placard above the baseboard by the door. In tiny lettering, it read: This room is for entertainment purposes only. It is not a substitute for a licensed mental health care practitioner.

Montserrat stared at the placard. She couldn't get mad. "You get what you pay for," Nana always said. Fifty-five hundred a month for high-tech therapy that had fizzled out after three weeks. Some lifetimes are shorter than others, E'lann had said.

Might have to give Dr Guntsworth a call on Monday. Montserrat headed toward the shower. She always felt embarrassed as she left the psychiatrist's office, had chided herself in the car for being so weak. Although the Built-in Blues Buster had dredged up those memories that had eluded her for so long, it was no match for the real thing.

As she left the house, she saw Elza and two other neighbors chatting at the end of the cul de sac. She honked, and they hailed her with animated smiles as she drove past. *Wonder what they're talking about*, she thought, waiting for the automatic gate to open. *Wonder if Elza knows about that little placard in her healing room.*

It felt good driving away from Heather Hollows. A square of sunlight beamed down through the open roof of her BMW. She stopped at a discount store on La Brea, buying sponges and cleaning fluid. Heading back to her car, she noticed a purple sign for a Japanese restaurant and stopped in for lunch. Montserrat felt just right sitting at her table, sipping a bowl of miso, feeling the fragrant brown soup warming her insides. She watched couples feeding each other with chopsticks, laughing as the sticky rice fell on the table. She stared at a cluster of women chatting at the sushi bar. It would be nice to joke with a friend over a meal.

She looked at her watch. Fentisha was coming over at two o'clock to use the sauna. It was five past. Montserrat didn't know her phone number, had never had a reason to call her. But the front door was locked. She wouldn't be able to get in. The re-You-thing sauna was linked with the healing room and the dBugn System, E'lann said. If the other two units had malfunctioned, that meant the sauna was probably defunct as well.

Montserrat flagged down a dour waitress, handing over her credit card. Once inside her BMW, she headed south, past a dollar store, past antique furniture stores with "Everything Must Go" signs in the windows. *It'll be alright.* But who was she trying to assure? Up ahead, she saw the wrought iron gates of her subdivision, with its trellis of delicate leaves and hardened vines. It looked like any other suburban neighborhood. What happened to the women in the community once they were "cured"? Did they just use the healing room every once in a while for maintenance? Did they throw "happy parties" and invite their morose friends over for a boost? Now that she was stronger, she wasn't sure how she felt still living amongst the neurotic. *Way too early to put the house on the market.* She drove inside the gates. She'd just have to adjust.

The cul de sac was empty. Montserrat pulled into her driveway behind the red Mustang. The front door of her house was ajar. She didn't remember leaving it unlocked. Had E'lann come by while she was out? And if so, why hadn't he closed the door behind him, or was the front door a part of the same system failure?

The smell of overripe grapes hit her as she walked inside. On the living room table, tiny black bodies had drowned in a bath of red wine. A Gucci tote bag was tossed carelessly on a chair, and a pair of platform shoes had been kicked off by the chaise lounge.

Montserrat ran to the patio, nervousness streaking her chest. By the time she reached the re-You-thing sauna, her neck was throbbing. The glass door was partly open, and a fine mist clung to the clay. A white sundress was crumpled on one of the salt benches. She squinted. Something black was visible on the thin material. She picked up the dress. In the middle was a dirty footprint.

"Fentisha!"

Her arm fell limp at her side as she backed out the door.

"Fentisha!"

Maybe her coworker had realized something was wrong with the sauna and had gone out to the backyard to sun herself, waiting for Montserrat's return. The rattan patio chairs were pushed neatly against the table. A squirrel scaled the fence, freezing at the sight of her. Birds circled her avocado tree.

Inside, she heard a faint noise. She stood in the living room, listening.

Yes, it sounded like a blur of giggles coming from deep within the house. Had the healing room somehow revived itself? Had Fentisha somehow triggered a switch that set the grinding sensors into motion?

By the time Montserrat reached the top step, she heard sobbing. How similar to laughter it sounded from a distance. A naked figure was curled up outside the healing room. Thick tangles of red hair swept the floor.

"Fentisha."

She looked up, and Montserrat stifled a cry. She was staring at a fat face damp with tears. Lineless. The small girl rose on chubby legs, the red beaded necklace hanging to her belly button.

"Fentisha? What did you do?"

The girl flinched. Her mouth opened in a soundless sob.

"I'm sorry, Fentisha. I didn't mean to scare you."

Montserrat reached for her, surprised at how light the child was in her arms. She couldn't have been more than three or four years old, and her breath was hot on Montserrat's neck. She carried her across the doorway of the healing room, not bothering to remove her shoes now, and sat in the chair in the middle of the sunny room. Mechanically, she began to rock. She heard the grinding of a white glider pushing away from its metal moorings. Soothed by the movement, the little girl quieted, sucking her thumb. Her blue nail polish was chipped. "Peace, be still," Montserrat said, rocking faster. The floorboards squeaked beneath her feet, as if bracing for a heavy foot. Montserrat hummed to herself, stroking the red hair. It felt as fine as corn silk, the luster restored at last. She rocked. Cinnamon burned in a steaming pan of butter, and from deep within the house she heard the bruised laughter of a child.

A Revolution for Black Maids

(Who Have Escaped Their White Female Authors)

The woman was cowering on the floor of my study, beneath the tented pages of a Kafka novel. When I flipped on the light and saw her thick black form dart under the open book, I suppressed a scream, thinking she was a large roach. But as I stood there in the doorway, trying to decide whether to run or face the thing I feared, she crawled out from her hiding place. No taller than my middle finger, the woman seemed to be rising from the carpet rather than sinking into it. She wore a black dress that swept her ankles and a white apron. Her body was enshrouded by a milky blue light, a fuzzy aura that seemed to be projecting from the bookcase behind her. A white bonnet the size of a toothpaste cap was perched on her head. She watched me watching her from the doorway for a few minutes, and then she shuffled toward me.

"Excuse me, ma'am." She bowed slightly as she spoke. Her voice, the drone of a dying housefly, helped put me at ease. "These your books?"

"Well, I didn't write them, but yes, they belong to me."

"You a writer, ma'am?"

"Yes," I replied after a pause. I had written several scripts since moving to L.A. seven years ago but hadn't sold any. To some people, I definitely wasn't a writer, at least not a working one. After that weak "yes," I felt like a fraud, but the woman clasped her hands in relief and moved closer.

"I needs your help."

What kind of help could I offer this miniature woman wearing a maid uniform? Somehow restore her to a normal size so she could clean my apartment? Outside my window, traffic whooshed by on Heliotrope Boulevard. The wind rattled my vertical blinds, and we both turned toward the sound.

Now that my fear had ebbed, I wondered how my tiny visitor and her weird wavy light ended up in my study. Maybe she was a hallucination. Sensing my unasked question, she said, "I cain't go back there."

"Go back where?"

"To her. You'se my only hope."

"I'm sorry, but I don't know how to help you."

"I needs you to write my story, ma'am."

I kneeled inches from her, taking in her taut brown skin and full lips. Tufts of knotty hair were visible beneath her maid's cap. Her tiny fingers were thick and swollen. She seemed like a poor subject for a biography. "Who are you?"

"Maisie, ma'am. Maisie Washington." She gave a little bow. "Missus Becky Hope White be the one writin' my story now, but I cain't go back there."

"Where?"

She shook her head so vigorously, I thought her bonnet would fall off. "I cain't go back to dat book, Miss … Miss –"

"Viola. Viola Jones."

"That sho is a pretty name, Miss Viola." It was the first time she smiled since materializing on my carpet. Then she frowned. "I hates my name – Maisie Washington – but it's the only one she give me."

"I'm sure your mother thought it was beautiful."

"No, ma'am. Not my mother. Missus Becky Hope White. My author."

Then Maisie told me her sad, strange story. She lived in a book about black maids called *The Domestics*. Her friends – Adelaide, Bertha and Hattie Mae – cleaned houses as she did "in a little town in Georgy you ain't never heard of called Motherwood." Maisie wanted to do more with her hands than scrub out crusty pots and hang wash on the clothesline to dry, but Missus Becky Hope White was determined to tell the tale of noble black cleaning ladies circa 1950.

"I jest had to escape, ma'am." Maisie gestured to the blue light encircling her, as if pleading to a foreign god. "But it's jest my spirit that done flew away. I'se still stuck here in the prison of these pages."

"If you're trapped, Maisie, how in the world can I help you?"

"Missus Becky Hope White, she still be writin'. The endin' ain't done yet," Maisie said. "But she got a lot of folks innerested in her story. I don't want her to tell it. I wants you to do it."

The defiant buzz in her voice stung my heart. What could I do to help this little woman, this maidling? No one was paying attention to my words. I stopped writing screenplays about the lives of women named Nia and Shawnetta – replacing them with characters named Libby and Heidi – to make my work more palatable to agents. Less ethnic. Now a fugitive from a white lady's novel on black maids and was begging me to write her story. I rose and booted up my laptop.

"I'm still not sure if I'm the right person for the task," I said over my shoulder. My visitor just stared at me, her fingers still knit in supplication. "But I'll do the best I can."

"You'se my only hope."

If not for her black skin and mammy dress, she could have been a holographic Princess Leia begging to be rescued from the Empire.

"Maisie, do you remember the last thing you were doing in *The Domestics*?"

"Yes, ma'am, Miss Viola –"

"Just Viola is fine. You don't work for me."

"Yes, ma'am, Miss Viola. I was in the kitchen makin' some mint julep to brang to Missus Priscilla Westenbury – she be the lady I work for in the book. Well, Missus Priscilla was fannin' herself on the porch, and I was standin' by the sink, stirrin' up dat mint julep, when I saw the sun shinin' through the kitchen window." With the grace of a pregnant dove, Maisie levitated, landing on the spine of the book. "And I looked at dat big ole yaller sun, and it looked like life to me, and I knowed I weren't meant to be nobody's maid."

"And then what happened?"

"Next thing I knowed, the kitchen floor was gone, and I was fallin' through a hole. I landed 'mongst all these books, then you came in and switched on the light."

I turned back to my laptop, studying the white page in front of me. I traced the keyboard with my fingertips, trying to pull courage from the black squares. Finally, I typed

Maisie Washington stood near the counter, preparing her employer's afternoon drink. The smell of mint filled the kitchen, clashing with the savory smoke of baking ham. As she watched the sturdy green leaves floating to the top of the glass, she was reminded of her grandmother, Sepal. It was an unusual name, but beautiful. Maisie's father had explained to her that a sepal is the tough leaf protecting the delicate inner parts of a flower.

Sepal – that's such a majestic name, thought Maisie. I think I'll adopt it as my own.

As she rechristened herself that summer afternoon, sunlight flooded the window, caressing her smooth brown skin. Emboldened by her decision, she pulled off her bonnet, tossing it to the floor. She toyed with the soft coils springing from her scalp.

"I feel like a new woman," Sepal said aloud. "Like I belong to myself."

As she uttered those words, her skin grew hot, as if scorched by an inner sun. Her hands reddened, and she stared at them in wonder, marveling as the thick knuckles and water-cracked skin began to smooth. Just as Sepal thought she was having a heatstroke, a plume of fire shot from her fingertips, demolishing a sack of flour sitting on the counter. She coughed, fanning away the fine white dust sifting down on her spotless kitchen. Grabbing a dishtowel from the sink, she moistened it and then swatted at the rising flames. Once the threat was doused, she stared at her hands again.

"Well, I declare."

A brittle voice floated in through the open window: "Maisie? You lazy nigra. My mint julep is supposed to be served every afternoon at 2:00, and it's five past. You better make haste, gal."

"Be there directly, Miss Priscilla," Sepal said. She hurried to the broom closet and retrieved a dust pan. As she swept up the mess on the floor, she marveled at her new power. Colored women can't set things on fire with their hands, she thought, dumping the ruined flour in the wastebasket. But I did. Yes, indeed. I held that heat. Nobody would ever try to cheat me or call me out my name if they knew what I had in these fingers.

"Maisie? I'm not going to call you again."

"Coming, Miss Priscilla."

A fly entwined in the kitchen curtain buzzed lazily, as if drunk on the pungent smell of mint. As Sepal placed her employer's drink on a stainless steel serving tray, she raised her finger. The curtain erupted in flame, and she headed out the door.

I read the passage aloud, then looked back at Maisie, not sure what I expected to see. She was still standing on the spine of the book, but her bonnet was gone, replaced by a cloud of kinky hair. "I do like the name Sepal. That's right pretty," she said. Maybe it was the wiry curls unleashed at last from the maid's cap, but she seemed taller to me. "What happened to Miss Priscilla?"

I shrugged. "Haven't gotten that far yet, but I'm pretty sure you go outside and zap her with your superpowers, and then escape through a field as the house burns down."

"Our house?" She gave a nervous laugh, pressing a hand to her chest. "Miss Becky Hope White ain't going to like you killing off Miss Priscilla Westenbury. She worked hard to get that woman's temper just right."

"There are plenty other women to replace her."

In spite of her hesitance, I felt a surge of joy in my chest, the feeling I always had when working on a story that moved me. I had been stuck on page twenty-four of my own script for the past several weeks, dying a little each time I tried to wade through Libby and Noelle's exploits at the Beverly Hills boutique. But now, I really had a reason to write. I felt more entitled to the story than Becky Hope White. My grandmother Reynalda had cleaned houses for a living, and I often accompanied her into the homes of the D'Angelos and McGoverns as she did day work. Becky may have researched the lives of maids like Sepal, Adelaide, Bertha and Hattie Mae for her story – may even have been raised by a black nanny – but her research couldn't compare with the stooped shoulders and arthritic fingers of Nana as she scrubbed toilets, as she washed and waxed floors on her bare knees.

"Yes, ma'am, Miss Viola. I 'spect you right, but I don't know what to do with fire in my fingers." She studied her palms. "I want to use these hands to make things – to plant a garden, paint, maybe even write."

I fought to conceal my skepticism at the thought of that uneducated black woman sitting down with a pen and paper. As if reading the disbelief in my eyes, Sepal said, "I got some book learnin'. I went up to the sixth grade, but Mama's eyes started going bad. I had to quit school and help out with the other children. I was only a girl myself, but I had five brothers and sisters to look after. Had to keep 'em busy. So I told 'em stories – oh, all kind of tales about God and the devil, about talking mules and a little baby chick that grew up to be a princess."

"So you're a storyteller."

"I reckon I am, ma'am."

She said it with such conviction that I felt sorry for doubting her. She had more faith in her budding ability than I had in a talent I spent years cultivating.

"I got a little money set aside. I want to go see my kin up north. Maybe start over. I don't have nobody to look after in Motherwood – no husband, no children – although Miss Becky Hope White trying to marry me off to some flat-headed man named Jerome Jenkins." She frowned at the thought of this would-be beau. "I like being by myself. I just want to do something different with my life."

Sepal sounded so much like me that she could have been a character from my own life. I didn't speak for a few minutes, trying to decide on a future befitting the maidling.

"Sure are quiet, Miss Viola. What are you thinking about?"

I fingered the dark squares of my keyboard again, loving the hardness of the keys. "Sepal, I'm thinking about a revolution."

Later that night, I tossed and turned beneath my comforter, too excited to sleep. I had left Sepal in my study, promising her that I would continue to work on her story in the morning before I headed to my job. But I sat up in bed, worried. What if she was gone when I woke up? What if I dreamed the whole thing and there was no black maidling standing on a Kafka book? Or worse, what if I had actually endowed her with superpowers and she accidentally incinerated my office?

My words changed her. Of that, I was sure. The bonnet disappeared; her speech was less mammified. More human. The only thing that had not changed was her domestic mentality. When I read her the short passage I had written – her new story – her first concern had been for the welfare of her boss, Miss Priscilla. My hand itched as I thought of the woman – with her splotchy skin and nasal voice, pink scalp showing through her wispy hair. She probably sat her plump bottom in a glider on the porch every day, fanning herself, as Sepal cooked, did laundry and washed and dressed her snot-nosed kids – all while calling her a "lazy nigra."

You wrote those words. I snuggled beneath the covers. A car door slammed outside my window, and I heard a woman's high-pitched laughter. It was after 1:00 a.m. One of my neighbors was probably coming home from a hot date. No man had asked me out in more than two years, and now this new project was one more distraction that would prevent me from having a social life. At least, that's what I told myself.

I was now the co-author of Sepal's story. I wondered how my "intervention" would affect Becky Hope White's writing of *The Domestics*. Would Miss Priscilla's pages disappear from the manuscript? Would Becky suddenly find herself with a bad case of writer's block while working on Sepal's character arc? What made her think she was qualified to write this particular story anyway? Did she care that she was contributing to yet another novel on servile black women – noble women, maybe, but domestics nonetheless -- that she was the god of yet another universe populated with cinnamon-skinned, saucer-eyed, full-lipped, buxom, crinkly-haired, bonnet-wearing, stooped shouldered, compassionate, English-slaughtering black women?

I hate her, and I haven't even read her book.

I adjusted my scarf, waiting for sleep to shutter my eyelids.

I jumped out of bed the next morning, hoping Sepal had not left me. As I walked barefoot across the hardwood floors in the living room, daylight streamed through my Venetian blinds. Now our whole conversation seemed silly beneath the glare of those fractured rays, and I was reminded of my inadequacy as a writer. I felt like a failure for having never sold a script. I'd been hawking my projects for seven years, and I knew people who had sold several screenplays after only living in Hollywood for half that time. *Maybe I'm not determined enough.* I turned the knob of my study.

Two maidlings perched atop the Kafka book, like old friends sitting on a riverbank, passing the time of day. Sepal rose to greet me, but her friend let out a squeak, sliding down to the floor.

"That's alright, Adelaide. This is Miss Viola that I was telling you about. She's writing my story."

Adelaide hoisted herself up, brushing off her black dress. Like Sepal, her body was encased in flickering blue light. She too wore a bonnet, which was askew on her straightened brown hair as the result of her fall.

"It's not just your story," she said, adjusting her cap. I hid a smile. Her voice hummed like Sepal's, except she sounded like someone with a cold giving a poor impersonation of a southern accent. I would fix that.

"That's true, but I'm the main story. Miss Becky Hope White spent more time on me. Said right in the beginning that I reminded her of somebody from her childhood."

Probably someone who nursed her. I powered on my laptop. I was surprised by my lack of surprise at Adelaide's appearance, that there were not one but two servile apparitions on the floor of my study. Maybe she had gone looking for her friend and fallen into the same hole. Whatever the case, I was eager to start writing. I had two miniature muses standing behind my swivel chair, and I wouldn't let them escape without creating a life fitting for them. The story began to move and breathe in my mind. I would dedicate it to my grandmother Reynalda, she of the metal-gray hair that was always hidden beneath a purple head wrap as she cleaned houses. I touched my own head, pulling off the silk scarf I slept in. The women watched as I shook out the jumble of kinky plaits.

"That hairdo looks right nice on you, Miss Viola," Sepal said. "Different."

"Thank you. But just Viola is fine."

"Yes, ma'am, Miss Viola."

As I opened the document I'd been working on the night before, I heard Adelaide say, "Why you trust her? You don't know her."

"She reminds me of somebody I know. And she's doing a mighty fine job on my story. Just need to change a few things."

"*Our* story. You trust somebody with hair like that to get it right? 'Sides, I likes my job. We live in a nice house."

"Ain't your house."

The little women bickered for a few more moments, then I said, "Adelaide, what do you do?"

"Ma'am? What you mean what do I do?"

I turned to face her. Even from where I sat, her scowl was visible, her arms akimbo. Whereas Sepal appeared to be around forty years old, Adelaide looked half her age. She was shorter too. She reminded me of my friend Daphne – all attitude and hair. In another world, she'd be playing somebody's sassy best friend on a sitcom.

"Well, I know that Maisie – I mean Sepal – works for Miss Priscilla. Who do you work for?"

"I am a live-in governess," she said, her lips stretched in pride. "I helps Missus Charity Vanderbilt take care of her two children – Scooter and Harper."

"Two boys must be a handful."

"Scooter ain't no boy. She a girl," she said, as if I'd insulted her own child. "And don't you be changing my name either. I likes Adelaide."

"It's beautiful," I said. "It suits you."

She gave me a half smile. "Missus Becky Hope White got a way with colored names."

Like she plucked them right out of the Ethnic Dictionary *sitting on her shelf right next to the* Catalog of Negro Women Features. I turned back to my computer, reading over what I'd written the previous night. "Can you tell me the last thing you remember, what you were doing before you ended up here?"

Although my back was turned, I detected a note of pride in the maidling's voice. "Scooter had just come home from school – she's nine, and just as feisty as she can be – and I had just laid out her cookies and milk. She likes to drink it with the clabber. I never could stand that sour stuff," Adelaide said. "After I finished up the dishes, I went up to Scooter's room to play with her dolls. I never had no dolls growing up."

"You don't know what you had," Sepal cut in, and I swiveled around in my chair. "Out of me, you, Bertha and Hattie Mae, I'm the only one so far with a childhood. I don't think Miss Becky Hope White got that far with you yet."

Adelaide fiddled with her apron. Her hands, I noticed, weren't as work-worn as her friend's. "I'm sure I had a perfectly lovely childhood. Just not no dolls. Maybe that's why I likes playing with Miss Scooter Ann's dollies so much."

I ran my index finger over the keyboard, trying to reclaim the magic of last night's storytelling. As the miniature woman continued to narrate the life that had been chewed up and fed to her, I typed away

Adelaide swept cookie crumbs from the table with the blade of her hand. Scooter was such a messy brat. Always expecting someone to pick up after her. She'd grow up to be a vile, lazy woman, just like her mother.

"When I was her age, I was cooking supper for my younger brothers and sisters until Mama came home," Adelaide murmured to herself as she soaped Scooter and Harper's plates. Although Mama was dog tired when she returned home from taking in wash, she always brought trinkets for the children – a game of jacks or a Raggedy Ann doll given to her by one of the ladies she did laundry for.

Adelaide climbed the staircase with a sigh. She was only twenty, but hers were the movements of a much older woman. She passed Miss Charity's closed door. The woman was probably in bed as usual, although it was only 3:30. Her employer attributed the many hours that she spent "resting" to anemia. As pallid as she was, it certainly seemed like she had poor blood. Too bad that scotch she keeps in her chiffarobe don't strengthen her system none, Adelaide said, opening the door to Scooter's bedroom.

The girl sat at a tea table by the window, her back to Adelaide. Long red hair hung down the back of her calico dress in a neat French braid. That's my doing, Adelaide thought as she closed the door. If not for me, I imagine it would look like her mama's – a messy bird's nest.

Scooter turned around at the sound of Adelaide's laughter. Freckles dotted her milky skin like the blood of a gutted animal. Her cold green eyes were huge behind her bifocals. She looked like an intelligent bullfrog. Adelaide stifled a giggle.

"What are you laughing at, Adelaide?" The teacup paused, midway to the girl's lips.

"Just happy, I guess, Miss Scooter." Adelaide walked around the canopy bed,

straightening the rose-colored chenille bedspread and fluffing the white pillows. She pulled out a little wooden chair and sat next to the child. The chair was tight, but she was small enough to fit. Maisie would never be able to get her backside in a chair like this.

"You darkies are always so happy, Mama says." Scooter took a sip of her imaginary tea, then stopped as if forgetting something important. "You can't sit down until I say so. I didn't give you permission."

Biting back a sigh, Adelaide grabbed the arms of the chair and pushed herself up. She stood to the right of the child, her fingers clasped in front of her apron. You 'bout the orneriest little girl in Motherwood. Wish I had a paddle, she thought. Then you'd have to worry about sitting down.

"Mind if I take a seat, Miss Scooter Ann?"

Scooter poured herself another cup of tea before addressing the maid. "Did you say something, Adelaide?"

"Yes, ma'am. I asked if I could have a seat."

The girl nodded. As Adelaide sank into the chair, Scooter asked, "Would you like some tea?"

"That's mighty kind of you. I reckon I will."

"Papa said no niggers can eat off our plates or drink out of our glasses. I hope you brought your own cup." Adelaide itched to slap the freckle-faced brat, but she tightened her hand into a fist instead and held it out. "Yes, ma'am, I did. Here it is. Thank you for giving me some of your tea." Rude hussy.

Scooter lifted her teapot, but then paused. "I don't serve nigger women," she said, setting the teapot back on the table. "You're my maid. You pour the tea."

Adelaide's jaws tightened. She felt heat rising from her cheeks to her temples. But it wasn't a feeling of shame, like that time in the junior choir when she forgot the words to "Precious Lord, Take My Hand." Something clicked in the middle of her forehead, as if her skull had cracked open, no longer able to contain the matter within. She looked at the girl to see if the noise was audible, but Scooter was still sitting there with a tight smile. Then her eyes widened.

The teapot flew across the table, bouncing off the window pane. Four pink teacups rose nearly to the ceiling, and then clattered against the hardwood flooring, as if dropped by an invisible hand. The child cried out, ducking her head as if she expected that same hand to slap her face. Her chair toppled over backward, spilling her to the floor.

Well, I'll be, Adelaide said to herself. Did I do that?

The rush of heat that had collected at her temples surged to the middle of her forehead. She focused her gaze on the child, who struggled to rise. Her red braid shot up stiffly, like an asp, transfixed. Then the girl flew backwards across the room, crashing into her pink-and-white canopy before falling to the floor. Adelaide jumped up and raced around the bed. Scooter landed with her back on the scatter rug. One leg rested on her chest of drawers. Her mouth hung open and her chest heaved, but she looked too startled to cry.

Satisfied that the girl wasn't too badly hurt, Adelaide reached down to pick up Scooter's bifocals. One black arm hung limp, and a lens was cracked. She tossed the glasses in the trashcan.

"Just look at this messy room. Glory be! Get up from there, pick up those teacups and straighten up that bed," she told the whimpering child as she opened the door. "I'm going down the hall to see about your mama."

"I don't see nothing funny about hurting a poor innocent child," Adelaide said after I read her the passage. She stood with her fists on her hips. "Scooter is just as sweet as sugarcane. She wouldn't never talk back to no adults, much less me."

"It's just a draft," I said, sitting back in my swivel chair, buckling beneath the whip in her voice. Outside my window, bottles tinkled in the shopping cart of a homeless man as he walked by, muttering to himself. "I can always change it."

Adelaide turned to Sepal. "Knew somebody with crazy hair like that wouldn't know nothing about writing no proper story," she mumbled.

"Gave me a chuckle. I kinda like the idea of being able to float things around with your mind – especially little bad behind girls." Sepal untied her apron and let it slide down the cover of the book. "Now what's that you said about my backside not fitting in that child's chair?"

"Maisie Washington. I never said nothing about your behind." The younger maidling rolled her eyes at me. "Just messing up our story. Missus Becky Hope White never wrote an unkind word about our hindparts. She made us all proper colored ladies."

Adelaide was having none of Sepal's transformation. It saddened me that the little woman didn't consider me a worthy writer, that she considered Becky more competent, more well versed in making her a "proper" colored lady. I squinted at my tiny visitors. The milky blue light surrounding them was losing its vibrancy. Their black dresses looked washed out. They were fading, and I had just begun to tell their stories.

"Don't leave," I said to them, but my plea was directed to Sepal. "I want to keep writing your story."

"We can't stay in this room forever," Adelaide said. "We got our own place."

Sepal stood at the edge of the book closest to me, extending her hand. "I do trust you, Miss Viola. You don't know us as well as Miss Becky Hope White – well, I 'spect you wouldn't since we belong to her – but I want to see where you and that machine can take us."

"I have to get ready for work now, Sepal, but I'll take you anywhere you want," I said, turning off my computer. "And everywhere you should have been allowed to go."

An hour later, I pulled into the parking garage at my job. I was running late – again. It was such a chore to get out of bed lately. I knew the feeling of dread that gripped me each morning I opened my eyes was one of the many signs that it was time to leave my job. There was no joy to be found in my cubicle.

I swiped my badge and pushed open the double doors leading to the studio lot. I worked at a production company for a teen sitcom, and my building was a five-minute walk away. A blonde wearing a pencil skirt and stilettos zipped past on a golf cart. Young women clad in tight jeans and sandals chatted as they headed down a pathway shaded on either side by Jacaranda trees. It occurred to me that I could be a character in someone's novel, one of the few blacks living in a production metropolis peopled by white women – the Motherwood of Los Angeles. *If I'm a character,* I thought, dropping my badge in my purse, *I hope no Becky Hope White is writing my story.*

I thought of the maidlings left behind in my study. Adelaide was probably pointing out to Maisie – Sepal – how dusty the room was. I'm the granddaughter of a cleaning lady, but I hate washing dishes or scouring grime from a tub. It's interesting how invested the characters seem in the lives of their employers – although I realize it's not actually their concern, but a concern their author imagines they would have.

Nana never talked about the people she cleaned up after, mainly because she rarely saw them. Her employers were working-class Italian and Irish families in her southwestern Pennsylvania mining town, and they left her alone all day to clean while they managed factories or taught high school. She didn't wear a maid's uniform either, just a checkered housedress and a pair of Papa's old shoes. Nana kept the keys to their houses on colored pieces of yarn that she hung around her neck and tucked down the bosom of her dress – green represented the McCrackens; blue for the D'Angelos. My grandmother wasn't known for wringing her hands. She would cuss you out in a minute if you tracked dirt on her floors. "I clean houses for twelve hours a day. Damn right my own house is going to be just as spotless," she always informed visitors as she told them to remove their shoes at the front door. She loved to laugh and play Bid Whist with her friends while drinking homemade whisky served with a slice of her famous orange pound cake. I missed her loud laughter.

As I rounded the bend, the familiar stone-gray building came into view. I will walk up the steps to my cubicle, nod and smile at the dozen or so writers that I pass, drop my purse on a stack of binders, sit at my desk and boot up the computer as yet another morning whines to life. I just clocked in, and I can't wait to get home, so I can continue writing for the maidlings. Their fabricated lives are so much more exciting than my own.

As I headed to the break room for a cup of instant coffee, I wondered how I would continue Sepal's story. Usually, when I sat down to write, I worked from an outline, or a character appeared in my head, and I followed her around to see where she would take me. But Sepal's story was different. She had not appeared in my head, but had materialized in my study, and she came complete with her own manuscript … that she was trying to edit herself out of. It made me wonder if some of my own characters had escaped my scripts and were out in the world somewhere, begging another writer to alter their narrative.

"Talk to me, Sepal," I murmured.

"Talking to yourself again?"

Tiffani, one of the production assistants, was bent over the water cooler filling her thermos. I hadn't heard her come in. The sullen redhead couldn't have been more than twenty-three, but her curly hair was beginning to thin in the crown. Even though she had a lower position than I did, there was always a note of superiority in her voice.

"Good morning, Tiffani." I stirred sugar into my coffee to hide my embarrassment. "You know writers – we always have characters on the brain."

"Speaking of which, I left a script on your desk for revisions. Crysta said she needs it ASAP."

"Will do." Usually, Tiffani's self-importance irritated me, but I swatted down her arrogance. I was too high from my morning writing session to allow her attitude to get to me.

Back at my desk, I sat down the coffee cup, thumbing through the script that needed to be checked for typos and continuity errors. I knew Crysta needed it soon, but I had other characters on the brain. It was risky, but I had to return to Motherwood. Sepal's life was more important to me than the exploits of some silly rich tween trying to reunite her celebrity parents.

Turning my monitor away from the entrance to my cubicle, I opened a new document on my computer. I pretended to revise the script as I typed

Sepal hurried across the pecan orchard which bordered her employer's property, apron flapping in the breeze. Several pods had fallen to the ground, and she stumbled over them. Her chest heaved, and she reached out to grab a sapling for balance.

After placing Miss Priscilla's tray of mint julep firmly on the fat lady's lap, she skipped down the brick steps. The woman's shrill cries followed her around the back of the house: "Maisie. Where are you going? You hear me talking to you, gal? Insolent nigra. What in the world is that smell?"

Now Sepal hid behind a pecan tree that was at least a hundred years old, trying to catch her breath. Everything on the Westenbury property had history. Behind her, the house where she'd been employed as a servant for the past three years was burning to the ground. Mr. George Westenbury was so proud of the white, two-story townhouse that had been in his family for several generations.

Two columns in the front were badly burned in the War, he told her once, but the house had been restored.

"As strong as the day it was built. Damn Yankee cannons couldn't damage it," Mister George always said, showing small yellow teeth as he blew into his coffee. "It's still standing."

Now she watched as the 200-year-old Greek Revival house blackened and plumes of smoke poured out of the windows.

Had Miss Priscilla gone back inside in an attempt to extinguish the flames? Had she run through the house to save her mama's good china and silverware, her mottled complexion made even redder by the exertion, to grab the gray short-waist jacket her husband's father had worn during the War?

"Gone," she whispered to herself. "It's all gone. My hands did that."

Sepal hoped her employer wasn't hurt, but it was too late to worry about that now. She had to leave Motherwood. Tonight. She'd head up north to visit her kin and start over from the ashes of domestic life. The only thing she regretted was that she wouldn't be able to say goodbye to Adelaide, Hattie Mae or Bertha.

At least I don't have to worry about Jerome Jenkins, she thought. *Never could see myself married to anybody with a misshaped head like that, I don't care if he is a colored man of property.*

A fire engine wailed in the distance. Untying the apron, she flung it against the bark of the old tree. Then she hurried through the orchard, taking the back road to town, the smell of smoke lingering on her black uniform.

At 6:30 that evening, I pulled into my garage. My head was pounding. There were too many ideas floating around in my mind. I didn't feel like running into my neighbors in the elevator, so I took the back stairs up to my apartment.

As I let myself in the apartment, I reflected on my horrible afternoon. Crysta had chewed me out for turning in a shoddy second draft of a script. "This is unacceptable. There are more typos now that when I dropped the thing off. And who the hell is Sepal?" she said, tossing the marked up script back on my desk.

Can't wait until I sell a script. I kicked off my heels at the front door, feeling defeated. That's one of the main reasons I want to be a screenwriter –

not just to see my stories come to life on the big screen, but to have creative and financial freedom. How great it will feel to sit at my laptop all day, churning out my own stories, without some rabid, micromanaging boss standing over my shoulder.

Free from the prison of stilettos, I wiggled my toes. I couldn't imagine standing on my feet all day. At once, I missed my grandmother. I missed the thickened hands that once ran a straightening comb through my hair, that smoothed menthol on my chest when I had the flu. I hated sharing her hands with others, especially those who did not appreciate them as I did. As I opened the door to my study, I blinked. In the lamplight, I noticed that the amount of visitors had doubled. Four faces stared up at me. *I might need to move to a bigger apartment*, I thought walking over to the women, *or else I'll have a village of miniature maids before long.*

"Good evening, Miss Viola."

"Good evening, Sepal. Looks like we have company."

Gesturing to her two friends, she said, "This is Bertha and Hattie Mae – my bosom friends from Motherwood."

Bertha, a thin, nut brown woman, gave me a nervous smile. Hattie Mae, the color of weak tea, curtsied slightly. I had to give Becky Hope White credit. At least she varied the size and skin-tone of her black female characters. They weren't your garden-variety dark-skinned, big-bosomed, fat-faced maids that Hollywood likes to churn out.

"Mighty pleased to meet you, ma'am," Bertha said. "We was so worried about Maisie. Missus Minnie Lovington – lady I work for – said she heard Missus Priscilla's house had burnt down. Well, as soon as I got a chance, I went looking for Hattie Mae – "

"I was polishing the china cabinet when I heard her calling from the back porch," Hattie Mae chimed in. She gestured with her hands as she talked – something my grandmother used to do. "Missus Dorothy Aberdeen – my boss – was off to her bridge club. Well, I left that rag right on the counter, and we went looking for Maisie. Nobody seen Miss Priscilla."

I sat in the swivel chair, mulling over the news. The threads of inadequacy that had settled in my stomach during Crysta's scolding began to dissolve. Something strange was happening – stranger than the presence of four finger-length fugitives on my carpet. I thought I was creating a new story for the maidlings. Actually, I wasn't sure just how my writing would affect the characters in *The Domestics*. But according to these new visitors, I was changing the outcome of Miss Becky Hope White's novel. I smiled, relishing this newfound power. My words mattered at last. But then the feeling of authority vanished. Did Becky think she had typed the words to incinerate Miss Priscilla's house – and presumably, along with it, Miss Priscilla? Would Sepal somehow be implicated in the crime and punished? And what about over at the closeted drunkard's house – Charity Vanderbilt? Would Scooter rouse her mother from her daily stupor and accuse Adelaide of assaulting her?

I had created two bonnet-wearing outlaws. Well, I hadn't created them, just infused these servants with superpowers. It dawned on me that if I had that much control, I could have caused all the maidlings to disappear, could have made Motherwood a ghost town with a few keystrokes. But even if my inferno scorched the red clay and consumed the Victorian homes in Miss Becky's village of happy darkies, another white woman author would one day feel the need to examine the lives of black female servants, would desire to broadcast to the world from her dominion atop the *New York Times* best-seller's list, the stooped nobility of her subjects.

As if black women didn't already know that we were superheroes in aprons and uniforms.

Fuck that.

"Listen up, ladies," I said, as my computer whirred to life. Four faces turned toward me, heads tilted at my tone of voice. "I respect Becky Hope White as a fellow author, and, I guess, for birthing you all."

Hattie Mae gasped, and Bertha pressed a hand to her chest. Adelaide shook her head, and Sepal just stared at me with a quiet smile.

"But there's a new mother in town," I said, opening my document. I hadn't thought of a title for the maidlings' story, had just saved my writings under the file name "Domestics." But the miniscule women were more than their moniker implied, were more than their relationship to their employers. If I had my way, they would be lightsaber-wielding Jedis, and the white folks they served – no matter how well-intentioned and kind – would be the

Siths they had to overthrow. But who would buy the story of black maids creating a new world order, saving the universe from the dark side of The Force?

It wasn't my story to tell anyway; it was Sepal's. No matter how servile she appeared, she'd found the courage to flee the back door of her existence, to search for the help she needed in creating a life that belonged to her. And she managed to hustle a few of her friends down the hole with her.

I turned to her. "Sepal – I mean Maisie – I want to do your story justice," I said. "No matter how badly I want to save you from the Empire, I can't fight for you."

"Call me Sepal. Suits me just fine, Viola." Her dress was a faded black flower, withered by the sun. "I trust your words."

I glanced at the multi-hued faces of her comrades. "Why? Because we share the same hair texture? Because only black women can tell other black women's stories?"

"No, because I kinda like this fire in my hands," she said, holding up her palms. "I could do a whole lot with this."

"Well, I don't need to be moving things around with my mind," Adelaide chimed in. "I like my house. If it's all the same to you, I'd just as soon be back there giving Miss Scooter Ann her cookies and clabber and playing with her little dolls."

Sepal turned to her friend. Even though her aura had dimmed to a faint blue glow, her face shone. It shone as I imagined it did the day she stood in the kitchen window with the sun on her skin, declaring herself a new woman.

"I'm going up north. We might not see each other again, you understand?" she said this to Adelaide, but she included her other two friends in the question.

Hattie Mae dabbed at her eyes. "Come back with us, Maisie. We need you in Motherwood. Who's going to be our fourth player at gin?"

"It's so cold up there, and you don't know nothin' about living up north," Bertha added. "What you going to do for work? Be a maid? That's the only thing your hands are good for."

"My hands are good for more than that, and I aim to find out just what."

Sepal glanced at me. Even though she had not left yet, I began to miss her too. For a minute, her body wavered, and I could see the bookcase through her skin. She was fading away.

"Sepal," I said, growing nervous. "I think Becky Hope White is trying to pull you back to the Westenbury house – what's left of it. She's probably restoring that old place brick by brick as we speak."

"Then make haste," the maidling said, a new confidence in her voice. "I told you first time I saw you I wasn't going back there, and I meant it. You're writing my story now."

You'se my only hope.

Facing the monitor, I typed

Sepal rested her head against the window, the cold seeping into her forehead. The steady, rumble of the train down the tracks disturbed her rest. Too nervous to sleep anyway, she said to herself. She wouldn't feel truly safe until she was up north at her sister Reena's house. She uncovered the basket on her lap, biting into a biscuit. The roll was hard and cold, but she ate it with relish. Sepal wiped her mouth, glancing around the car. Her compartment was half full. The other colored occupants were either talking with their families or asleep. She felt her hand growing warm.

No, she said to herself, putting the half-eaten bread back in her basket. I'm going to save my fire for the time I really need it. Besides, these hands are going to be writing hands.

She was anxious to see new houses, new flowers, new people. Motherwood was a memory. What a crazy-sounding town anyway? She was heading to Phoenixville, Pennsylvania. Now that was a name that sounded good, solid. Phoenixville. Just the kind of place I need to start over.

Sepal leaned back in her seat, listening to the whistling train, thinking of the friends she'd left behind. Yesterday morning, she awakened in a field on the outskirts of town, dried grass brushing her cheek. She washed her face and hands in a small stream, waiting until nightfall. Then she walked the two miles to Adelaide's house, carrying her shoes in her hands. Adelaide lived in a small brick house in back of her employers' property that once served as the slave quarters.

"A governess," Sepal chuckled to herself as she approached the building. As much as her friend loved the Vanderbilts, they would never let her sleep under their roof. A light was on in the maid's bedroom, and Sepal scratched at the window. Adelaide's face appeared, her brow creased in surprise. She opened the door, glancing around to make sure they were alone.

"Sheriff's looking for you," Adelaide said in a whisper. She fiddled with the belt of her gray flannel nightgown, a castoff from Miss Charity. "They want to talk to you, see if you know anything about Miss Priscilla's house burning down."

Sepal glanced at her hands, saying nothing.

"I would let you stay here, Maisie, but I can't take no chance like that. I got to live here. This is my job." She glanced at the large white Victorian house across the yard. "I can't talk for long. Miss Charity might hear us."

Adelaide stepped back inside her small home, closing the door. She returned with a basket of bread and several pieces of chicken. There was no recognition in her eyes, no knowledge of having ever stepped foot outside of Motherwood. "I won't tell nobody you was here. Be safe in your journeys. I'll pray for you, Maisie."

Now, as she listened to the rugged melody of the train panting down the tracks, Sepal pulled the skin off a chicken breast, chewing quietly. She still loved Adelaide, her bosom friend. But some people didn't want to be free. The rhythm of the train made her sleepy, and she turned her head to the window, closing her eyes. When she awoke, the train was pulling into the station in South Carolina. Some of the colored passengers got off and new ones boarded. A woman wearing a black pillbox hat walked down the aisle, the veil masking a hazel eye. She carried only a small purse the color of an eggplant. After glancing around the compartment, she stopped at Sepal's seat.

"Mind if I sit with you?" The stranger's voice was deep like a man's but clear. "I'm traveling by myself. Be nice to have someone to talk to, if you don't mind."

"I don't mind at all," Sepal said. Grabbing her basket, she moved aside so the stranger could take the window seat. After the woman settled in, she offered her a biscuit.

"Thank you, ma'am. Sure am hungry," the stranger said. "I rushed off and didn't have time to pack much. Got a long way to go."

"Take as much as you want. Where you headed?"

"Up north. Staying with my relations in Pennsylvania. A coal-mining town."

Sepal smiled. "I'm heading to Pennsylvania too. What'd you say your name was?"

"I didn't, but it's Reynalda." The woman extended her hand. "Reynalda Jones."

Sepal shook her seat-mate's hand. It was smooth to the touch, not cracked like her own. Maybe it would only be a matter of time. Maybe it wouldn't. "Pleased to meet you, Reynalda. I'm Mais – Sepal. Sepal Rose."

"That's a pretty name – Sepal."

"Thank you kindly. It's my grandmother's name."

They rode in silence for a few minutes, then Sepal said, "You said you rushed off. Didn't have time to pack."

Reynalda kept her face turned toward the window. "Yeah. That's what I said."

"I don't mean to be nosing in your business. I had to leave town in a hurry too."

Reynalda turned to her, a question on her plum-black lips. But before she could ask, Sepal said, "I used to be a maid, but I got in some trouble with the lady I worked for. Now I'm starting over again up north. I want to be a writer."

"Anything beats cleaning up after folks," Reynalda said. She scrunched up her nose. "I did day work once, but I couldn't get through the week. Those were some nasty crackers. 'Sides, there's more things in life for me to do with my hands."

"What you plan on doing up north, if you don't mind me asking?" Sepal said. She offered her new friend another piece of bread, and Reynalda nodded her thanks.

"I'm going to band together a group of colored lady superheroes."

Sepal cocked her head to the side. "What'd you say, Reynalda?"

"I'm going to make a name for myself, Sepal. I don't know how yet, but I'm doing to do something special. Just watch me."

Was it Sepal's imagination, or did the woman's skin seem thinner. Her eyes widened. She could almost see the passing countryside through Reynalda's body, as if she were transparent. Then her skin returned to its dark brown color.

"Biscuit sure is tasty. Would go good with a nice jar of corn liquor," Reynalda said as she swallowed. "Too bad it's a little cold."

"Here," Sepal said, reaching into the basket. Something pulsed red beneath the cloth napkin, a glowing heart. "I'll get you another one."